PRAISE FOR THE WORKS OF ALYSON RICHMAN

The Lost Wife

"Staggeringly evocative, romantic, heartrending, sensual, and beautifully written, Alyson Richman's *The Lost Wife* may very well be the *Sophie's Choice* of this generation."

—John Lescroart, *New York Times* bestselling author

"Daringly constructed, this moving novel begins at the end and then, a fully realized circle through the most traumatic event of the twentieth century, returns you there in a way that makes your heart leap. Richman writes with the clarity and softness of freshly fallen snow."

—Loring Mandel, Emmy Award–winning playwright

"Begins with a chilling revelation and had me hooked throughout. A love story wrapped in tragedy and survival, I read *The Lost Wife* in one sitting. Tense, emotional, and fulfilling: a great achievement by Alyson Richman."

—Martin Fletcher, special correspondent, ABC News,
winner of the Jewish National Book Award

"Richman . . . once again finds inspiration in art, adding evocative details to a swiftly moving and emotionally charged plot . . . this is a genuinely moving portrait."

—*Publishers Weekly*

The Last Van Gogh

"*The Last Van Gogh* is a balanced symphony . . . Richman's style is gentle and sober. With clear, undulating prose . . . it is as evocative as one of Van Gogh's paintings. Richman proves she can travel through time to re-create the past."

—*En Route Magazine*

"*The Last Van Gogh* paints an intricate portrait of a woman's life at the end of the nineteenth century . . . it is a powerful and poignant love story."

continued . . .

Swedish Tango

"An engrossing examination of the prisons people create for themselves and the way they accustom themselves to suffering until liberation seems as painful as captivity. This is an ambitious exploration of political and personal struggles." —*Publishers Weekly*

"A heart-wrenching story of loss and love in the lives of people affected by war and political upheaval . . . [marked by] sharp resonance." —*Library Journal*

"Places an Ayn Rand lens on societal ethics against personal loyalty and safety . . . deep, thought-provoking philosophical questions on the needs of an individual and a family against the demands of deadly leadership and a nation." —*Midwest Book Review*

The Mask Carver's Son

"Recalls Arthur Golden's *Memoirs of a Geisha* . . . Her sense of Japanese culture is subtle and nuanced." —*San Francisco Examiner & Chronicle*

"This reverent, formal, and ambitious first novel boasts a glossy surface and convincing period detail." —*Publishers Weekly*

"Richman has successfully drawn upon her historical research and her own experience . . . filled with historical detail and strong characterization." —*Library Journal*

"A meticulous profile of a man struggling against his native culture, his family, and his own sense of responsibility." —*The New York Times Book Review*

Also by Alyson Richman

THE LOST WIFE

The Last Van Gogh

ALYSON RICHMAN

BERKLEY BOOKS, NEW YORK

THE BERKLEY PUBLISHING GROUP
Published by the Penguin Group
Penguin Group (USA) Inc.
375 Hudson Street, New York, New York 10014, USA
Penguin Group (Canada), 90 Eglinton Avenue East, Suite 700, Toronto, Ontario M4P 2Y3, Canada
(a division of Pearson Penguin Canada Inc.)
Penguin Books Ltd., 80 Strand, London WC2R 0RL, England
Penguin Group Ireland, 25 St. Stephen's Green, Dublin 2, Ireland (a division of Penguin Books Ltd.)
Penguin Group (Australia), 250 Camberwell Road, Camberwell, Victoria 3124, Australia
(a division of Pearson Australia Group Pty. Ltd.)
Penguin Books India Pvt. Ltd., 11 Community Centre, Panchsheel Park, New Delhi—110 017, India
Penguin Group (NZ), 67 Apollo Drive, Rosedale, Auckland 0632, New Zealand
(a division of Pearson New Zealand Ltd.)
Penguin Books (South Africa) (Pty.) Ltd., 24 Sturdee Avenue, Rosebank, Johannesburg 2196,
South Africa

Penguin Books Ltd., Registered Offices: 80 Strand, London WC2R 0RL, England

This book is an original publication of The Berkley Publishing Group.

Cover design by Annette Fiore Defex.
Cover photographs: Landscape © Malgorzata Maj / Trevillon Images; Woman © Yolanda de Kort / Trevillon Images.
Text design by Tiffany Estreicher.

PUBLISHING HISTORY
First Berkley trade paperback edition / October 2006

Library of Congress Cataloging-in-Publication Data

Richman, Alyson.
The last Van Gogh / Alyson Richman.
p. cm.
ISBN 978-0-425-21267-7 (trade pbk.)
1. Gogh, Vincent van, 1853–1890—Fiction. I. Title.
PS3568.I3447L37 2006
813'.6—dc22

2006045957

PRINTED IN THE UNITED STATES OF AMERICA

10 9 8

For Rosalyn Shaoul for her infinite wisdom
And to Zachary and Charlotte with love

ONE

A Folded Red Poppy

I WAS the first to see him, small and slight, with several canvases under his arm, a rucksack slung over one shoulder, and a straw hat pulled over his eyes. That was my first secret—from behind the blooming chestnut trees, I saw him first.

I had gone out to do my errands, as I always did in the early afternoon. It was a warm, radiant day in May. The sky was cornflower blue, the sun the color of crushed marigolds. I have to confess that I walked a little slower that day when I passed by the station. I knew approximately which train he would be arriving on. So I walked with smaller steps than usual, carrying my basket of eggs and my loaves of bread.

I heard the sound of the locomotive's whistle and the screeching of its brakes as the train came to a halt. I walked over and stood behind the trees that bordered the platform.

I remember how he stepped down from the carriage; he was impossible to miss compared to the formal gentlemen in their black suits and top hats. He looked almost peasantlike in his white collarless shirt, broad straw hat, and unbuttoned vest. At first, the brim of his hat prevented me from making out his features. But finally, as he gathered his canvases and slung his satchel over his shoulder, I saw him clearly.

In a strange way he resembled Papa. I was surprised when I first saw him because their likeness was so strong. It was as if I were seeing a glimpse of my father, thirty years younger. Vincent's head was the same small shape—tapering ever so slightly by the temples. He had the same red hair and small patch of beard as Papa, the identical curved nose and furrowed brow that framed deep-set, blue eyes. He moved like a small bird, with quick, deliberate gestures, the same way my father moved when he was nervous or excited. But, unlike Father, he struck me as handsome.

To be sure, he was not classically beautiful. His complexion was pale. His cheekbones protruded; his red whiskers stood on end. Still, he intrigued me. He seemed so determined as he walked along with his head cocked high and his paintings loaded on his back. As he surveyed his new surroundings, I could see the eagerness and the energy in his eyes. And just by watching him, I could see what subjects he anticipated painting. He seemed to be assessing the rooflines of the village, the spire of our church, the clock tower of our town hall. Yet, as engrossed as Vincent seemed in his new surroundings, he seemed oblivious to the people passing him, hoisting their valises onto trolleys, struggling to make their way to their waiting carriages. He made no effort to move out of the way as he stood in the middle of the platform, his gaze now firmly planted on the river Oise.

He was like a sweep of yellow that afternoon in the rural landscape of Auvers. The sun gravitated toward him and in its warm, soft glow he appeared illuminated. I stood there and waited, watching as my father's patient began to make his way into the village. I didn't see him again until later in the day, when he arrived at our front door.

PAPA had spent much of the day preparing for Vincent's arrival. He canceled his appointments in Paris and spent the early hours of the morning in the attic, looking over the paintings and prints he had not yet framed. He took his lunch upstairs and, around two o'clock, as I was heading out to do my errands, I saw him descending the stairs.

I tied my favorite kerchief under my chin and walked to the hallway to find my basket. Papa was now at his desk, unrolling one of his prints and flattening it with four paperweights.

"Papa, I'm going out," I said.

He looked up at me, acknowledging my departure with an absentminded nod. I saw him turn to his bookshelf and withdraw a ceramic brush jar and a small Asian vase that Cézanne had given him a few years before. He held one in each hand, turning them around in the light and examining their patterns, seeing his own reflection in their glaze.

I knew that my father would place those two porcelains within arm's length. It was part of his act when meeting people he wanted to impress, and I was certain he'd incorporate them into his first conversation with Monsieur Van Gogh.

* * *

IT had been a weary winter, and I was deriving enormous satisfaction from seeing my garden in bloom. I was one month shy of my twenty-first birthday and I had recently spent all my energy with my knees pressed to the ground and my fingers plunged into the soil. My labors, however, had not been in vain. For now the rosebushes were flourishing, the bulbs were sprouting into tall sturdy irises, and, just beyond our house, the fields were alight with red poppies, anemones, and white daisies.

Vincent's arrival signaled not only a new addition to our village, but also a guest that Father felt was worthy enough to welcome into our home. We had few visitors, except for a handful of select painters. Camille Pissarro, Paul Cézanne, and Emile Bernard had all come to visit our home, but I never remember him inviting a single person from our village. The cobblers, the bakers—they were of no interest to Papa. But by opening our home to his various artist friends, Father was able to perpetuate the life he had enjoyed in Paris.

He often spoke of his time in the capital. After graduating from medical school, Papa joined his childhood friend Gautier—an aspiring painter—where they lived *la vie bohéme* among the burgeoning stars of the art world. And Father, who considered himself a dabbler at painting, was able to establish a thriving clientele of artists, writers, and musicians eager to exchange their work for his medical services.

Papa had written his dissertation on melancholia, taking the position that, historically, all great men—the great philosophers, poets, and artists of the world—suffered from that illness. Thus, he always had a sympathetic ear for those artists who considered themselves depressed or affected by a malady, and was quite eager to experiment with his medical obsession—the practice of

Hahnemann's homeopathy—in order to cure them. With the money Papa inherited from his father's estate and the substantial income brought by Mother's dowry, Father was free to pursue the unconventional methods of medicine that fascinated him most.

It had actually been Pissarro's suggestion, to Theo van Gogh, that Vincent come to Auvers so that Papa could look after him. "With your background in painting and psychiatry, you'd be the perfect doctor for him!" Pissarro had told Papa one afternoon in our garden. I remember they were all in agreement that the fresh air and rural surroundings would both soothe his spirit and inspire Vincent's painting.

But despite the bucolic surroundings of the village, ours was not the particularly light and airy home one might envision a country house to be. I remember wondering what this delicate painter would think of our narrow, cluttered living quarters. Would all the black furniture and bric-a-brac offend him in some way? And what would he think of Father and his homeopathic remedies? I wondered if he would come to our house frequently, the way the other artists had years before, and whether our home would come alive again.

He arrived at our door around teatime, bounding up the long narrow stairs with such energy that I heard his footsteps from inside my bedroom window. Father greeted Vincent and brought him into the family room. I had seen him take out one painting by Pissarro and three by Cézanne that afternoon and I knew he would be showing them to Vincent upon his arrival.

"Ah, yes, that is one of my favorites, too," I heard Father agree with Vincent. I suspected Vincent was talking about the Pissarro, a lonely painting: a red house in the distance, a mother and child shivering in the foreground, and three chestnut trees covered in frost. "Most of my collection is upstairs," Father continued. "And I have a print-making machine that I would be happy to lend to you. Cézanne used it often when he lived in Auvers." Father paused and then switched to a more reverent tone. "You see, Cézanne gave me this small vase and ceramic brush jar as a token of his appreciation. I was of great assistance to him and his painting!"

I shook my head, overhearing all this. With each passing year, Father was becoming increasingly more inventive with his tales. His desire to be a painter himself seemed to overshadow his efforts as a doctor. The two men spent a few more minutes discussing various artists before I heard my name called.

"Marguerite!" Father summoned me. "Monsieur Van Gogh has arrived. Could you please bring us some tea?"

Madame Chevalier, the woman who had arrived in our home after Mother died and become the governess for my brother Paul and me, was reading in her bedroom. She spent most of her time now either sewing or fussing over Papa. I was the one who was responsible for the majority of the household chores.

I was wearing a new dress that afternoon. It was pale blue with small white flowers embroidered into the hem and neckline. I remember that at the last minute, just before I was about to descend the stairs, I turned back to fetch a white ribbon for my hair. It wasn't something I normally did, as I usually wore my hair quite plainly around the house and kept it covered. But today I took the thin strip of ivory silk and tied it purposefully. I arranged one of the ends to rest against my collarbone, the other trailing against my shoulder. Against the backdrop of my father's art collection and the shadows cast by our black furniture, I yearned to be seen.

By the time I brewed the tea and arranged the small yellow cakes I had made earlier, Father and Vincent had retreated to the garden. Vincent was seated next to Father, the large red picnic table stretched before them. The bending branches of our two lime trees framed their faces. Father's body relaxed as he sat there in the garden talking about art, the joy his printing machine gave him, and his own dabbling in oils and pastels. And Vincent, too, seemed at ease with Papa. How I wished that day that I had been invited to partake in their conversation. But they sequestered themselves among the flowers and the shadows of the trees as I remained shuttling between the garden gate and the kitchen.

I was not misinformed. Father had spoken of Vincent's talent and unique use of paints even before his arrival. I knew Vincent had come to Auvers to be Papa's patient, but that fact did not deter my interest in him. He did not appear sick. He was fair, but not ghostly. He was perhaps a bit rough around the edges, but that only increased his magnetism. I can tell you now that he possessed something I have never experienced since: a rare blend of vulnerability and bravado. How I envied the bees on my rosebushes, overhearing everything Father and Vincent were saying. I wanted to study his face more closely and see which of my flowers his eyes fell upon. Did he think my violet anemones were beautiful and worthy of painting? Was he intrigued by the medicinal plants that Father kept near the front door? Did he notice the wall of ivy that cloaked one of the two caves on our property? The one where Papa stored all his wine and cheese? Later on, during the war, it would house the most precious paintings in his collection: the ones by Vincent.

I could hear Father's voice booming over the sound of the chickens in the yard. He was leaning close to Vincent, who seemed to nod in agreement as Papa lectured about his views on painting and the healing of the mind.

"Artistry and homeopathy are both sciences. Both are passions, Vincent!" Papa's face was radiant as he spoke to his enraptured audience of one.

Having watched him closely, I could see why Papa was drawn to both medicine and painting. He mixed his elixirs as though they were rare pigments; a drop of hyssop was as precious to him as a thimble of cobalt. He relished the tinkering and the measuring. He enjoyed the satisfaction of creating and using his hands.

Although I shared little of Father's penchant for herbs and tinctures, I did resemble him in one way. I, too, was intrinsically interested in artists. I wanted to understand what they saw, what they deemed worthy of their canvas and paints. I wanted to learn why they chose carmine and crimson madder to paint the red flesh of strawberries, how they managed to paint both eggshells and the fluff of clouds against a nude, white canvas.

Unfortunately over the years I had little opportunity to ask such questions. Even when Pissarro and Cézanne visited I seldom saw them unless it was over an informal lunch. Even then, I was cooking or clearing the plates, not free to engage in conversation or observe them as they set up their easels and paints.

But Father's assistance would be keeping Vincent in our village indefinitely and I was hopeful that we'd have an opportunity to become friends. I knew he would be visiting our house almost daily. And although it was evident from his arrival at the station that he was far less polished than the other men Papa had entertained in our house, he intrigued me endlessly more.

"Marguerite, the tea!" Again, I heard Father summon me. I hurried into the garden carrying their refreshments. As I put the tea set down, my hands trembled from the weight of the silver pot, causing the porcelain cups and saucers to rattle on the table. Neither of them appeared to notice. They were so engrossed in their conversation that they hardly realized I had placed the tea before them.

"You must paint as much as possible here," Father was insisting. He was using his hands to demonstrate his enthusiasm, and speaking to Vincent as if they were old friends. "That is the cure to your illness . . . when you paint your symptoms will disappear."

"But I painted in Arles—at the sanitarium—and my symptoms returned. Dr. Péyron sometimes forbade me from painting because he felt it contributed to my relapses."

"Nonsense," Father said, shaking his head furiously. "You simply did not have the peace and quiet that you needed. In Arles, you were surrounded by sick patients who distracted you from your work. You were not in a village like Auvers. Did you have access to air as fresh as this?" Father made another sweeping movement with his hand. "Did you have such a peaceful, unadulterated view of thatched cottages and sugar beet fields? Could you perch your easel next to endless rows of apple blossoms or on the shores of a rambling river like the Oise?"

Vincent shook his head no.

"And, lest we forget," Father said, touching the table to reaffirm his conviction, "there you didn't have me!"

Vincent managed to smile.

"Auvers-sur-Oise is where artists come to retreat from their hectic and troubled city lives. These men are my friends and I have treated them successfully with my herbs." Father's voice was exuberant. "Did you know that Pissarro himself is such an enthusiast for my homeopathic remedies that I have treated almost every member of his family? I should show you all the paintings he's given me over the years in payment for my services! Nearly thirteen works of his are in my collection!"

I cannot forget Vincent's eyes at that moment. He looked at Father with such hope, such adoration. It was as if he truly believed my father had the capacity to cure everything that had ever hurt or troubled him for his past thirty-seven years.

And so I thought that it didn't matter that Vincent had never seemed to see me that afternoon—either at the station or in our garden. I had seen him.

As I retreated back to the kitchen, I stopped by a patch of poppies growing by the gateway. I paused for a second, fingering their petals lightly. They were tall and vibrant, their red skins opening like the horn of a trumpet.

I suppose I was so caught up in their beauty, I did not realize that, evidently, Vincent had, indeed, noticed me that day. For, as he came to bid me farewell that afternoon, Vincent opened up his palm and revealed a small poppy flower he had folded in half. He extended his hand toward me and with his eyes firmly planted on mine, he said: "For you, Mademoiselle Gachet, a tiny red fan."

TWO

Two Altogether Different Shoes

I WAS barely three years old when we moved from our apartment in Paris on the rue du Faubourg Saint Denis to the village of Auvers-sur-Oise. By that time, Mother had already been diagnosed with tuberculosis; my brother was not yet born.

Paul arrived the following year, on the morning of my fourth birthday. The strain of a second birth clearly hindered Mother's recuperation, and she did not remain long in the house after Paul's arrival. A few months later she traveled to the south of France to seek a more curative climate. She returned a year later, still sick and very displeased that she was no longer surrounded by the comforts and social distractions of a bourgeois life in Paris.

I knew, in the way a child intuitively senses the moods of each parent, that my mother was unhappy. I don't remember there being laughter in our house, and I certainly have few memories of my mother playing with Paul or me.

Still, I did my best to please her, and so as a young child, I cultivated a willingness to please and an aversion to asking unnecessary questions. I never doubted my father when he told me we were moving to Auvers-sur-Oise because of Mother's health.

"Fresh air and clean water will be good for your mother," he said, as our housekeeper packed up my clothing and toys.

HE had bought the house only a month before from Monsieur and Madame Lemoine, he a retired housepainter and she, a schoolmistress. The house had been both a boardinghouse and a school for years.

The morning we were to move, we loaded our trunks and valises from our apartment in Paris onto our carriage and started out for Auvers. The crates of carefully wrapped porcelain and silver, the dark ebony furniture—her rosewood bed, her intricately carved Louis XIII commode—all the things that Mother loved and which came from her dowry, were loaded in a separate wagon and followed behind.

I can still see Mother clearly in my memory from that afternoon. Her face is in profile, etched like a perfect cameo; her ruby mouth, her snow-white skin. She holds in one hand a lace handkerchief that she presses to her face to bury her cough. The long, pale fingers of her other hand push nervously into the crimson upholstery of the coach; her rose-cut diamond flickers in the glass.

Father leans toward her as the carriage comes to a halt, telling her that this is to be our new home. She turns her head toward the pane. The house is high on a hill, a long climb to the front door.

She will have to walk up a steep incline of stairs to reach this very unremarkable house; the one with the tiny shuttered windows, no balcony, and a small slit of a door. She turns to him and shakes her head.

The coachman opens the carriage for her to alight and she stands on the pavement. She sees the small painted sign hanging from an iron lantern at the gate: BOARDING DAY SCHOOL FOR YOUNG LADIES, HEADMISTRESS MME. LEMOINE.

"This is the house, Paul-Ferdinand?" she asks.

My father nods his head, looking up at his latest investment, his face full of satisfaction.

He is not looking at my mother as her face falls. He is already bounding up the flight of stairs. My mother is in her satin dress, the collar high around her neck. It is like a saucer around a ceramic cup, capturing the trickle of tears.

SHE unpacked little by little, as her health was frail and too much would exhaust her. She had Papa put the dark wooden couch with the velvet seat and matching chairs in the parlor. The piano had been placed in the corner with a lace coverlet over its wooden top. I imagine Mother saw herself playing for guests while they sipped coffee, from china that had been her mother's, nibbling on pastries she pretended she had a chef to make.

The marble pendulum clock was placed on the mantel; the boxes of Japanese porcelains, the unglazed earthenware, the decorative vases, and the tall tapers in their elaborate candlesticks were arranged neatly on shelves. The kitchen, although small, was able to accommodate her limited collection of pots and pans. The oak cupboard that housed her two sets of hand-painted dishes was in the dining area. A curtain of Algerian stripe was hung over the open kitchen door.

After the house was unpacked and arranged, so that it resembled a proper bourgeois home, my mother still seemed weary and unhappy. Much to her chagrin, Father continued to maintain our apartment in Paris, where he stayed a few nights during the week, supposedly with late appointments. He would not, however, allow us to join him, citing Mother's failing health as a reason for the two of us to remain.

Mother grew increasingly resentful in our new home. She often complained about the countryside's dampness, the distance from Paris, and the lack of people with whom she thought she could socialize. She hated the symmetry of the house, and the way it towered high on a hill, with nine shuttered windows on an impenetrably plain stucco façade. It had not one small flourish, not a single carved cherub, not a single stitch of fancy ironwork. She said it still looked like a boardinghouse and it made her weep.

Things only worsened after she gave birth to Paul. She had still not recovered from her illness. On one rather miserable evening after she had returned from her aborted respite in Provence and Paul and I were playing quietly in my bedroom, we heard her drag herself from her bedroom and yell at Papa.

"For you! For you, Paul-Ferdinand, we've moved here! Not for me! You use the income from my dowry to serve yourself!" He tried to calm her down, taking her by the shoulders and pleading with her. She had a vial of one of Father's tinctures in her hand and she threw it on the ground, the glass shattering on the floor.

"I want to see my own doctor!" she shouted. "I would rather drink arsenic than one of your bilious concoctions! I am not a fool! I know the real reason that you want to keep me away from Paris!"

Her voice traveled through our tall, narrow house, and I remember trying to press out the sound of my mother's shrill voice by covering my ears. But, even after Father had succeeded in silencing her, Mother's discontent permeated deep into our house's damp, plaster walls and her suspicion regarding my father was firmly planted in my mind.

Less than a week later—two days before she would die—Mother dressed herself from head to toe in all her Parisian finery. She powdered her face and applied too much rouge, layering her makeup in the way sick people do who believe they can paint away their illness and mask themselves into good health.

She did not listen when her nurse tried to stop her from taking a carriage to the station. Father had left earlier that morning for his appointments in Paris, and Mother was insistent that she needed to join him.

She did not kiss my brother Paul or me good-bye. She descended the stairs in a whirl of black, the silk material trailing on the ground. But when she lifted up her skirts and ducked inside the coach, I noticed that, in her haste, she had put on two altogether different shoes. A black calfskin and a black silk faille. The ribbons dangled untied on both.

Mother never returned to our house in Auvers. She died not in her rosewood canopy bed, as Father had intended, but in our original apartment on the rue du Faubourg Saint Denis. I was six years old at the time. My brother only two.

Less than a week later, Madame Chevalier arrived. We were told that this woman would be our governess. But strangely, even after Paul and I had grown to adolescence, she still remained.

She arrived with little more than a suitcase, her dark hair swept up in a loose chignon. She wore a common black dress: boiled wool with silver buttons. A winter dress in the beginning of spring. There was no lace collar, no fluted sleeves with decorative trim. The bodice, however, was tight so that the material accentuated her narrow curves. Just above the yoke of the skirt, one could see the pointy nobs of her hipbones poking through the heavy cloth. She kissed Papa on both cheeks when she arrived, her lips leaving a trace of pink on his skin.

He opened his green parasol to shade her from the sun. She tipped her head so it remained under the umbrella as they walked up to the house. I remember the sound of her boots against the garden stairwell, the drapery of her skirt brushing too close against Papa's leg.

I was suspicious of Madame Chevalier from the moment she arrived. She was not our mother and yet Papa encouraged her—almost immediately—to take the position of mistress of the house.

My brother Paul, on the other hand, had had little chance to become attached to our mother. Thus, in his eyes, Madame Chevalier was a welcome addition to the house. She nurtured him with great tenderness, showering him with affection and coddling him as if he were her own.

From almost the moment she arrived in our house, she had felt comfortable holding him in her arms. I remember watching her as she swept him up like a basket. Several strands of black hair fell from her chignon, and my tiny brother extended his hands to tug at her tendrils as if they were reins to an imaginary horse.

It was clear that Father also seemed to be affected by Madame Chevalier's arrival. His transformation was apparent almost immediately after she arrived. He traveled to Paris less frequently, spent more time at the house, and began inviting his artist friends over from Paris to paint with him in the garden.

He even took the opportunity, after Mother's death, to redecorate part of the house. Opting to rebel against what he considered Mother's haute-bourgeois taste, a quality he deemed to be wholly nonintellectual, he placed among her antiques odd mementos he collected from his artist friends. Formal perfection was replaced by eccentricity. An empty bamboo birdcage hung in one corner of his sitting room. A stringless violin was pegged to the plasterboard wall. He lined the glass-covered doors of his étagère with prints and etchings he liked but felt were not technically strong enough to be framed.

He replaced the muted tones my mother had chosen for the walls in both his master bedroom and the room where Madame Chevalier slept with vibrant colors and intricately patterned wallpapers. He painted one of the doors near the staircase bright red with large black Chinese letters down the side and covered the hallways with a wallpaper full of reclining Roman nudes.

Still, he maintained the dark taupe and pale green walls in the formal rooms on the ground floor and kept the heavy dark furniture that Mother had brought from Paris. So, on the outside, and to those who visited after Mother died, our home maintained the same somber quality. In the narrow floors upstairs, however, the change was remarkable.

At first, I liked the bright turquoise and scarlet palette Father had selected for his and Madame Chevalier's rooms, separated from each other by a floor. But as I grew older, my opinion changed. I began to see them as vulgar—even garish—and I avoided entering them because they bothered me so. Even the nude illustrations on the hall wallpaper began to embarrass me.

I learned to retreat to either the sanctuary of our rear garden or the comfort of my own small room. It was the tiniest and most modest one in the house, but I preferred it. I enjoyed the fact that the room was set back so my walls did not buttress Madame Chevalier's. It was the one thing in the house that was mine completely. The little decoration my room did have came from a few old pieces that had been my mother's, including a rosewood nightstand and bureau and a few china figurines.

My favorite was a young girl in a brightly colored gown. The stiff porcelain skirt was painted with small scarlet dots, the nipped waist in pale blue. Her delicate white hands extended outward, as though she were permanently accepting an invitation to dance, and I would stare at her as I drifted off to sleep, her black eyes and ruby mouth smiling at me as I dreamed of late-night Parisian soirees and a trail of names filling my dance card.

THREE

A Delightful Young Woman

ALTHOUGH Father told us that Madame Chevalier would be our governess, it was clear almost from the start that she had little training as a teacher. She brought with her no readers, no pencils, only a few samplers for me to do in needlepoint.

What would begin as a lesson after breakfast always ended with her holding my brother on her lap and me copying the letters of the alphabet on a few sheets of paper that she had torn from my father's sketch pad.

After both my brother and I learned to read, she had little else to offer us. She would sometimes bring down two books from my father's library and have us spend the afternoon reading them. "Your father says if you read, you'll be able to answer all your questions regarding the world," she told us. But strangely, I never saw her bury her head in any of their pages. She preferred to sit by the fire, looking at the sewing patterns she had ordered in the mail.

What she lacked in intellectual enthusiasm, she made up in attending to our father. There was little doubt how much she idolized him. Unlike Mother, who seemed perpetually annoyed with Papa, Madame Chevalier never tired of him. Her admiration appeared endless. When Papa was busy cultivating his herbs, she would pull up a garden stool and watch him for hours. When he would arrive home late and tired from a full day's work in Paris, she would tell Paul and me to remain quiet, and she would go upstairs and draw him a warm bath, bringing him a glass of sherry on one of Mother's silver trays.

She would often tell us how smart our father was, and remind us how lucky we were—that there were so many less fortunate children than we. "Plenty of children in Paris would cut off their right arm to have what you have," she said on more than one occasion. "A home with a garden full of animals to play with . . ." Every time she told us this, her voice trailed off wistfully.

No matter how hard she tried with us, I still thought very little of her. She clearly lacked the grace or sophistication of my late mother, and it bothered me even more to see just how enamored Papa was of her.

Papa began calling her by her first name, Virginie, quite early on in her residence with us and although I found it shocking at first, I could often hear her speaking in a hushed voice with him in his bedroom upstairs. There were murmurs and stifled giggles in the late evening when Paul and I were supposed to be in bed. There was the occasional wink over dinner, when Papa thought I was heading toward the kitchen.

Nothing, however, could prepare me for the scandal that

would arise six years later. Just before my twelfth birthday, Papa announced that Madame Chevalier had a daughter close to my age.

"The girl's been living with her grandmother in Paris for the past six years," Papa said, his lips slipping over his wineglass. "But there's been some sad news recently. Madame Chevalier's mother has fallen ill and can no longer take care of the child."

Papa took another sip of wine and looked Paul and me squarely in the eyes. "She's just returned from a stay on the Côte d'Azur, where she helped friends of mine from medical school with their two young children. I had hoped that when she returned from her employment with the Lenoirs, her grandmother would have recovered. But it seems she hasn't."

Paul and I both stared at Papa, wondering why he was telling us all this.

"Therefore, I have done the decent thing." He cleared his throat. "I have invited Louise-Josephine to come live with us."

Paul and I looked at each other with disbelief.

"She will come to stay here in Auvers, Papa?" Paul's face was quizzical. Even though he was only eight years old at the time, he too thought the arrival of another child into our household was peculiar.

I, however, could barely contain my shock.

"Louise-Josephine is fourteen years old now. I had the pleasure of meeting the girl while I was in Paris and she is a delightful young woman. I think you will enjoy having another girl in the house, Marguerite. It will be nice for you to have some female companionship and she will help you care for your brother. Dr. Lenoir tells me she proved herself extremely helpful around their house this spring."

My mind was spinning. How could Father even contemplate

such an arrangement? How was Papa, who was always so protective of his privacy, going to explain to the villagers that his alleged governess was living under his roof with a child: Whether the child was born out of wedlock, or Madame Chevalier was just a widow with a young daughter in tow—either version would bring about its own thread of village gossip.

I needn't have worried about such details as, minutes later, Father was instructing us on how he was going to ensure that there would be no gossip at his expense.

"We will need, of course, to keep this our little secret. Madame Chevalier would not want the villagers to gossip about her." Papa paused. "The girl already knows that she will not be allowed to journey outside the home."

I remember Paul glancing over at me. His face was visibly puzzled.

Wasn't what Papa was proposing a bit ludicrous? How could this girl remain a secret? But I knew how little contact I had with the outside world. So she would not get a chance to go to the market or to church, but otherwise, I suspected her life would be quite similar to mine.

SHE arrived on a sunny afternoon. Papa picked her up at the station, while her mother remained at home. She was slender, with chestnut hair and dark brown eyes that looked like molasses. Her skin was a shade warmer, her eyes much darker than mine.

Just as he had appeared when Madame Chevalier first arrived, Papa seemed strangely familiar with Louise-Josephine. He helped her into the house with a paternalistic affection, showing her every room and urging her to feel at home.

As her mother's arrival had done years before, Louise-Josephine's entry into our household seemed to invigorate Papa. He repapered her room a few months after she arrived, allowing her to select a pattern from a large decorator's book that he brought back from Paris one afternoon. It did not take her more than a few seconds to choose a pattern of three-pointed flowers with a border of trumpet lilies. The shades were reminiscent of something in a pastry store—a palette of sherbet pink and cocoa brown. I remember Father complimenting her on her "fine taste" once she had made her selection.

At first, I did not mind when Louise-Josephine came to live with us. I enjoyed the idea of another girl close to my age. But she was cautious when she arrived. She showed no interest in befriending me, preferring to keep to herself. Sometimes, at her mother's request, she would care for Paul, drawing him a bath or mending his clothes when he tore them in the garden. These were all chores that I had done before her arrival, but now it seemed Madame Chevalier felt more comfortable asking her daughter to do them than me.

I had assisted Madame Chevalier in the kitchen for so many years that now I was beginning to cook many of our family's meals as well as do the shopping. I felt as though I was finally able to take over where my mother had left off, rearranging her knick-knacks when I dusted the shelves, polishing the brass girl that adorned her marble pendulum clock, drawing the curtain over the door when I began the preparations for supper.

Over the coming weeks, Louise-Josephine slowly became absorbed into our house, much like one of Father's newly acquired canvases. She blended into the plaster walls like sponge paint, rarely speaking unless spoken to, never making unnecessary noise, silently gliding through the house like a piece of transparent cloth.

She busied her days making small découpage boxes or looking at magazines she had brought from Paris. But sometimes I would pause and notice her doing things that I had believed were my responsibility. When I saw her taking Paul's hand to usher him into his warm bath, I saw in his eyes the same sense of adoration he had had for Madame Chevalier when she first appeared after our mother's death. And, again, I felt the same swelling of resentment that I had when Madame Chevalier first arrived.

I soon abandoned any thoughts of befriending Louise-Josephine. I acknowledged her in the hallways, when we passed to sit down at the table, but otherwise our contact remained distant.

REGARDLESS of mutual lack of affection, Louise-Josephine learned quickly how things were done in our household. She adapted to the distinct difference in how we acted as a family when we were alone and when guests were present. In those latter cases, she retreated to the upstairs. Even during visits by Papa's artist friends from Paris—who, oddly, seemed familiar with Madame Chevalier, in the way one knows a long-lost friend—Louise-Josephine was never introduced.

Sometimes Madame Chevalier was also instructed to remain upstairs. If Papa had a guest from Paris come for lunch, he would tell Madame Chevalier that it would be awkward to explain why his grown children still needed a governess, and she would simply nod her head and go upstairs as if she understood the situation fully. She had obviously taught her daughter everything she knew in the art of being unseen and unheard. They both knew how to tiptoe, as well as how to occupy themselves for hours at a time, for we never heard a peep from either of them when Papa had a guest. High above the muted parlor, in the brightly painted rooms upstairs, Papa's secret life remained far from prying eyes.

When we were alone, however, and outside the public eye, we existed as a strange family of sorts, with Madame Chevalier and her daughter not acting as servants but living among us essentially as family. Often, our father even seemed more affectionate with Louise than he did with either Paul or me, stroking her arm tenderly when she passed by his side. And although he did not pay for private lessons on the piano for her, as he did for Paul and me, he yet held a certain tenderness for Louise-Josephine. If Papa could have arranged his children as he did the paintings on his wall, Louise-Josephine's would have been the unsigned canvas that remained closest to his heart.

FOUR

Awakening

I HAD inherited my love of music from my mother. In her healthy days in Paris, she had played the piano daily, even composing her own melodies on occasion. As I became more accomplished over the years, Father would ask me to play when one of his artist friends visited our home.

He had hired a piano teacher shortly after my mother's death in the hope that I would show talent like she had. Madame Dutreau was one of the few people that I remember being allowed inside our home who was not associated with Papa's artistic circle. She took a liking to me right away, as I always studied my weekly assignments diligently, unlike my younger brother, who seemed perpetually distracted.

I adored her. She was tall and elegant. She smelled of freshly cut roses and the faintest trace of mint. When she played the piano, she was mesmerizing. Her slender fingers looked like stalks of firm, white asparagus fluttering over the ivory keys.

How I longed for her weekly visits! They were a rush of fresh air for me. She was not only my piano teacher, but my thread to the outside world. She knew just the sort of novels a girl my age would want to read and she would bring them to me and slip them between the sheets of music.

Sometimes after she had finished giving Paul his piano lesson, I would ask her to stay for tea. We would eat some cake and discuss one of the novels she had lent me. Often, she might ask me about my gardening or suggest a recipe I might enjoy.

Papa, however, was suspicious of our friendship. When he discovered that she was bringing more than just sheet music into the house he was furious. "I pay her to teach you to play the piano, not to choose what romance novels you read!" he grumbled over dinner one evening. I begged him to maintain my lessons but he shook his head. A few days later he terminated her employment, telling me only that I had "learned enough from Madame Dutreau." As he saw it, she was no longer necessary in my education—I now had the skills to teach myself.

Although I was heartsick that I no longer had the visits from Madame Dutreau, I continued to play the piano over the years. When Vincent returned that second afternoon in 1890, I was playing Chopin in the parlor. I had recently been practicing the soft, fluid notes of the Impromptu in C Major, and had become so enamored by it that I had little interest in practicing any of my other pieces. I found that my fingers naturally took to the melody, and I was transported when I played it. No longer was I restricted to the confines of my father's house, forced to be a dutiful daughter and obedient servant to him and his whims. No longer was I limited to the fields and small narrow streets of our village. When I was at my piano, I was in a different world; one where I was free to travel, where I felt beautiful and charming. There were only two places in the world that I felt completely at ease, my garden and my piano. In either of those places, I was not the daughter of Paul-Ferdinand Gachet. I was simply me.

WHEN Vincent arrived that second afternoon, he did not come with a house gift or a bouquet of flowers. He simply arrived carrying his easel on his back and a box filled with paints. This time, I was the one who answered the door, as Vincent was one of those visitors that Papa did not want Madame Chevalier or Louise-Josephine to meet.

"Good afternoon, mademoiselle. Your father said I might come over and paint in the garden. . . ." He spoke quickly, but his French was formal and polite. From beneath the brim of his hat I could see the smoothness of his skin, the fawn-colored freckles that reminded me of a blue jay's egg.

"Oh, yes, of course," I replied shyly. I touched my fingers lightly to my chest. "Father is out this afternoon. He has consultations in Paris."

He looked clearly disappointed not to find Papa at home.

"Can I give him a message for you?" I asked.

"No, that's quite all right," he replied.

He looked almost childlike in the doorway. His clothes were too big for his slight build, and his voice was shaky. It was evident that he felt a bit awkward around me. He was clutching a canvas loosely at his side—tapping it gently against his thigh. It looked like it was a painting of one of the many fields behind our village church.

"I had hoped I might be able to paint in your family's garden," he finally stammered. "But with your father away it's probably not a good time."

"You're welcome to come in," I said and I felt my heart racing as the words fell from my lips. I knew I should never have made the offer, as I knew Papa would be annoyed if I let Vincent come into the house when he was not there. He would tell me it was wrong to invite a gentleman—a patient of his, no less—into the house without his supervision, but I could not help myself.

Vincent seemed to think about my offer for a second before refusing it. "No, that's very kind of you," he said. "Please just tell him I came by to see if he was available for a short visit. Next time, I shall try to make more formal arrangements."

"Papa will be home tomorrow. Why don't you stop by then?" I suggested. I took a few tiny steps closer to him so I could see his features from underneath the brim of his hat. The sun over the past few days had already made its mark on him. Now all that remained of his former pallor were the delicate white lines around his eyes.

He seemed slightly uncomfortable in my presence, which made me feel strangely more confident with him. I enjoyed the fact that I did not feel intimidated, something I always felt when I was with Papa. I suddenly felt brave and let myself look straight into his eyes.

I did not expect him to meet my gaze, but he did. His blue eyes were in stark contrast to his pale red lashes. His dark pupils were small and intense, while mine were wide-eyed and full of excitement.

"Mademoiselle," he said, his eyes still firmly fixed on mine. "I shall come tomorrow, then." A small smile crept over his face. "I look forward to your gentle greeting at the door."

I smiled and nodded. Stepping back, my hands clutched the brass handle of the door.

I watched as he hoisted his rucksack on his back and switched the canvas to his other arm. Again, his eyes locked with mine and my heart began to quicken once more.

As he turned to walk toward the street, I could not refrain from staring. I could hear the patter of his shoes, the sound of the leather soles slapping against the cobblestones. There was something endearing about it. As if it were the metronome atop my piano, I could not erase it from my head. And for the rest of the afternoon, it made me smile.

HE arrived the following day and, again, I answered the door. "Papa's already in the garden," I told him. "He's feeding the animals, and will be most pleased to hear that you've arrived."

He fidgeted slightly as he stood there in the vestibule of our house. "I am anxious to paint," he said quietly. "The light is good today and I really should be working, as your father suggested."

I nodded, relishing another opportunity to study him. The sun was radiating through our stained-glass window and it cast a kaleidoscope of colors on his white linen shirt. For a moment, he struck me as one of the figures that lined the windows of our church. His thin fingers protruded from the length of his sleeves, and his head was surrounded by amber light.

I found his shock of red hair amusing. Like the stiff bristles of a porcupine, the ends stood up and alternated between deep scarlet and pale strawberry. His beard, however, appeared softer in texture, the fiery red tufts rounding out his otherwise angular face. It was a face that looked as though it had been carved by a chisel—

the sharp cheekbones, the high forehead, the narrow bridge of his nose—all of his features lending themselves to dramatic shadows and reflections of light. I could have looked at him for hours. Vincent's expression, his features, every part of him seemed to contrast with the men I saw at church! Those men whose eyes were as lifeless as river stones and whose cheeks were plump like oozing slices of Camembert. Vincent was so much more handsome in comparison.

I hoped he did not realize that I was staring at him once again. Trying to gather myself, I let out a little cough and motioned for him to come through the house.

"You will like painting in our garden," I told him softly. He lowered his eyes when I spoke. I could not believe that this person who had appeared so bold and confident when he handed me the folded red poppy was actually quite shy. Just like the day before, I found myself feeling more at ease knowing that he, too, had bouts of awkwardness.

"Please, come this way." I made a small gesture with my hand. He collected his things and followed me through the long corridor. We passed the parlor and then the kitchen, where it was clear I had been busy baking.

He took in a deep breath. "There is nothing more comforting than the smell of baking bread," he said softly to me. "Except, perhaps, the odor of turpentine."

I found him charming, and let out a small laugh. "Bread and paint thinner are an artist's milk and honey," I said as I opened the back door that led to our lawn. We stepped outside and discovered Father busy feeding the peacocks and the goat.

"Papa, Monsieur Van Gogh is here!"

Father turned and looked up. He was wearing his blue smock,

and the tufts of red hair around his ears appeared almost orange against it.

"Ahh . . . Vincent! I'm so glad you could come this afternoon." He came over to Vincent and extended his hand. "I see you're taking my advice and are ready to paint today."

As I saw the two of them standing there in profile, I again could not help but notice their physical resemblance. Father's hair, too, was closely cropped, the pale red color achieved through a shampoo of crushed henna leaves. They both had the look of an ascetic, with their sharp cheekbones and close-set eyes.

But whereas Papa could barely contain his energy, Vincent seemed to be keeping his in close reserve. I suspected he saved all his strength for his painting. He stood perfectly still, while Father gestured feverishly to the various parts of our garden, like a maniacal conductor without his baton.

There is truth in the saying that the less one says, the more mysterious he becomes. And so was the case with Vincent. I watched transfixed as he stood in Papa's shadow, his brushes and wooden stretchers extending from the open corner of his rucksack. He didn't move or utter a word as Father chattered on. In contrast, he remained almost frozen. Like a garden statue set against our flowers and trees.

I imagined that as Father rambled on, Vincent was no longer listening, but was busy deciding where he would place his easel, at what angle he would adjust the level, and what colors he would use to paint. He seemed far more interested in painting than talking; that was perfectly clear. I could not help but feel embarrassed that Papa's egotistic nature prevented him from seeing that.

"I will leave the two of you," I said as my father took a breath between sentences. "I'm sure Monsieur Van Gogh is anxious to paint."

"Yes, I'm sure he is!" Father nodded to Vincent. "But I'm sure he would like some tea before he begins. How about picking some lime leaves, Marguerite? Certainly Monsieur Van Gogh will appreciate the fragrance."

I acknowledged my father's request and began to walk toward the house.

"Actually, if you don't mind, Doctor . . ." I could hear the faint whisper of Vincent's voice behind me. I slowed down my steps so I could hear more clearly.

"I'd prefer not to have any tea now but to get to work at once, if that's all right with you. I got up early and painted behind the Château Léry, but the light has changed and I think my paintings here this afternoon will be all the better for it."

"You're absolutely right, Vincent!" Father said, clasping his hands. "I think you'll find the light in our garden to be perfect!"

I collected the lime leaves anyway, as I knew that Father would ask Vincent to stay for tea after he finished his painting for the day. Also, collecting the leaves allowed me another chance to watch him from afar.

From behind the trees, I studied Vincent intently, just as I had the day he arrived in Auvers. He walked around for several minutes before settling on an area with a patch of yucca plants and blooming geraniums. I thought it a wise choice, for from that corner, one could see over the garden wall and view the entire panorama of the village: the tops of the thatched cottages, the tile chimneys, and the blue ribbon of the horizon.

Even at four o'clock, he did not take tea with Father. This surely must have upset Papa, but Vincent was so engrossed in his painting that he seemed to have little time or patience to stop for idle conversation. He painted vigorously, as if he were in a mad race against the setting sun. From the rear window of our house, I caught him looking up at the sky on more than one occasion. With a gaze of competitiveness, he seemed to be challenging the daylight to a race, striving to capture one more image before the sun began to descend.

By five o'clock, he had painted the twisting branches of the apple trees, the spiny blades of the yucca, and our narrow terrace, which he had painted replete with marigold bushes and aloe plants.

Father offered to store the canvas upstairs so that the thick paint might have a chance to dry. Vincent declined.

"Might you join us for dinner and afterward a little music played by my children?" Father asked.

"I am afraid I am too weary this evening, Doctor," Vincent answered quietly. "But perhaps another time."

"You must come for lunch, then," Papa insisted, "when you have your energy about you. Perhaps later this week?"

Vincent smiled and lifted his head. He appeared almost celestial, as if his skin were merely a veil and his eyes and flesh could barely contain the enormity of his spirit.

"It would be my pleasure to join you and your family for lunch," he answered politely. And as he finished his sentence, he looked up at me and I was sure that I noticed a certain flirtation in his eye.

FIVE

Paul van Ryssel

THAT Saturday, two days after Vincent painted his first canvas in our garden, Papa took the train to Paris to meet with Vincent's brother, Theo. I had not known of his plans until Paul mentioned it in passing.

"They're going to discuss Vincent's cure," Paul said, as he leaned against the wall. I was rolling out a sheet of pie dough and tried to hide my curiosity.

Paul had arrived home that afternoon from his studies in Paris. It had been his first year away from our home and his semester had nearly come to an end. He would be returning home full time in only a matter of weeks.

"Well, I'm certainly glad Papa didn't invite Vincent to live with us this summer," Paul muttered as he fumbled in his pocket and retrieved his small pipe. "He's quite a curious little man. But I wouldn't want to share the same roof with him."

I looked up and smiled at him and said nothing. In truth, I thought my brother's comment a bit ironic. At that point in our lives, Paul was not full of bitterness toward me. In fact, he was a rather benign young man in his youth, albeit a bit odd. Much to my chagrin, his first year at school had only accentuated his oddness, not curbed it as I had hoped it would. I suspected he was having quite a hard time adjusting to life in the city after such a sheltered existence in Auvers.

I tried to change the subject between us. "You shouldn't smoke here while I'm cooking," I chided. "My pie is going to taste like tobacco!"

Paul ignored me, and lit his pipe anyway.

"Have you seen him yet, Marguerite?"

"I was here the day before last, when he painted in our garden," I said, trying to sound disinterested.

Paul, however, was making no attempt to conceal his curiosity about Vincent's arrival. "Just today, when I arrived from the station, I saw him painting in the field behind the church. He was dressed like a beggar, and had paint all over his face."

I scooped up some flour from my ceramic bowl and spread it on the countertop. "He seems perfectly nice to me. Perhaps a bit eccentric, but that just makes him more interesting than the others. . . ."

"Eccentric?" Paul laughed, shaking his head. "Madame Chevalier told me that Papa said he cut off his ear in Arles!"

I suddenly felt the color drain from my face.

"I don't believe you, Paul. You shouldn't make up such terrible things."

"It's true! Next time you see him, take a good look at his left ear. He cut off the bottom part!"

I shook the flour off my palms and wiped my hands on the front of my apron.

"We shouldn't be gossiping, Paul. He's a patient of Papa's." I tried hard not to seem affected by what my brother had just said, but, inside, I felt my stomach turning. I reached for a glass of water. The stove was making the room unbearably hot and it was difficult to breathe.

"Whether Vincent is ill or not, he's immensely talented. I saw the painting he began of our garden. The colors were so vibrant, and the paint was applied so thickly that it seemed almost sculptural." I paused for a second, remembering how I'd been impressed by the canvas. "Truthfully, Paul, I think he's better than Papa's friends Pissarro and Cézanne put together."

My brother's face suddenly changed. He was capable of instantly becoming morose, as he had inherited our father's mood swings. "You really think he's that talented, Marguerite?"

"Yes, I do."

Paul began to sulk, chewing on the side of his mouth while pulling on the chain of his pocket watch. "You always seem to be around when there's excitement in the house," he grumbled, still playing with the watch.

"Paul, that's because I'm always here. Consider yourself lucky you're not in the kitchen half the day!" I said. To emphasize, I smacked him on his thigh with my dishrag.

I managed to get a small smile out of him, but it quickly vanished. I knew this year had been a difficult adjustment for Paul. Over the past several months, while doing my dusting, I had glanced at some of his letters, which were often left opened on Papa's desk. He complained that his classmates had not been kind to him, that he often felt like a lost ship among those steadier and sturdier than he.

My heart actually ached for my little brother when I read these letters. He was almost seventeen years of age now but his upbringing had been quite unconventional. I could see how he might be a target for certain secondary-school bullies.

The fact that, over the winter, he had decided to grow a small goatee like Father's probably didn't help things. The narrow tuft of beard only accentuated his sharp angular face. Tall and thin, he appeared almost sickly. Like a fragile duck, with a long neck of blue veins. I could almost hear the taunts echoing in my head.

Recently, when Paul returned home for the weekend, he began to show less and less interest in adapting to the lifestyle of his peers. Perhaps in a reaction to their rejection of him, he began to cultivate an attitude of eccentricity just like Papa's. At first, it began quite benignly. He would withdraw after his Saturday dinner to his room, where he proceeded to dabble with some borrowed paints of Papa's. Then he started to imitate our father's style in other ways. He would wear similar smocklike jackets and brightly colored cravats.

He began to mimic Papa's way of walking, the way he held one hand under his breast pocket, the other dangling awkwardly with a pencil clutched between his fingers. He memorized Papa's gestures and expressions, even the odd way he tied his tie.

But whereas Father's quirks were the eccentricities of an aging doctor, they seemed particularly worrisome in a boy of school age.

At dinner one Sunday, Paul announced that someday he would be a famous painter. I knew he was trying to impress Father with the idea that his only son would fulfill the dream he had been too bourgeois to devote himself to.

Papa looked up from his lamb chop, holding his fork steady on the bit of meat, and smiled. "There will always be space on the walls here for your paintings."

It was a far kinder response than I had expected, though Papa said little else to encourage him.

Still, Paul threw himself into his newfound ambition. He would return on weekends not with textbooks, but with a stack of sketch pads and a tin full of pastels. He set up an easel in the corner of his room and spent several hours a day drawing or painting with his window wide open.

He took the name Paul van Ryssel as his "painter's name," as Father had painted under the name Louis van Ryssel since he was a little boy. He copied paintings out of Father's books, trying to imitate Cézanne. Even I could not help but admire his determination, though I did wonder how well he was devoting himself to his other studies.

That afternoon, as I rolled pie dough in our hot, crowded kitchen, he chirped confidently: "I doubt anyone will ever hear of this Vincent van Gogh in years to come, but they will surely have heard of me!"

"Paul, I hope the world hears of both of you," I replied sweetly. I wanted to share his confidence, but I had seen his sketches and paintings. They were awkward and revealed little talent.

I looked over at my brother. His eyes were cast downward, his fingers were still nimbly fiddling with his watch. I could not help but remember him when he was just a little boy of seven, playing with me in the garden. He wanted to be special even then, begging me to weave him a crown of laurel leaves so that he could be the ruler of the forest. So that he, in our tiny little realm, could be king.

SIX

Gachet's Secret Water

THERE was little doubt in my mind that Father must have seemed odd to the villagers of Auvers. Every Sunday, he walked through the streets with our pet goat—whom he had affectionately named Henrietta—on a leash. "She's the town's lawn mower," he would tell those who looked at him puzzlingly as the goat grazed on the long grasses that grew alongside the road.

Father stood out against the rustic farmhouses like a fauvist painting among a sea of Brueghels. He would wear one of his white button-down smocks and festive cravats tied in a voluminous bow and carry a green parasol even when it was cloudy. He was surprisingly amicable to anyone who approached him during the course of his promenade, though he would never engage and socialize with them beyond that or invite them into our house. On more than one occasion, people asked him for medical advice on how to cure their aches and pains. "Take my elixir," he would tell them and hand over a bottle from one of his pockets. He never asked for money, as it was his great pleasure that he could give them (or so he thought, anyway) the secret to long life in a small glass bottle with a handwritten label. Though they never seemed to come back for more.

Papa had begun making "Gachet's Secret Water" several years earlier as part of a personal experiment. He had a secret recipe that he planned on taking to his grave. He cultivated homeopathic herbs in our garden and distilled his elixir with great reverence and care. As children, we were taught to take a spoonful of it every night before we went to sleep. Our personal bottles of it still stood on our nightstands as a constant reminder.

But the winter before Vincent arrived, I had decided to stop drinking it. It was my secret way of rebelling against my father, and even though he would never know of my silent dissention, it pleased me anyway. For although my mutiny was passive and perhaps one might even say cowardly, I did it to satisfy myself. From that spring on, every night before I went to sleep, I would open my window slightly and pour a few capfuls out into the garden.

Paul, however, continued to take his daily dosage of Father's curative water, even boasting that he sometimes took two capfuls a day. His blind idolization of our father bothered me, and I soon bemoaned the fact that there weren't more years separating us so that I—rather than Madame Chevalier—could have been more involved with his upbringing after Mother died.

I had wished on more than one occasion during my childhood that our family was a more typical one, like those I imagined our neighbors having. Not one that isolated itself and strived to cultivate an air of mystery or drama. I wanted to be like the other young girls, who had girlfriends of their own. I would often see the other girls my age walking arm in arm around town. They would giggle to each other behind a fan of fingers or run after each other in the park. I longed to be like them. To have such companionship. But I knew such relationships were impossible. Father limited my movements and was adamant about maintaining our family's privacy. So the only contact I had with anyone my age was my brother and the daughter of a purported servant who carried on more like a country doctor's wife than my own mother ever did when she was alive.

My contact with boys was similarly limited, basically only to Paul. As my birthday approached, I prayed that Father would at least acknowledge that I was approaching a marriageable age. There were obviously few options for the daughter of a Parisian doctor to find a suitable match in Auvers, but I was nearly twenty-one and Father had still not mentioned any social events that might afford me the opportunity to meet eligible suitors. Indeed, he had yet to speak of making any arrangements at all for me or my marital future.

I worried that Father might approach my matrimony very much the way he approached education for both Paul and me. He refused to bring a teacher into the house even after we had exhausted the limited teachings of our alleged governess, Madame Chevalier, and it was very reluctantly that he let Paul enroll in secondary school. And even that had been delayed until only this year.

"One must learn everything on one's own! Instruction is useless, a joke! One learns only when it is voluntary," my father boasted to a distant aunt who visited us once after Mother died.

"There are hundreds of books in my house, and if my children are curious, they can read and do their own investigation!"

But marriage and love could not be found in a library of old books. And I wondered if Papa realized that, but preferred to have me wait—on him and his household. Me, the child who reminded him of his late wife, but with healthy lungs and a quiet demeanor.

FATHER arrived home the following evening, and went straight to his office to tell Madame Chevalier the reason for his good mood. His meeting with Theo had apparently gone well and, as Papa made no effort to stifle his voice, it was easy for me to hear the details of his afternoon. "Vincent is lucky to have such a devoted brother. The boy idolizes him, will do anything for him. . . . He's confident that the art world will eventually recognize Vincent's genius." Madame Chevalier did not answer Father. I imagined that her head was down and she was concentrating on her knitting. "He's entrusting me to maintain Vincent's health and to make sure that he's able to paint." I could hear Father dropping his cuff links into the ceramic box he kept on his mantel.

"We ate a wonderful lunch at La Coupole," Father continued. "I told him how I was not unfamiliar with the artistic world. He already knew about my collecting but he had no idea about my 'Wednesdays at the boulevard Voltaire.'" Papa chuckled. He was referring to the address of the pastry chef Eugène Murer, who hosted a weekly salon at his apartment that was frequented by the painters Pissarro, Sisley, Monet, and Renoir. Somehow, Papa had always managed to get himself invited.

"I told him I'd pay him a visit at Goupil's and take a look at the other artists he's representing."

"You might want to invite Theo and his family here to visit Vincent," Madame Chevalier suggested quietly. "It might make him feel less isolated in Auvers."

"I will—it's an excellent idea." I could hear his footsteps treading over the floorboards. "And that reminds me," he continued. "There was a note from Vincent saying that he would accept my invitation to lunch this Sunday. Make sure Marguerite prepares something appropriate."

I could not believe my ears. Did Father think I wouldn't make something appropriate? I wouldn't have that much time to prepare my menu, but I would certainly never make something that would embarrass Papa or insult our guest.

I felt my entire body stiffen with annoyance. I was more than capable of making a meal that Father wouldn't be ashamed of!

Irritated by his words, I tried to distract myself. I walked over to my window and opened the shutters. Outside, the sky began to fill with stars, and I could hear the grasshoppers down below chirping at the moon.

I opened my journal and found the folded red poppy that Vincent had given to me a few days before. It was still damp between the pages.

I picked it up carefully and studied its scalloped edges and crimson petals.

When folded, it was like a fan. I imagined it as a miniature opera fan that, had it been larger, might have accompanied a woman who wore black gossamer silk and an enormous bustle attached to her skirt. One who was chic and elegant. One who alighted from her carriage with creamy white skin peeking from her collar and fingertips gloved in black satin.

That night, I fell asleep with the pages of my journal open, imagining my mother as I had last seen her, though in my dream she wore two matching velvet shoes and held a magnificent scarlet fan.

SEVEN

Like Two Eagles

SUNDAY morning, I awakened early and began my preparations for the luncheon. I didn't ask Louise-Josephine to assist me because I thought that might appear a bit cruel, considering that neither she nor her mother would be invited to eat with us. It was at times like these that I didn't know how to treat her or Madame Chevalier. In name, they were servants and, truth be told, the ones that should be making the lunch. Yet Father treated Madame Chevalier more tenderly than he did my late mother, and he certainly appeared to shower Louise-Josephine with affection. He never asked either of them to do the errands or the cooking. The only housework she or her daughter really did was a little dusting or light sweeping. They didn't even do the laundering, as Papa insisted that it be sent out.

I would be lying if I said that I did not suspect that Louise-

Josephine was his daughter, born out of one of his long visits to Paris when my mother was alive. She had a sense of entitlement that I would otherwise think peculiar in a typical servant's child. However, I never questioned it out loud. Just as I never mentioned my suspicion to Paul—though I'm sure he, too, heard Madame Chevalier's footsteps, the tiny patter that echoed through the house as she routinely walked down the stairs at night to visit Papa in his room.

As I trimmed the tough ends of the asparagus stalks, I found myself wishing that I had secrets of my own so that I could distract myself from the ennui of my everyday life. I thought about how my mother must have felt quarantined in this house, distanced from her beloved Paris. No place to dress up in the silk gowns that lined her closet. No boulevards to promenade down or damask-upholstered salons to visit, where one could gossip for hours and sip tea. It would have been a painfully lonely life for her—remaining indoors all day with few or no distractions. But now I realized that my late mother was not the only one who led that life. So, clearly, did I.

Shortly before Vincent was scheduled to arrive, Paul came into the kitchen. "Do you think Father would mind if I showed Vincent some of my paintings?"

I was stirring some poached pears, trying to ensure that I didn't get any red wine on myself. "I don't know, Paul," I replied. "Perhaps you should ask Papa."

He looked crestfallen. "He's been in the studio all morning, and I think he's preparing to show Vincent some of his paintings."

"Well, lunch is supposed to be for Vincent and Papa, not really for us," I reminded him. "We should be happy that he's including us at all."

It would never have occurred to me to be so brazen as to show Vincent my watercolors. I would have been embarrassed to show him something that I knew he would consider amateurish.

"Do you think he might like them, Marguerite?" Paul asked. For several moments I ignored him. I was trying to focus on the food preparations and making sure that the table was set with great sensitivity—silently hoping that Vincent would notice my efforts to create some semblance of beauty in our otherwise crowded, dark house. Paul, however, was too absorbed in his own dilemma to notice my concentration on matters besides him.

He clanked one of my pot lids down and the noise startled me. "Paul!" I cried. I poked him with the wooden spoon I had been using. "Vincent will be arriving in a few minutes and nothing is done yet!"

"But what about showing him my paintings? I am going back to Paris this evening and I won't have a chance to see him all week!"

I let out a loud sigh, unable to conceal my growing impatience with him. "I don't know, Paul. . . . Papa wants us each to play him something on the piano. See how much he enjoys that. If he likes that and shows enthusiasm, then you might ask him if he'd also like to see your paintings."

Paul straightened his back and beamed.

VINCENT arrived twenty minutes late, huffing and puffing like a laborer who had been in the fields all day. He had changed his clothes and wore a jacket and hat, but the cloth seemed worn and his shoes were scuffed and tracking mud. "Mademoiselle Gachet," he said when I opened the door, "your father has been most kind to invite me for lunch."

"Yes," I said. "We'll be eating in the dining room this afternoon." I motioned for him to come in. "It's unfortunate about the rain," I murmured apologetically. "The garden would have been nicer."

"One appreciates the sun so much more after a bit of rain," he said as he took a peek out the window.

For a second, I thought I caught him staring at me, his eyes traveling from the lace on my collar down the front placket of my dress.

"How true," I said and I was unable to prevent a small smile from appearing across my lips. I was happy that he seemed to be taking notice of me. Then, as if suddenly freed from the insecurity that plagued me, I uttered, "An artist sees the beauty in the world, but I suppose a woman often only sees its limitations."

He looked at me quizzically as if surprised that I had the capacity to speak.

"What a curious thing to say, mademoiselle." He reached into his pockets. "I suppose the same thing can be said about the impoverished. A day for the poor is full of hardship and limitations, but the rich man and the artist only see its possibilities."

I smiled. "That is probably the *only* place they overlap."

He seemed amused by my answer, and I noticed that he continued to stare as he took off his hat and coat and handed them to me. They were damp from the rain, but they felt nearly weightless in my arms. I thought about Papa's cloth coat and Paul's as well—they were both so heavy in comparison, with silk lining and tortoiseshell buttons. Vincent's, however, seemed like it was made from muslin. As I hung it on one of the wooden pegs near the vestibule, I noticed that I could see my hands through the threadbare cloth.

I was just about to take Vincent into the parlor when Father's voice interrupted me. "Vincent!" he said, his tone revealing his great enthusiasm. He had heard Vincent's footsteps and was now rising from his chair and rushing toward him.

"I'm thrilled that you could join us today." Vincent nodded and thanked him quietly for extending the invitation.

"How are you feeling today?" Papa asked him, while patting him on the back. "Terrible about the weather . . . I bet it's been difficult to paint this morning."

"I began a sketch of an old vineyard this morning," Vincent replied. "But my mind is still not at ease."

"You need to paint as much as possible," Papa reminded him. "It will help keep your head clear."

"I am restless." He spoke softly. "You are right, the painting helps. . . . But when I don't have a paintbrush in hand, I am filled with anxiety."

Papa chuckled. "I hear similar complaints from other artists. It is not unusual."

I could see flashes of Cézanne and Pissarro go through Papa's mind. A smile crossed his face just to utter those names in passing.

Vincent nodded and glanced down at his fingers. I noticed the skin spotted in paint, the faded patches of pigment—cobalt blue and thin lines of cadmium red. It looked as though he had tried to scrub them raw but, still, traces of the pigment remained.

"You know, Vincent, I have a saying written in Chinese letters by my office and outside on one of the walls on our cave. Translated it says: Work and you will be happy. I believe strongly in that saying. It's good advice for you."

"I want to paint—I am painting. It's just that when I'm in my room at night and my fingers are so tired I can barely lift a comb to my head, I find myself staring at the ceiling and then a flood of fear washes over me . . . the fear my blackouts might return, the fear of another attack. . . . There was a time when a glass of absinthe would send my demons away but my doctor in Arles has strictly forbidden it. . . ."

Papa nodded. "This is all completely understandable. You had a terrible time in Arles. But we will keep you away from absinthe, Vincent, and get you stronger so that you produce what you are meant to. Genius needs to be nurtured with clean air, rest, and healthy exercise. I have promised your brother that I will make sure you are well taken care of out here. And should you need a little something at night, I'll make you a tincture of passionflower to calm those nasty nerves of yours!"

Vincent made a face at Papa's remark about the tincture. "Well, I am happy to hear my brother is asking you to keep an eye on me. I have not heard from Theo in days, have you?"

"I saw him a few days ago in Paris. We had lunch together." Papa went over to the server and withdrew a bottle of wine. "You're lucky to have someone as devoted and dedicated as your brother. He's convinced that your day of public recognition is not too far off." Papa turned the corkscrew as he spoke, holding the tall green bottle with his other hand. "We talked about you and some of your colleagues. I think he mentioned a man named Paul Gauguin."

Vincent's brow furrowed slightly. "We lived briefly in Arles together before my headaches returned." It was obvious he wanted to change the subject. "I'm a bit anxious to have my things shipped to me. . . . I left a few paintings with Tanguy back in Paris and have some furniture still in Arles." Vincent cleared his throat. "Did Theo mention anything about this?"

"No, I'm afraid he didn't." Father shook his head. "Don't worry. I'm sure it will all get sorted out soon. Your responsibility now is to concentrate on your painting and on regaining your health."

"Yes, I know," he replied softly. "I nearly finished the painting I did in your garden the other day, and I've begun three more."

"Good!"

"And you're right, when I paint things are much better. . . ."

"Then just continue to paint and I'll have a look at my various herbs. We'll make you another tincture so that you can sleep better at night and be refreshed in the morning." Father cleared his throat. "Remind me after lunch—I will give you another tincture to take home with you."

FATHER and Vincent continued to talk in the parlor before I called everyone for lunch.

I had spent the early part of the morning preparing my favorite dishes. I had gotten up early so I could get the first pick of the market. I filled my basket with chicory and small fingerling potatoes, several heads of garlic, and a generous bunch of carrots. I handpicked the chicken from Armel, the butcher, insisting that I have the largest, juiciest one from that morning's slaughter. The herbs in my own garden had been paltry that morning, so I indulged in buying fistfuls of rosemary, marjoram, and thyme. I never tired of the fragrance of fresh-picked herbs and as I walked home, I inhaled their heady perfume, eager to begin my preparations.

The entire house now smelled of my crisp roasted chicken and creamed, buttered potatoes. I could not help but smile as I emerged from the kitchen with the large platter in my arms. I had placed a few more sprigs of rosemary on the chicken for decoration, and the colorful contrast of the carrots and chicory made it look as though it were made for a king. I believed all eyes were on me. But just as we were about to take our seats at the table, Paul appeared. He was wearing a bright red cravat and black waistcoat, his gold watch dangling from his vest pocket.

"I've been painting today up near Chaponval, Papa," Paul announced loudly as he sat down. "I'm sorry that I'm late."

Papa shook his head, then turned from Paul to Vincent and asked, "Have you been up to Chaponval yet? The trees are over a hundred years old. . . . Cézanne liked to take his easel there to paint."

I stood at the table slicing the chicken before dishing the vegetables and creamed potatoes onto everyone's plates. I served Vincent first, trying to arrange his plate as artfully as I could. He, however, didn't seem to notice.

"No, I haven't gotten that far yet. I've been mainly painting near the Ravoux Inn and near your home."

"Well, you are lucky that you are here indefinitely. There will be countless opportunities for you to paint these landscapes. And when the autumn comes you'll see how it will all change before your eyes!"

I took my seat, smoothing my dress underneath me as I adjusted myself into the chair.

"Yes," I said. "You'll have a wonderful time painting all the colors of the leaves. . . ."

I could see both Papa and Paul staring at me from above their perched silverware. Like two eagles, they sat hunched, glowering at me with increasing suspicion.

"If you want, Monsieur Van Gogh, I can take you to one of my favorite painting spots in Chaponval. You can see over Oise River and to the fields beyond." Paul was speaking quickly and I could tell how eager he was to impress Vincent.

I could immediately see Father's brain latching on to Paul's idea of accompanying Vincent while he was painting. Just as I suspected he would, Father added: "I could always take you around as well and show you the best vistas in the area. I could bring my easel and we could paint side by side."

Paul's face suddenly fell. He could not conceal his disappointment.

Vincent shook his head. "It's so kind of you both to offer your assistance, but I prefer to paint alone. Even when I lived with Gaugin, we rarely painted at the same spot." He cleared his throat. "My creative work is better suited for solitude."

FOR the rest of the meal, my brother remained unusually quiet. I could see that he tried on more than one occasion to look surreptitiously in Vincent's direction and that his preoccupation was clearly a result of schoolboy curiosity. With a series of unsubtle movements, he shifted in his seat and cocked his head awkwardly to the side. I knew what he was up to—he was trying to confirm whether the information Madame Chevalier had told him about Vincent's missing left ear was correct.

Papa, however, seemed oblivious to Paul's macabre curiosity, and in between his enthusiastic eating, he continued to engage Vincent in conversation.

"I was thinking, Vincent. We could invite your brother and his family over for an afternoon . . . to have lunch in the garden . . . .

and you could see your young nephew. Paris isn't that far," he continued. "They could come out for the day."

Vincent smiled. He seemed to brighten immediately at the thought of his brother and his family coming to Auvers.

"What a kind invitation, Doctor." Vincent looked genuinely pleased. "I had wanted them to join me here for the entire summer—bring the baby with them and get some fresh air—but Theo has just written me telling me it's impossible. But a lunch—that would be wonderful."

Vincent cut off another piece of chicken, washing it down with a large swallow of wine. He cleared his throat and turned to me. Again his gaze was intense. Those two pale blue eyes framed by the ledge of his forehead. The eternal arching of his copper brows. Then, unabashed by Father's presence, he turned to me and announced: "As long as it is no trouble to Mademoiselle Gachet."

I don't think I even managed to reply, so overcome was I by my blush. To hide my embarrassment, I turned my head and caught sight of my brother's face. It took me off guard. He looked as though someone had stolen his only slice of birthday cake.

WE all waited for Vincent to finish eating. Paul had already eaten two helpings of everything and was still looking wolfishly at the remaining bits of chicken on the decorated Limoges plate.

"Was the food to your liking, Monsieur Van Gogh?" I asked.

"Oh, yes . . . I rarely eat so well . . . my stomach isn't used to it."

I attempted to smile as I stood up to clear the table for dessert. Still, I worried as I exited toward the kitchen that the menu I had prepared was perhaps too rich for his digestion.

After I served the poached pears, Papa clasped his hands and announced that both Paul and I would play something on the piano in honor of Vincent's arrival.

"Paul will play first," he said.

I cleared the table as the three men went into the parlor. I could hear Paul saying he was going to play a piece by Bach. It was an ambitious choice on my brother's part, and I knew he had chosen it because he wished to impress not only Vincent, but Papa as well. He was starving for Papa to notice him (something I had long given up on) and hoped that though Papa failed to notice his paintings, perhaps he would take notice of his piano playing.

But the piece was far too difficult for him. He hadn't been able to practice when he was away at school and the selection he made required tremendous precision. I wished that I could have taken him aside and gently suggested that he choose something a little easier for such a spontaneous recital. But I had been so busy and preoccupied over the week with the cooking and cleaning of the house that I hadn't had the chance. Later on, I would feel guilty that I hadn't been more inquisitive, that I had not asked him what music he was planning to perform. Certainly, had I known it was Bach, I would have tried to encourage him to perform something less complicated.

But it was too late. By the time I walked into our living room he had already taken his seat at the keyboard. His nervousness must have gotten the best of him, for as he played his fingers shook like fluttering pine needles and he was incapable of striking all the correct notes.

It was painful to watch. It was equally painful to listen to. Knowing that he was failing publicly—in the eyes of my father and his esteemed artist guest—Paul's cheeks flamed with embarrassment. His ears turned scarlet as well, and it looked as though he might faint from the sound of his own blundering at the keys.

When he finally finished, I tried to clap as hard as I could. But it was little consolation. He sat sulking as I stepped up to the piano to play Chopin's Impromptu, which I had practiced each day since Vincent first arrived in Auvers.

I settled myself at the piano. If I looked to my left, I could see both Vincent and Papa reflected in the gilded mirror on the wall so I looked straight ahead toward my sheet music and the point of the metronome just beyond.

Papa let out a small cough and I knew he was signaling for me to begin.

I smoothed out my dress and placed my fingers at the keys. I placed my foot on the pedal and took one last, deep breath.

I began tentatively, cautiously approaching the first few notes, but soon I forgot that I was playing for an audience and the melody took over.

No longer did I need to read the music; I knew each stanza by heart. My body swayed as I connected each note. My diaphragm rose—my breasts lifted—as I breathed and exhaled into the melody. I felt as though I were a fir tree shaking off a winter's worth of snow.

The crescendo approached and as I struck the final notes, I felt a few stray locks of hair come loose from my chignon. They fell over my eyes and I fought hard not to push them back.

My fingers now felt as though they were being pulled by a spirit not their own. With lightning speed they danced over the keys.

Vincent was already on his feet clapping as I lifted my foot off the pedal.

"Such artistic passion," I heard him gush. He was clapping so feverishly that even Papa seemed embarrassed by his guest's enthusiasm and his sheer inability to mask his delight.

When I sat down, I could feel Paul's eyes glaring at me. He wouldn't be showing Vincent his paintings, and I felt sorry for my little brother. He had wanted so desperately to impress our guest.

"I NEED to get a tincture for Vincent," Papa whispered to me after the recital. "Your brother is clearly upset about his performance. Why don't you take Vincent to the parlor and entertain him for a few minutes. . . . I'll only be a moment."

Papa's suggestion took me by surprise but I could not protest. After all, wasn't this what I had been hoping for—a chance to be alone with him?

I motioned for Vincent to follow me into the salon. Inside I was shaking. I knew I was ill prepared to engage in small talk, let alone flirtation. For several days now my mind had been bursting with questions for him. I wanted to ask him how he chose his palette, how he learned his craft. Had he ever envisioned himself as something other than a painter?

But now conversation eluded me and my tongue failed to utter a single word.

"You play Chopin beautifully," he finally said as we entered the room.

"Thank you," I said with a small laugh.

Outside I could hear Henrietta making sounds at the chickens. It was strangely comforting to me, especially when Vincent smiled when one of the roosters cackled.

"When I hear you play, something about you transforms. I have been trying to place it exactly. . . . It's not that your hair becomes more golden . . . or the fact that your hands flutter like two white doves. . . . It's—it's just—" He stopped himself. "I am sorry, the right words are difficult to find. I only want to say that I was so moved by your performance."

"Oh, you are most kind. . . . But really, I lack the talent that my mother had. She was the most magnificent pianist."

Vincent's brow furrowed when I said this, as if he was troubled that I was selling myself short.

"That is rather inconsequential. Your talents are real—as real as the blood in my own blue veins!" He tapped on his forearm to reinforce the dramatic tone in his voice. "When I saw you in the garden that first afternoon, I noticed there was something special about you. Underneath that milk-white skin of yours, there is great passion for life. I can see it."

"Monsiuer Van Gogh, hush! If my father hears you going on like this I will never be allowed at the piano again!" Again, I giggled nervously, as I had never had anyone flatter me before.

"Ah, so you are not used to this attention," he said, and a small smile crept over his face. He was still sitting a comfortable distance from me but I could feel his gaze begin to intensify. Now he was staring.

I felt my face growing hot from his stare. "What you say is true. It is strange for me." My blush now spread: a stroke of pink on a wet page.

Vincent stood up from his chair. He was suddenly more confident and his voice was stronger. "I look around your father's house and I see all this bric-a-brac." He pointed to the ebony pedestal in the corner, the shelves lined with porcelains. "There is too much distraction. But, you, mademoiselle, stand out among all this dark furniture and gilded ormolu."

"You are much too kind," I whispered, my voice catching in my throat.

"No, I am not," he insisted. "A painter yearns to paint that which others fail to see. If someone tells me the sky is full of clouds, I am the artist that rushes outside to find what is hidden behind." He now came closer to me so that he was standing only inches from where I sat. And even though I tried to force my pupils to burrow into my lap, his eyes were still planted firmly in my direction. His gaze began to fixate on my features and I began to suspect he was studying my face, imagining how he might build the flesh from layers of thin, blended pigment.

When I finally did raise my head, I could now make out each of his lashes, the creases at the corners of his eyes, the follicles of his whiskers.

His mouth remained perfectly still. The feather-soft lines in his lips looked like the tiny veins of an autumn leaf, and the sweep of skin below his eyes was so pale it appeared almost blue.

"I would not be so distracted if I could paint you, mademoiselle."

I looked up at him. The irises of his eyes were not solid aquamarine as I had believed, but speckled with gold and apricot.

"Monsieur Van Gogh," I stammered. My skin felt as if it was burning right through the silk of my dress. I had never been so close to a man before and I was trembling.

"You will need to ask my father," I finally blurted out. "He will be here any moment!"

He let out a small laugh, obviously charmed by my awkwardness.

"Don't worry, Mademoiselle Gachet, I intend to ask permission from your father. I would not do it any other way."

He was now pacing while I sat there with my limbs frozen. And although I could hear Father opening and closing the drawers in his study upstairs and I could smell the yeasty perfume of my dough browning in the oven, I still sat there motionless, staring at Vincent as he moved in slow steps around our parlor.

It was he, again, who broke the silence.

"You should know that I do not take my portraits lightly. I choose my subjects carefully. Deliberately." He remained by the window with his face turned away from me.

"I want the people who see my portraits in a hundred years' time to see them as I did when I first painted them—as apparitions—as selected slivers of the divine."

I desperately wanted to tell him how honored I was that he wished to paint me, but before I could manage the words, I heard Father's footsteps bounding down the hall. He entered with a great flurry, his hands stretched outward as if he were making an elaborate delivery.

"Here, Vincent. Take three doses of this daily. It should help calm your nerves."

Vincent turned directly to my father and took the glass flask from his hand.

"I don't have the passionflower prepared, but take this; it's mugwort," Papa said. The vial contained a moss-colored liquid which was almost translucent when Vincent held it up to the sunlight. "The Saxons believed it was one of the nine sacred herbs. Even I take it every now and then when I'm feeling depressed."

"I told you," he stammered nervously, "I've been trying to wean myself from the green-eyed devil for several months now. . . ." Vincent returned the vial back to Father. "I don't think I should take it."

Papa shook his head and pressed the tincture back into Vincent's palm. "No, this isn't absinthe, Vincent." He let out a small laugh. "It's medicinal. I've been prescribing homeopathic remedies to my patients in Paris for years."

Vincent looked at him skeptically. "I don't know. . . ." He appeared agitated and there seemed to be genuine fear in his eyes. "I don't want to get addicted to anything again, and if there are side effects . . . I couldn't bear that."

"These tinctures will only help you get better, Vincent."

Still, Vincent hesitated.

"No, I am going to insist you take it, Vincent." Father's voice now sounded stern. "I doubt Theo would be pleased to learn you're not taking instruction from me. After all, I'm your doctor."

I was sure Vincent then cast his eyes in my direction, as if he thought an approving nod from me might assuage his doubts.

I did not, however, acknowledge him in any way.

It wasn't that I didn't want to. I desperately wanted to meet his gaze and interpret his expressions more clearly. But I was afraid that Papa might see me and suspect I was trying to undermine his authority. I wasn't a doctor. I knew little about the curative powers of plants and flowers. And I was fearful of igniting Father's wrath after Vincent left.

"Take it. . . ." Papa's voice was more persistent now. There was an urgency to it that made it sound like an order.

I saw Vincent take the flask from Father, place it in his side pocket, and reluctantly acknowledge his instructions with a nod.

EIGHT

A Female Model

I HAD difficulty sleeping that evening. All I could think about was Vincent's eyes heavy on me. I had been right that the first afternoon, when he had handed me the red poppy, he *had* seen something in me. Now, he had articulated his desire to have me sit for him and I was dizzy from the anticipation.

The following morning, Father mentioned in passing that Vincent was eager to have a female model and had asked if I could pose for him.

"Modeling is not an easy task, Marguerite," Papa warned me. "You will need to act like a professional."

"Yes, Papa," I said in my most serious voice. I had to fight hard not to show just how elated I was.

"Some people would frown on my decision to let you sit for him, but I promised his brother I would do all that I could to help Vincent continue his painting. And anyway, this will not be as though you are modeling for an art class." Papa laughed to himself. "No, I would never allow my daughter to do that sort of modeling!"

I blushed when Papa made this off-color remark. "No, of course not, Papa. Of course not."

I, on the other hand, could not have been more pleased that Vincent had made good on his promise. As a child I had posed for Armand Gautier, another painter friend of Papa's, but that was a long time ago.

I wanted to tell someone that I—Marguerite Gachet—had inspired a brilliant painter. That he had chosen to immortalize me in canvas and his luminous paint. My head was now filled with questions. Would Vincent use vibrant colors or choose the muted ones I feared my plain countenance deserved? Would Papa let him paint me unchaperoned or would I be allowed to sit with him alone?

But I had no one to discuss this with but my diary and myself. Paul had chosen to postpone going to Paris until Tuesday as the school was engaged in a reading period before exams. And although he remained in the house, he still had not spoken to me since his piano debacle. By that evening, he still had made no effort to speak to me, or even acknowledge me when I went into the parlor to do my needlepoint. He sat on one of Papa's armchairs with his head buried in one of his schoolbooks, his legs extended like two strips of timber, never looking up at me once.

I was used to his bouts of moodiness. He had been petulant even as a child whenever he didn't get his way, but it bothered me that he was angry with me because I had performed my piano piece without error and he had heard that Vincent wanted to paint me and not him.

"How's your painting going?" I finally got the courage to ask him. "Perhaps you can ask Monsieur Van Gogh for some instruction; I'm sure he could offer you some sound advice."

"He has little interest in me, Marguerite. You know that." His lip was curled up in a nasty little scowl.

I spent several minutes trying to reassure him. "If Vincent can't assist you, I'm sure Papa's other artist friends might be able to offer you some guidance on their next visit."

He shook his head. "Papa will monopolize them so, I will have little opportunity."

"We must remember, Paul," I said as I sat next to him and gently took his hand, "Vincent is one of Papa's patients, and we cannot push too hard with him. He is here to recuperate and to get himself back to his painting."

Paul nodded.

"I too am anxious to get to know him," I said, lowering my voice. "It will happen over time. Once you're home for the summer in a few weeks I'm sure you'll have ample opportunity."

Paul smiled. "Yes, perhaps after my exams are over and I'm here full time, he'll give me some pointers."

"Yes, I'm sure he will."

I touched Paul gingerly on the knee and made my way to the kitchen. I had left a pile of potatoes in the sink. When I slid open the Algerian striped curtain, I found Louise-Josephine standing over the potatoes with a bowl of water in front of her and a peeler in one hand.

"Oh, thank you," I said. I was surprised to find her there. I quickly reached for a knife and began helping her. We stood next to each other, aprons tied, the ribbons of potato skin falling into the sink. She hummed softly as she worked, a smile permanently fixed on her lips. After a moment, she turned to me and said, "Mother tells me you are to be painted by Monsieur Van Gogh."

My heart stopped as she spoke as if the fact that she knew about Vincent's request cemented it in stone.

"I'm sorry"—she hesitated—"perhaps I shouldn't have said anything."

I didn't answer her at first. I was still holding one of the potatoes in my hand. I expected her to look away from me out of shyness. But Louise-Josephine did not waver. She stood there staring at me, her eyes dark as claret.

"Yes," I finally said. "It's true. He's asked Papa if he can paint me."

She nodded her head and placed one of the potatoes in the bowl of cold water. "I suspect there will be some excitement in this house this summer." A faint smile crossed her lips. "It will be a pleasant change, don't you think?"

I looked at her as if I didn't know what she meant by such a comment.

She turned away from the table and brushed her hands on her apron. Looking directly in my eyes, she said rather matter-of-factly, "Of all the treasures in this crowded house, you're the thing that has caught his eye."

I wanted to embrace her when she said that. It was probably the kindest thing that anyone had ever said to me in my twenty-one years.

"You really think so?" I said to her as I inched closer. I was like a starved child desperate for any other morsel of flattery she could give to me.

"Oh, yes," she said. "He would never ask to paint something that didn't inspire him. It must be a wonderful feeling to know that someone finds you so beautiful."

NINE

Secrets

For years now I had tried to convince myself that Madame Chevalier and Louise-Josephine were just visitors in passing, that one day "Chouchette," as my Father affectionately called her, would pack up her one suitcase and take her daughter and leave.

I imagined her leaving as she had arrived. Wearing that memorable black dress, the silver buttons still shiny, her figure still poking through the cloth. It was a ridiculous fantasy, now that I look back on it. For I knew early on, though I didn't want to accept it, that Father never had any plans for her to be a real governess to us.

I am not sure if it was because I was looking for someone to reaffirm my suspicion that Vincent might be attracted to me or because she seemed to be taking notice of my feelings for him, but I suddenly welcomed Louise-Josephine's overtures of friendship toward me.

She was twenty-three now. Although she had lived nine years under our roof, I had never formed a close relationship with her. Over the years we had been polite to each other, and we had worked occasionally in the kitchen together when I needed assistance. She had helped me with the spring cleaning, even when her mother remained in her room doing needlepoint. She tried perhaps on more than one occasion to speak kindly to me but our exchanges rarely went beyond common pleasantries.

Though our lack of common interests had something to do with it, another part, I realize now, was my own snobbery. I resented the two of them living with us while their responsibilities remained unclear. Paul and I were old enough that we no longer needed Madame Chevalier's supervision. I did not expect to be waited upon, but I did not understand, either, why Father, who clearly had feelings for Madame Chevalier, went to such lengths to pretend that she and her daughter were living here to assist Paul and me—when clearly they were not.

Now, however, I began to welcome the idea of having a girl close to my age in the house. Louise-Josephine no longer seemed preoccupied with coddling Paul—he was too old for it now, and I'm sure she noticed, as I had, that he seemed to be going through an awkward stage of wanting to do everything like Papa.

I felt myself beginning to warm toward her. After all, she was kind to tell me she believed Vincent thought I was beautiful—and I yearned for a few moments alone with her to ask her why she believed that to be so.

I began to observe her routine. I noticed how she tried to stay out of our way, how she did little things to try and be helpful. I had never noticed before that she would often snip the dead flowers off my arrangements so that they appeared fresh for longer periods of time. Nor would I appreciate it when I sometimes lost track of time and Louise-Josephine would rescue my baking so it didn't burn.

Her comings and goings now intrigued me as well. Although Louise-Josephine remained sequestered on the grounds of our house, there were rare occasions when she ventured outside with Papa's permission. A few years after Louise-Josephine began living with us, Madame Chevalier had suggested that she might take her daughter into Pontoise once a month in order to buy her a few necessities. Papa had agreed, as he knew that Madame Chevalier and Louise-Josephine could take the small roads behind our house into the next village where their activities would go unnoticed.

When they returned from their monthly excursion together, their arms would always be filled with new bolts of cloth, their satchel filled with glass buttons and ribbon. Papa had given Madame Chevalier a small allowance and I knew she saved it for these excursions with her daughter.

I had never shown much of an interest in their purchases before, but now there was a sort of exuberance about me. I wanted to inquire what style of dress Louise-Josephine intended to sew for herself. I wanted to help her select the buttons for the bodice. And although I said nothing to either of them as they gathered their packages and slipped upstairs, I made a promise to myself that I would try to befriend Louise-Josephine.

I found myself over the next few days making more eye contact with her and smiling at her as I passed her in the hall—just what I had refrained from doing in the past.

With my brother away in Paris, I tried to reach out to this quiet, slender girl, whose life was perhaps even more difficult than mine.

TEN

Queen of the Weeping Willows

I HAD spent an entire childhood imagining places far away from our house in Auvers. I read all the time, as if to glean as much as I could from those leather-bound tomes about worlds other than my own. I also learned that the borders of our house had their own enchanted corners. Past our garden, far behind Father's garden shed and the chicken coop, was a most magical place, a limestone cave half exposed by sunlight, half cloaked in leafy green ivy. In this secluded grotto in our backyard, where the ferns grew wild and the vines hung down like majestic ropes waiting to be climbed, I first realized that if I used my imagination I could escape the loneliness of being a quiet child in a dark and melancholy house.

Sometimes Paul would accompany me as I wove the wild grasses into garlands for my hair. At his request, I would crown him King of the Dogwood Trees, and myself Queen of the Weeping Willows, as we stomped over velvety moss singing imaginary songs. It was also there, in the emerald green light of our little hideaway, that I first nurtured my love of flowers. I picked the blossoms of the pink mallow bushes and the tall delicate umbrellas of the Queen Anne's lace. I emerged from the grotto with bouquets of tiny violets in one hand and a large fern in the other, fanning myself as if I were a Grecian princess, kicking the heads off the dandelions as I danced barefoot in the grass.

I suppose back then I must have thought myself beautiful, or at least imagined myself to be. I likened myself to the heroines in my fairy tales, the princess who was bound to discover her prince; the sleepy maiden who would continue to slumber until her first kiss.

I no longer thought myself a princess as I grew into my teenage years. I pinned up my hair rather unartfully, telling myself that there was little time for vanity or personal indulgence. The sense of adventure that I had cultivated as a child had left me. Yet there were times over the years, most often when I was sitting at my piano, or digging my hands deep into the earth, that I felt my spirit return to me. It found its way back in the oddest ways; perhaps the smell of lime leaves wafting through the window or the yellow cap of a dandelion tumbling on the lawn. And every time it happened, I'd hold my breath, hoping that if I didn't let go of the air in my lungs, somehow I would fool that feeling of sheer exhilaration into staying. That for a few hours longer, it might still remain.

By the spring that Vincent arrived, I had other distractions. My imagination had grown fat on all the novels I had read that involved romantic courtships and full-blown love affairs. If Quasimodo could find love within the shackles of his tower, then certainly I could, too. I vowed to myself that I had to convince Father that I was ready for a husband and family of my own. The possibility that I would remain in our dark, crowded house in Auvers for the rest of my life terrified me. At night, I was plagued by the image of my mother restless in her sickbed, crying out for her former life in Paris. I'd try to find solace in one of my novels, but it was futile. I would only awaken the next morning full of frustration.

I wanted to experience everything for myself rather than through the characters of my books. I wanted to do more than pinch my cheeks to give them some color. I wanted to apply lipstick and rouge as Madame Chevalier did. I wanted to wear colorful dresses. I wanted to regain that joy I had known as a child when I climbed over ivy and stuffed petals under the laces of my shoes.

And perhaps, when Vincent arrived that summer, he noticed that nascent stirring about me. He saw that I was bursting to come to life again. Twenty-one years of age, and for the first time since I was a young child, I wanted to dance in the garden and sing. The words of Louise-Josephine kept repeating in my head: *You're the thing that has caught his eye.* Reliving the memory of those words, I could hardly suppress my urge to smile.

ELEVEN

The Cellar

"I WILL cure him," I heard Father say as he gathered a wicker basket and a pair of shears. Then there was the ebullient rustle of Papa in the garden, the incessant humming, and the inexhaustible sighing. I looked out the rear door of our house and saw him kneeling on the ground, the red tuft of his goatee brushing against the tall plumes of shepherd's purse and elderflower.

Ever since I was a little girl, I had watched him prepare his herbal medicines. When I began cultivating my various roses in the garden, he took special pains to show me where I could not plant. A few steps from our house, he had sectioned off a plot of the garden where his medicinal plants—chickweed and horsetail, cowslip and primrose, among others—grew in abundance.

Although Papa had trained as a medical doctor in Lille, he became intrigued with natural medicine after making the acquaintance of the Baron de Monestrol, a leading homeopath, while living in Paris. Papa had long considered himself a Positivist, believing that scientific knowledge was based primarily on observation. Thus, the school of homeopathy intrigued him. The fact that a substance that can cause symptoms in a healthy person can actually cure similar symptoms in a sick one, was one of the tenets of homeopathy. A small dosage of coffee crudea, for example, could alleviate insomnia. A little pill made from bee venom could reduce the swelling from a wasp bite.

Over the years, Papa began cultivating various plants and herbs in his garden to use for his tinctures. He experimented with many of his remedies on himself, and sometimes he gave his tinctures to Paul, me, and our mother in order to prove their effects. He would give us dulcamara when the weather changed from dry to wet in order to prevent colds. When Mother had trouble sleeping, he would give her a tincture of belladonna. For Paul's recurring sore throat, he'd make a special remedy using bryum moss.

I knew that if Father were up early collecting his herbs, he would be devoting the rest of the day to making tinctures. It was a monthly event. He would gather his flowers, roots, and special leaves and then soak them in alcohol. After two weeks he would press the herb-steeped solution through a wine press and funnel the liquid into flasks. It would be only a matter of hours before he'd be asking me to gather his various supplies.

In an effort to appease him, I decided to find the necessary mason jars and empty vodka bottles in advance. I adjusted the stove's temperature and then made my way into the root cellar, where, aside from the various bushels of apples and potatoes, Father kept all the accoutrements for making homeopathic remedies. He also kept all of Mother's possessions from her former life in Paris there.

I am not sure why Father did not sell or give away the boxes of assorted menageries Mother once collected. Aside from the crates filled with fragile glass pieces blown in the shapes of elegant swans and giraffes, tall crystal vases, and pitchers rimmed in gold, there were other odds and ends from her dowry. Standing against one of the cellar walls was a bookcase of carved oak, as well as several rosewood pieces, a box full of Japanese porcelains, and a wardrobe full of pristine white silk petticoats, camisoles, and a French cashmere shawl.

I knew her wedding dress was stored in a cedar chest in the far corner of the basement. I purposefully avoided it when I went down there to retrieve the alcohol and jars. I did not want to try it on—or even touch the silken layers—until I knew to whom I was betrothed. I did not want to cast bad luck on myself in a childish indulgence.

Instead, I walked to the opposite side of the cellar and gathered the dark glass containers, placing them in my basket while carrying the jug of alcohol in my other arm. When I returned to the kitchen, Papa was still in the garden and I heard him intermittently talking to the chickens and Henrietta, the goat.

I had nearly finished making a quiche when he walked into the kitchen and announced: "Marguerite, I'm going to need to sterilize some glass jars for my tinctures." He placed his basket on the pine buffet and took one of the hyssop stems to his nose. "I've decided to make a few remedies for Monsieur Van Gogh . . . I'll be needing my supplies."

"I thought you might be needing your mason jars, Papa, so I took the liberty of boiling them in advance." I removed a lid from the large cast-iron pot that was boiling on the stove and showed him.

He stood there in the kitchen as the first morning rays of

sunshine came through the window. Papa always looked weary in the morning, and the bluish mottling under his eyes and the golden shadows cast by the summer light made him look like a slightly bruised pear.

"What a nice surprise, Marguerite." He lowered his head for a moment and sifted through his basket of herbs. "I am planning to make a tincture for Monsieur Van Gogh's anxiety. A little passion-flower, a little hyssop and skullcap flower . . ." He placed the herbs on the countertop and a flurry of tiny bellflowers dangled off their stems. "In the meantime, he'll be taking his daily dose of my elixir and a couple doses of the mugwort."

"Yes, Papa," I responded softly. "If it works for you, I'm sure it will for Monsieur Van Gogh."

Father nodded and tapped his breast pocket. He always kept his silver medicinal flask close to him, taking an occasional swallow of his self-prescribed tincture throughout the course of the day. He had not made it a secret in our house that he was medicating himself for his own depression. After all, he had written in his dissertation that all great men of the world were affected by one form of melancholy or another.

"Artists are sensitive, Marguerite," he said and his voice drifted slightly as if he were imagining he were speaking about himself. "Painters, perhaps more so. A sculptor can find relief in his clay. He can claw into the clay and channel his frustration into the earth and mud. But a painter . . . he has a far more arduous task . . . he must always fight against the gap between his vision and his canvas."

"Yes, Papa."

"If your brush fights against you, you are helpless. You are always at the mercy of your brush!" He was shaking a stem of skullcap at me and I could see the tiny seedpods fluttering to the floor.

I remembered seeing Vincent painting in our garden the other day. He had painted so vigorously, with one spare brush sticking out of his mouth, and the other wielded with an outstretched arm. I watched him as he applied one color over another on his canvas. I could see the traces of where his brush swept the pigment across, how he sometimes took his palette knife and carved away the paint to reveal an underwash of another shade. Watching him, I was hypnotized.

I looked at Papa as he began removing the stigmas and anthers from the passionflower. His hands were deeply lined, the knuckles large and chafed. But still, he was nimble. He worked carefully but briskly. Within a matter of minutes he had a pile of pristine, carmine-colored petals in a jar.

"I was watching Monsieur Van Gogh painting in our garden," I said. "I wonder, do you think what he paints resembles the images in his head?"

"I suspect it does," Father said rather absently. He was now stirring the mixture of the herbs and alcohol.

"What colors he sees, then. . . ." I sighed. "Lapis blue and tangerine . . . " My mind was spinning.

Papa raised an eyebrow. My comment had obviously disturbed him. He looked at me quizzically. "Why are you thinking such thoughts, Marguerite?" he asked. "You have little experience with the complexity of an artist's mind." He lifted his finger and waved it at me cautiously.

"Papa, I meant nothing by it—it's only—" I stopped myself midsentence.

He looked at me carefully, as if trying to gauge the root of my curiosity. Then he spoke with a soft voice, but one full of warning. "Marguerite, you must realize I am in a unique position and one that requires tremendous sensitivity. Artists come to me because they know I will understand them. I may not have succeeded in my own painting career but I have great compassion for them." He paused and straightened his back. "I have *great empathy*."

"Yes, Papa." I managed to get the words out. My bottom lip was trembling.

Father placed the tinctures on a tray. "Vincent is not well, Marguerite. You should realize that. Before he came to me, he was in an asylum in Saint-Rémy."

I looked at Father blankly, trying hard to disguise my disbelief.

"He is under my care now. Let it be just that. He is a great painter, and I want to see him fulfill his potential. His brother Theo believes he is a genius, and I am beginning to suspect he is right." Father took a deep breath. "Regardless, you must accept that a man such as Vincent does not see the world like most people do."

I nodded and bowed my head.

There were pockets of time when I did see the world as Vincent's paintings portrayed—stitches of bright colors, voracious strokes of malachite green and peacock blue. I might be lonely in my solitude but my garden afforded me a palette of crimson and pale yellow in the summer and it made me appreciate the changing colors of the outdoors. Even after my rosebushes were cut back and our hedges trimmed for fall, I still rejoiced at the October foliage, when our chestnut trees turned copper and our tall oak trees swayed with red and gold leaves.

It was at the thought of November, however, that I could no longer share his vibrant vision. The wet stones of winter, the naked, shivering boughs weighed heavily on me. Our house became even darker, the walls even damper, and the lack of access to the outside world seemed even more intolerable.

I was curious how Vincent painted the winter. Did he continue to paint in colorful hues? Did he forsake his reds and greens, trading them in for a palette of the palest shade of blue and marble white? And how did he paint while he was in Saint-Rémy? Although Father had initially shocked me with his divulgence of Vincent's time in the sanitarium, the longer I thought about it, the less disturbing it seemed. For after all, Vincent appeared perfectly sane in my company. Perhaps he was a bit socially awkward on occasion, but his odd choice in clothes and his enthusiasm for painting seemed no less eccentric than my father's own behavior.

Papa continued to methodically work on distilling his tinctures. Hunched over the wooden table, with the stems of flowers before him, he could have been an artist arranging a still life. The long-nosed bottle of spirits might easily have been filled with turpentine; the mason jars could have been holders for his brushes and water. Watching Papa, I shook my head. I could not help but see yet another similarity between Papa and Vincent. They both seemed to have a genuine disregard for what others thought of them. Father pursued his homeopathy and love of painting with a passion I could not help but respect. He thumbed his nose at the classically bourgeois life and, much like Vincent, nothing else seemed to matter to him as long as he was doing what he loved most in the world. And although Vincent's paintings were infinitely better than Papa's, their enthusiasm for their respective passions was undeniably the same.

TWELVE

A Slip of Paper

On Tuesday, he arrived again at our house. I had heard Papa saying that Vincent might come that day, so I had spent most of the morning trying to make myself look beautiful.

I put on my pale green dress with the yellow ribbon at the hem and brushed my hair until my wrists grew tired. I took special pains to arrange the curls around my face, twisting and plumping them until my coiffure resembled one of the porcelain dolls I had been given as a child. I pinned my cameo on and sprayed some perfume behind my ears and neck.

As I had done nearly two days before, I bounded down the hall when the bell sounded his arrival. I could feel my heartbeat sounding through my bodice and my breath quickening as the bell rang again.

"Monsieur Van Gogh." I smiled as I opened the door for him. "We're delighted you could join us for another visit."

He looked frazzled, far more unnerved than the last time I had seen him. He was missing his overcoat and the smock he was wearing was soiled with paint stains.

"Finally a good day! Finally some sun . . . I painted Père Pilon's house in the rain and have been feeling under the weather ever since." He placed his paint box on the floor and adjusted the canvas that was strapped to his back.

I stepped aside so he could walk into the vestibule. He seemed slighter when I gazed at him from behind, as if he had the shoulders of a young man, perhaps Paul's age. I could see the perspiration beading on his neck, the tiny patch of freckles above his collar. I stepped closer to him.

"I've made some corn cakes this morning . . . would you like some before you paint?"

"Unfortunately, I must decline, mademoiselle. I've already had several cups of coffee and I'm eager to begin working."

"Oh, I see," I said, trying not to reveal my disappointment.

He turned to face me; the red bristles of his hair were matted in clumps and his eyes looked straight into mine.

"I want to finish the painting I began in your father's garden last week. I want to take advantage of the sunlight."

"Oh, yes," I tried to reply, though inside my stomach was churning. I worried that he might find the way I dressed silly. "Let me show you out." I motioned for him to follow me into the garden.

"Vincent!" Papa shouted as we walked through the gate. "So good of you to come by. It pleases me that you think my house a worthy perch for your easel." He patted Vincent on the back and I could see how the sheer force of Papa's hand caused his entire body to catapult forward. Papa turned to me. "We'll be taking our lunch outdoors today, Marguerite."

I nodded and excused myself. When I reached the door, I turned to see if Vincent was looking at me. But he was busy setting up his canvas. He hadn't noticed I was gone.

FROM the living room I watched them. Papa stood only steps from Vincent, his shadow blending in with that cast by the long, dark legs of Vincent's easel. His arms were crossed before him as he watched Vincent assemble his palette, squeezing the bladders of paint onto his large kidney-shaped board. The flicker of Vincent's palette knife—a flash of bright silver—moved vigorously over the pigments, blending them in what I imagined was a smooth, opaque consistency. The way melted chocolate or satiny lemon curd coats the back of a spoon.

I envied Father's proximity. No doubt he could see Vincent layering the colors, carving out the highlights with the tip of his blade. The other day, he had painted the cypress tree first, like a tall violent flame in dark bottle-green and olive strokes. Next came the spiky branches of the yucca in turquoise and sea-foam, the jagged edges outlined in Prussian blue.

Now he again painted with the same fury. He did not hesitate to apply the pigment directly onto the canvas, to drag it across until he had created the intended shape of leaf or flower. He painted wet on wet, until I could not tell where one color began and the other ended. That afternoon he added a flash of orange—painting the roofline of the houses on the street below. The sky he imagined was a thousand tiny strokes of cobalt and azure. It looked as though he had penetrated the impenetrable blue of the horizon, caught the impossible drizzling of rain.

I marveled at how someone could paint with such speed. I had watched other painters who came and visited Papa in our garden, and they all had devoted several hours to a single tree or a bush or even the bell outside the garden gate. But Vincent painted as though in a trance, the color leaping from his brush.

THEY ate their lunch alone, two men under the shade of our ancient trees, the summer light illuminating their helmets of strawberry-colored hair. Vincent tore hungrily from the baguette and seemed to eat far more heartily this light summer fare I had casually put out than the meal I prepared a few days before.

After coffee was served the two men excused themselves. Father informed me that they were going to the Ravoux Inn to look at some of Vincent's paintings, so I shouldn't expect him to return until late.

Vincent walked behind Papa, the soles of his shoes stepping delicately over the floorboards. Even his footsteps sounded like poetry to me—so much that they had a rhythm and uniqueness all their own.

I stood back next to the floral centerpiece in our hall, bursts of pink geranium and green belles of Ireland poking into my long cotton sleeves.

"Have a lovely afternoon," I said softly as Vincent approached my side.

He did not look up at me, though I noticed he seemed to slow his pace slightly.

I was unsure what was happening when I first felt his fingers reaching out to me, searching to find my own trembling hand.

"Take it," he whispered.

He slipped a piece of paper into my hand.

"For later," he said and his lips barely moved as he uttered the words.

I closed my fingers around the folded piece of parchment, the blood running through my veins with such velocity that I thought I might faint from the force.

By the time my eyes lifted, he was already down the hallway, close to Papa, who was now swinging open the front door. The daylight seemed blinding as I stood in the shadows of our dark, tenebrous house. I grasped the sight of him descending the stairs, enveloped by a single beam of light. I clutched the piece of paper to my breast and hurried, as fast as a hummingbird, to my room.

THIRTEEN

Muddied Hem and All

I WAITED to open the letter until after I looked out my bedroom window and saw that Papa and Vincent were well down the street.

I was trembling so much that the thin slip of paper nearly fell from my hands.

It did not take long to read it as there was only a single sentence.

I still intend to paint you, it said, in a perfectly scripted hand.

He left it unsigned but had drawn a small butterfly on the lower right-hand corner, coloring it in with a fingerprint of yellow paint.

That night I found I could not sleep. I left the letter on my nightstand so I could see it in the light of the moon. When morning came, I slipped it into my diary alongside the pressed poppy, each of its edges papery to the touch.

* * *

THREE days passed with no other word from Vincent. I began to doubt whether he would ever come, or whether his letter had been sincere.

But that Saturday the doorbell rang. I had been outside most of the afternoon sprinkling bonemeal on my rosebushes.

My breathing was heavy when I answered the door. There he stood as he always did with his spotted smock and his box of paints.

"I was wondering if you might sit for me this afternoon, Mademoiselle Gachet."

I had not been expecting him; I looked down at my dress. The hem was muddied and my hands were soiled from digging in the earth.

"I'm afraid I'm ill prepared to pose today, Monsieur Van Gogh. As you can see, I look like a potato farmer!"

He looked amused by my comment. "Not that you do, mademoiselle, but I've painted more than a few of those!"

"You'll have to let me change," I insisted. "Father would never let me pose looking like this. . . . I think the charwoman must look more elegant than I do today!"

"Your dress is white as those flowers," he said, pointing down the corridor to an arrangement of camellias in a blue and white Chinese vase.

"I've been meaning to paint you. . . ." He was stumbling over his words. "I hope you did not think I had forgotten." He took a deep breath and looked straight into my eyes. "It's only that I've been feeling so dark recently. This morning, when I awakened, I imagined you out there in your garden, you wearing a dress just like the one you have on now."

He extended his hand to touch the fabric of my skirt, and I, not being used to such forward gestures, found myself tripping over my hem as I backed away.

"Monsieur Van Gogh"—my awkwardness overcame me—"I don't think I could live up to your expectations as a model."

"Don't be ridiculous. If your father grants me permission, I will paint you just now. Muddied hem and all."

I THINK Father was taken off guard, just as I had been. Neither of us was expecting Vincent that afternoon, so his sudden appearance took us by surprise. Paul had been sketching Henrietta the goat since breakfast, and several pieces of paper were crumpled next to the garden chair where he had been sitting for most of the morning. His textbook remained on the low wooden stool untouched.

He stood up and greeted Vincent just as Father had. He carried his sketch pad with him, cocked under his arm, and wore a soft felt hat that flopped as he moved. Looking at him as he walked all gangly-limbed toward Vincent, I thought my little brother looked like a caricature—an awkward imitator of Vincent and Papa.

"Good afternoon, Monsieur Van Gogh." He tipped his hand to his head as though he were about to remove his hat, but then failed to do so. "I see you will be enjoying the visual delights of our garden." He swept his hand across the air as if implying that he was responsible for the beauty of the surroundings.

My brother sounded ridiculous using such formal language and adopting such airs, but I could see from the throbbing of his Adam's apple that he was nervous and trying, in his own way, to appear sophisticated.

"I, too, have been sketching," he said, extending his sketch pad. Vincent took a quick look at one of the pictures of the farm animals, and mumbled something about all things taking time and practice. I saw Paul's eyes fall.

"This isn't the time, Paul." Papa clicked his tongue to show his annoyance. "Monsieur Van Gogh has not come here to teach, but to paint and to recuperate. Isn't that right, Vincent?"

"I plan on painting Mademoiselle Gachet today," Vincent said, smiling back at me. "As long as the doctor doesn't mind."

Paul's left eye began to twitch, the lid fluttering like the wing of a magpie. I saw him kick the ground with his shoe.

"I'm insisting that she does not change. I want to paint her just as she is."

Papa suddenly looked alarmed. "You can't possibly want to paint Marguerite today!"

"Yes, I most certainly do."

"But I thought . . . I thought you might want to do a more formal sitting . . . a more—" Father stopped in midsentence. "Where do you want to paint her?"

"In the garden, near the rosebushes and the geranium blossoms."

Father nodded his head and sighed.

HE painted me in the midst of the garden, between two sections, where the turgid rosebushes intermingled with the vines. I covered my hair with a yellow bonnet and stood waist high among the blooming tendrils, my muddy hem cast behind a veil of forgiving shrubs.

That afternoon the light was golden, with the shadows of the chestnut trees casting long fingers on the lawn. I stood against one of the blue-stained posts that divided the terrace, staring into my garden. I knew where each bush began, where each set of roots mingled with its neighbor, and where one stem was blooming and the other was just about to bud. I felt the soft warmth of summer on my face and a soft breeze rustling across my bodice. I suddenly couldn't help myself from smiling. I was elated that Vincent had asked to paint me among the very things that I had spent years cultivating, toiling and tending with my own hands.

"Could you extend your hand, mademoiselle?" he called out from behind his easel.

I raised my right arm and opened my fingers slightly.

"Yes, that's it. . . ."

It was difficult to remain in this position for a sustained period of time, but I didn't want to disappoint him. So for nearly three hours I stood there, lowering my hand on occasion to avoid a cramp, but careful to resume the exact position I had held moments before.

He painted quickly, as he always did, his head popping out every now and then from his easel. His palette was suspended in front of him, the mounds of pigment piling over the canvas like rosebuds, his wrist flexing in an exuberant dance.

I wished that I could be in two places at once, still maintaining my position as his subject, but also seeing how he was progressing with the painting. I could not stop wondering what the finished canvas would look like. Would he simply try to capture my physical resemblance, or would he try to go beyond that and reveal something in me that I had not even seen in myself?

Father and Paul came out to the garden just as the sun was beginning to dip under the clouds. I could feel the moisture beginning to penetrate the air. The daylilies were beginning to close, and the crickets were beginning to chirp.

Vincent remained hunched behind the canvas. His oil rag was dropped on the ground and his brown boots were spotted in paint.

I felt as though my legs were about to crumble. I was exhausted but I refused to give in to my weary limbs. I would wait until he was done.

He did not announce when he was finished, though I knew both Papa and Paul were expecting a wild *"Fini!"* to emerge from his lips. Vincent did as I suspected he would. He placed his brush on the lip of his easel and stepped away and looked at the canvas. He nodded to me, then wiped his hands with a rag.

"Thank you, Mademoiselle Gachet," he called out. "I hope I haven't exhausted you."

"Oh, no," I gushed and I began walking toward him.

I came closer, my feet treading softly over the grass.

I was silent for several seconds as I examined the painting. It was not what I had expected. He had not taken pains to draw in my features, or to show the various planes of my face and the dips and curves of my figure. But he caught something of me, something more private—and less obvious than my physical countenance. He had portrayed me as I saw myself—waiting in my garden, my arm outstretched as if I were inviting someone to accept my hand.

The painting was quiet. Almost painfully still. I stood alone, my white dress submerged behind an audience of flowers and leaves, my hair and yellow hat flaming above my head like a halo.

"Does it please you, mademoiselle?"

I felt my body shiver as I tried to find the right words to reply. I did not know what I could say. I could not tell him that I thought he had made me look beautiful. I could not tell him that he had rendered my features in a most exacting manner. All of that would have been untrue.

"I look lonely," I said.

Before I had even finished, I saw Father's eyes condemning me. "Marguerite!" he blasted. "How dare you insult our guest!"

"I'm sorry, but . . ." I felt my face grow hot and the tears begin to pool in the rims of my eyes.

"You shouldn't be sorry," Vincent said to me quickly. Then he stated, "She's right. I have painted her alone." His voice fell hard against the last word. "A white pillar among a sea of vines and flowers."

Paul came closer to the canvas and squinted.

"Monsieur Van Gogh, I think you've forgotten to paint in her mouth."

Vincent looked sharply at my brother and his annoyance was palpable. "I have not forgotten anything! There are reasons for such omissions!"

I could see Paul's embarrassment immediately. Red streaks radiated up from his collar and his cheeks were flushed scarlet.

"Yes, yes," my father said appeasingly. "Of course there is a psychology to your paintings that might not be apparent to a less sophisticated eye. Please excuse my son's naïveté when it comes to painting. He is learning, after all."

Papa patted Paul on the back. "Vincent has done a marvelous painting of your sister."

Vincent's paint box snapped shut. He was kneeling on the grass collecting the odds and ends that went in his rucksack. But instead of acknowledging my father's remarks, I saw him look up from his things and sneak one last peek at me.

I was standing only inches away from him. His body was curled like a fiddlehead fern over his wooden painter's box and sack of things. As he rose, he reminded me of a sunflower, his straw hat rising as he straightened his spine.

"I would like to give you this portrait of your daughter," Vincent said reverently to Papa. "And also the painting I did last week of your garden."

The expression on Father's face suddenly changed. He was beaming at the prospect of obtaining some new paintings for his collection.

"You've been so kind in helping me here in Auvers. Since I cannot pay you your normal wage, I hope you'll consider these canvases a token of my appreciation."

Father took a firm hold of Vincent's hand. "It would be my honor," he said as he clasped his fingers around Vincent's. "I will display them proudly."

"I would also like to begin a portrait of you, Doctor. Perhaps an interior scene with you sitting at your desk. . . ."

Now Father's face became as rosy as a child's. He could not contain his delight.

"Oh, I'm so happy you asked, Vincent!" he said. "You just tell me the time and I shall make myself at your complete disposal."

"And perhaps another opportunity to paint your daughter again," he said, this time with a voice that was softer, perhaps a bit more nervous than when he asked Papa to sit for him.

"Marguerite? Again? You wish to paint Marguerite again?" Father was visibly perplexed. "Why, if you wish to paint another portrait after mine, Vincent, why don't you paint Paul's? He will be done with his exams in only a few short weeks."

Paul had been standing there the whole time almost motionless. After Vincent had seemed irritated by his comments about the painting of me, Paul had not uttered a word. Now, suddenly everyone went quiet waiting for Vincent's response.

"Out of no disrespect to you, Doctor, I hope you will allow me to pick who I wish to paint."

Father suddenly turned red, clearly embarrassed not only by his error, but also for his young son, who now seemed more pained than ever.

At that moment I too felt quite badly for my brother. I knew Father had embarrassed him with his presumptuous request, but even more humiliating was Vincent's obvious lack of interest in painting him.

But there was also something in me that felt strangely gratified to be the recipient of Vincent's attention. Paul had had years of coddling from Madame Chevalier, while she had treated me with complete disregard. And Papa's affection had always leaned toward my brother, especially now that he was trying to cultivate a certain artistic talent. So Vincent's kindness toward me was something that I relished, even if it did appear to upset Paul.

"Will you be needing anything else this evening?" Father was the one to finally break the awkward silence.

"I just want to thank you for allowing me to paint your daughter. It has been such a pleasure to be able to get back to my work and finally be inspired again."

I could feel Vincent's eyes stealing a glance at me.

I wondered if Father noticed, too, as minutes later, he motioned for Paul and me to go inside. "Children, if you'll excuse Vincent and me for a moment, I need to speak to him in private."

"Of course, Papa," I said demurely. I curtsied in Vincent's direction and said good-bye. Paul followed awkwardly behind.

Upon reaching the house, I turned to close the door behind us, but as I did, I noticed Papa reaching into his breast pocket and retrieving a glass vial. He pressed the flask into Vincent's hand. I saw Vincent shake his head and try to push the vial back into Father's hand, the two of them going back and forth like that for several seconds. Eventually, Vincent acquiesced. He placed the vial in his breast pocket and then he and Father walked down the garden stairs.

FOURTEEN

Foxgloves

It always amazed me how, despite the lovely weather we had in spring and summer in Auvers, the first floor of our house always seemed dark. The heavy wool drapes allowed little light to penetrate the rooms. The bric-a-brac of Father's keepsakes—his brass compasses, his antique stethoscopes, the left-behind figures that Cézanne had used in a still life—littered the shelves. There were canvases painted by Pissarro. One of chestnut trees poking through the fog, another of a ferry gliding through pewter waters. Crowded next to them were studies by Cézanne—a table full of apples and pears, a vase overflowing with white dahlias—and a painting of the houses on our street, the terra-cotta rooflines set against a blue-white sky. Father had hung these canvases so closely together that the room resembled the basement of the Louvre.

When sitting in our parlor, I always felt my lungs struggling to breathe. But Father's gloom was often more stifling than the clutter. There were times when no one from our household—including Madame Chevalier—could rouse him from his despair.

"I need my solitude! Can't a man have any peace?" he would holler at Paul or me if we disturbed him. He would sit for hours in the same parlor chair with the lamps unlit, a book half-opened on his lap, and his face turned away.

In the months before Vincent arrived, Father's bouts of depression appeared more frequently. If Father was truly as depressed as he appeared, his self-medication was obviously not working, and I could not help but wonder how Father could treat patients if he failed to successfully treat himself.

Sometimes his tinctures did prove effective and he would rebound with tremendous energy. He'd be so ebullient that neither Paul nor I nor even Madame Chevalier could match his desire for constant activity. But other times the medicine had the opposite effect: he would appear more agitated and nervous after taking his self-prescribed medicine. On more than one occasion, I caught him trying to control his shaking hands.

I noticed that, in the few weeks since Vincent's arrival, Papa had been making his foxglove tincture more regularly. I was not sure if he was making the herbal remedy for himself or for Vincent. But due to the volume of his production, I suspected it was for them both.

He would get up early in the morning and get out his jar of powdered leaves, his bottle of chloroform water, his solution of sodium carbonate. I would wander downstairs and find him at my worktable, shaking the solution under the haze of a kerosene lamp before eventually passing the liquid through a flannel sleeve.

The foxglove always made him temporarily energetic. He

would have bouts of productivity, when he would feel the need to rearrange his library or organize his collection of prints with an almost maniacal frenzy. I suspected he had given himself another dosage the night after Vincent painted me.

I had made a small quiche, with tiny roasted potatoes and haricots verts. It was not unusual that Father failed to compliment the meal. He rarely did, and I did not expect this time to be any different. What was different was how he continued to stare at me throughout the course of the dinner.

I noticed he lifted his eyes from his plate every few seconds. But he squinted as if scrutinizing me. I knew he was straining to see why Vincent had been so intent on painting me.

I kept my eyes firmly on the table and gave him no reason to find annoyance with me. Yet when the time came for me to clear the plates, he looked at me again, this time saying in a clear, sharp voice: "Have you heard, Marguerite? Vincent has promised to paint me, too."

I nodded to him and told him how pleased I was to hear such good news.

"He will do a portrait of me."

"Such an honor, Papa."

Madame Chevalier clasped her hands. "How wonderful, Paul-Ferdinand!" I could see her foot tapping against her daughter's leg underneath the tablecloth, prompting Louise-Josephine to applaud Father's good news.

"Yes, congratulations," Louise-Josephine said to Papa. She turned her head in his direction and lifted her eyes demurely to his. "*Maman* is right, it is quite an honor." She nodded her head to him and smiled before lifting her napkin to her lips, blotting them daintily before returning to her meal.

Papa nodded his head to Louise-Josephine and smiled back at her. He looked quite pleased with the respect that Louise-Josephine showed him.

"When does Vincent intend to come?" Madame Chevalier asked.

"He wants to start tomorrow. Last night when I walked him home he asked me to sit a few moments at the inn. He came downstairs and within a few minutes produced a brilliant etching of me on a tiny scrap of metal!"

"And again he wants to come tomorrow?" Madame Chevalier clucked her tongue. "He can't wait to paint you!"

She poured more wine into Father's glass. The black cloth of her sleeve dangled close to the rim. I could smell her toilet water—as her hand reached across to Papa—a combination of roses and clove. It was far too strong.

"He certainly is prolific," Papa continued. "He's been here two weeks and already several canvases completed!"

I saw Paul twist his mouth in a sour expression. "Doesn't seem quite normal to me," he said underneath his breath.

"One can never understand the artist's mind completely." Father looked squarely at him. He had obviously heard what Paul had muttered. "It is not for us to judge. . . . Anyway, I've just given him a dose of digitalis and that should help prevent any epileptic fits."

"Epilepsy?" I gasped. It was the first time Father had mentioned it and I couldn't hide my alarm. But the remark about the digitalis confirmed that he was giving the foxglove to Vincent as well. After all, I knew he made the medicine from the plant.

"Yes," Father said gravely. "He had several bad bouts of it back in Arles. Though it might have been a lingering effect of his absinthe addiction." Papa sighed. "Regardless, I promised his brother

I'd tinker with a little preemptive medicine. A little digitalis will help soothe his nerves . . . even I take it now and then."

He took another swallow of wine.

"I'm just relieved he seems to be so contented here. And now with another portrait in the works . . . of me, no less . . . he seems to be well on his way to complete recovery. I'll have to take a little credit for that!" He placed his glass down and winked at Madame Chevalier.

Father's boasting unnerved me. I stood up and began to clear the dishes. I had only made my first steps into the kitchen when I heard Louise-Josephine's footsteps behind me.

"You should be careful," she said. "Your father's possessive of Vincent. He suspects he's attracted to you." She was standing unusually close to me and her eyes seemed to reveal wisdom of someone far beyond her years.

I looked at her incredulously. "Why do you say that?"

"It's human nature." She tidied up the cutting board, brushing up the crumbs.

I wanted to ask her what she meant, but she answered me before I could.

"Your papa will make it difficult for any man to love you. He doesn't want you to ever leave this house. He relies on you more and more, and it will only get worse."

A few months ago, I would have been furious that she had the audacity to speak to me that way. But now I knew better. While our conversations were still infrequent, I now listened to her carefully. I was beginning to realize that when Louise-Josephine spoke, what she said usually ended up being right.

FIFTEEN

Stealing into the Night

My heart nearly stopped beating the evening I caught Louise-Josephine crawling out her window.

I had been in my room reading when I heard the sound of a window opening, then the crack of footsteps teetering on the ledge. I put my novel down and listened again. There was a rustle in the trees, yet it wasn't the sound the wind makes as it passes through branches, nor the sound laundry makes as it flutters on the line. If anything, it sounded like a small animal scampering to the ground.

I stood up and looked out the glass. There in the dark, I saw Louise-Josephine, clad in nothing but a housedress, crawling down the trellis of our front garden.

The white linen of her gown was whipping at her heels as she undid the latch of the gate. Her chestnut hair was undone and the wind blew it upward, exposing the nape of her neck, the cleft between shoulder blades. She was slighter than I and not as tall either, which made her appear much younger than her twenty-three years.

I remember she cast her eyes up toward the window of her bedroom before she slipped away. She did not turn around after that. She ran down the rue Vessenots, the white of her dress flashing like lightning against the sky.

I stood there gazing at her from my window, my breath forming clouds of steam over the pane. For a moment, I couldn't believe my eyes. Had Louise-Josephine really just escaped from her bedroom window and stolen off in the middle of the night?

I knew that she was not running away. She would not have left for good in such informal dress. She would have thrown on an overcoat and packed a bag if she were truly leaving us.

Suddenly, I was seized by the possibility that she had found someone in the village. I imagined her falling into his arms, his hands running down the back of her linen gown, her hair let loose like the sinewy fingers of seaweed. I wondered who he could be and where she could have met him. Hadn't her movements, her interactions with the villagers, been limited as mine and Paul's had? I was incredulous that she could have even had the opportunity to meet someone. Did she, a girl only two years older than me, already have a lover, when I had not even had my first kiss?

I found myself in her room that evening searching for clues. I had been inside her bedroom on very few occasions, never looking at anything too closely or staying for more than a moment. But as I now stood in her quarters, I noticed how, in contrast to my sparse room, she had littered hers with several collections she had accumulated over the years and had managed to decorate it in a unique style that was all her own.

I walked over to the simple pine chest where her toilette accessories lay. There was a small tortoise comb, a wooden brush, and a needle cushion. All of these objects were rather unremarkable, but next to them rested a small, beautiful box that Louise-Josephine had made in découpage. She had cut out small pictures of butterflies from old magazines, and applied them to the little case, varnishing them over with shellac.

On closer inspection, her room was full of curious things. There was an old rabbit with only one glass eye; a small ceramic turtle with a moonstone on its back. Then there was a small photograph of her mother on her nightstand. Its frame had originally been a simple wooden one, but Louise had glued several small glass marbles around its perimeter so that it now looked like it was bejeweled in aquamarine and amethyst stones.

I was overwhelmed by her obvious creativity. Despite her lack of schooling, she had managed to be far more inventive than either Paul or me.

I sat down on her bed and stretched my limbs. I felt the stitched pattern of the coverlet beneath my nightdress and the moonlight on my naked toes. I could hear Madame Chevalier's breathing coming from the adjacent room and marveled at either Louise's good fortune or her cleverness in choosing a night in which her mother wasn't shuttling off to Father's room.

I walked over to the window and noticed that Louise-Josephine had kept the pane slightly ajar. There was no rope, no ladder. Nothing except for the trellising that flanked the stucco façade of our house. How would she manage to return? Would she climb up the trellis or would she walk in through the front door?

Up until this evening, I had thought I was the only young girl in our household with a secret love. But now, I realized I was far from alone. Father, Madame Chevalier, and now Louise-Josephine all had theirs.

The irony was not lost on me. Our household, which took great lengths to maintain an appearance of bourgeois correctness, was in actuality teeming with clandestine love affairs and scandal. I cast my eyes around Louise-Josephine's room, pondered her empty bed, and felt as though I had just watched a party boat depart on the water while I had been left to remain alone on the dock.

It was at that moment I came to a decision. If I wanted Vincent to think of me as more than an acquaintance, I'd have to take my cue from the other women in my household. I had no choice, I would have to learn how to be more bold.

SIXTEEN

A Handful of Fireflies

LOUISE-JOSEPHINE returned at half past five, walking up the flight of stairs with velvetlike steps. I was barely awake when I heard her turn the doorknob to her room, and I had to rush to make it look like I hadn't been sleeping in her bed.

When she walked in and found me sitting on her bedspread, she nearly cried out from the surprise.

"Marguerite!" She forced her voice into a hushed tone. "You frightened me!"

"I'm sorry," I whispered back.

She remained at the threshold of the room. She had removed her housecoat and her nightdress fell over her body like a Grecian robe. Her chestnut hair was long and full over her shoulders, and her cheeks were flushed from the night air.

"What are you doing here?" Her right brow arched quizzically as she shut the door. "It's almost dawn."

"I know, I know," I responded sheepishly. "I saw you go out, and I waited up for you to return."

"You shouldn't have done that, Marguerite."

I could tell by the inflection of her voice that she was annoyed at me. She must have thought I had been spying on her.

"I only noticed you leaving by accident. I heard you climbing down the trellis, and when I approached my window, I saw you running down the street."

She was facing her nightstand now and quickly braiding her hair to put into her sleeping cap.

"I have less than two hours left to sleep, Marguerite," she said, turning now to face me. "I really don't need to explain myself . . . unless you're going to sit here and tell me you're planning on tattling to my mother."

"No, no," I hastily told her. "I would never dream of telling anyone."

She sat down on the bed and motioned for me to slide over.

"Then tell me," she whispered as she nestled into the covers, "why are you here?"

I was nervous in her company. I felt intimidated, though I knew that I should be the one who commanded respect. It struck me as ironic that I would feel more confident around Vincent than I would around Madame Chevalier's daughter.

I smoothed out my nightdress over my knees and slowly met her eyes. "I have come to you for advice," I started. "I have no one else to confide in."

Louise-Josephine's eyebrow arched quizzically. "Yes?" she asked. "What is it? You've succeeded in piquing my curiosity."

"I . . . I want you to tell me what it's like."

"What *what's* like?" She shook her head.

I placed my arm underneath my cheek. "Tell me what it's like to have someone to love."

I DID not allow Louise-Josephine to get much sleep that night, so exhausting was my bombardment of questions.

At first, she started out cautiously, revealing few details. But as the night progressed and she saw how little exposure I had had to such affairs, she began to relish telling me the details. She whispered as she told me about her love's stolen kisses and secret meetings, and the lustful feelings that overwhelmed her when she was by his side.

"Sometimes I feel like I can't breathe," she whispered. Her fingers traced her collarbone as she turned to face me.

"It was like that the first time I saw him. Your father was in Paris that afternoon and Mother had told me that I could wander in the fields behind our house." A mischievous smile crossed Louise-Josephine's lips. "But I had no desire to wander in the fields! I took the opportunity to go into town!"

I smiled. I was glad to hear that she had broken both my father's and Madame Chevalier's orders.

"I decided to buy a bar of lavender soap at the pharmacy. I had only a few centimes and that was all I thought I could afford." She took a deep breath and then exhaled as if she were relishing reliving the memory of their first meeting. "He was standing next to me at the counter. I turned and our eyes locked. His felt like a hot iron searing past the cotton of my dress, tiny needles tingling on my skin."

Her description sounded familiar to me. I didn't want to reveal that I, too, had felt the same way when Vincent first gazed at me, but I was desperate to confirm what I had experienced.

"I paid for the soap and tried to avert my gaze from him while I left the store," she continued.

"He followed me. Through the Place de Marie, even past the *boulangerie*. When I approached the hill near the Château Léry, I turned around and faced him.

"'Why are you following me?' I asked him. I was nervous someone might suspect I was living with your father and I knew how angry he'd be that I had betrayed his orders, so I looked him squarely in the eye and tried to sound intimidating. Inside, however, I was trembling. I clutched the package of soap to my chest in order to calm my nerves.

"'Because you're the most beautiful woman I have ever seen,' he said. 'Imagine I'm a honeybee, following my chosen flower. . . . Théophile Bigny,' he said as he took my hand and slowly pressed it to his lips. 'It is a pleasure to meet you.'"

A small smile crossed over Louise-Josephine's face as she recalled their first meeting. Her dark eyes reminded me of silky chestnuts, slick after the rain. And though most of her hair was pinned behind her nightcap, several soft brown ringlets now peeked through the sides. She looked beautiful.

"Have you seen him many times since?"

"Yes," she whispered, her pink mouth turning up slightly at the edges. "But you must swear on your honor that you'll never discuss what I've told you with anyone. Not Paul, not anyone!"

"No, no, never," I promised, pressing two of my fingers to my chest.

She curled deeper into the bed, and I could feel her breath close to mine. "Sometimes, one can't wait for love to find you. Sometimes one has to pursue it."

I smiled, implicitly thanking her for the advice and encouragement.

Her eyes were beginning to close now. "I need to get some sleep now, Marguerite," she said. My mind continued to race as I lay next to her. I suddenly felt guilty that I had never accepted Louise-Josephine as a sisterly presence—even a friend—all these years. I wanted to wake her up and apologize to her. Tell her how grateful I felt that she lived in our home.

I listened to the rhythmic undulations of her breathing and could not help but feel less lonely than I had when I tossed and turned in my own room. Still unable to sleep, I found myself observing her as she slumbered. I looked at her delicate profile. Her small upturned nose, her brown hair piled into her nightcap. She was so beautiful. Quite different from her mother, whose features were so severe.

Fearing that Madame Chevalier might grow suspicious if she saw me departing her daughter's room in the morning, I decided I should return to my bedroom. I carefully unrolled myself from the covers and tiptoed across her room.

From the window where Louise-Josephine had escaped a few hours before, I could now see the sun rising over the beet fields. The light in the sky was the color of ripe apricots and the thatched cottages looked aflame against the dawn. It would make a beautiful picture, I thought to myself as I turned back before leaving. I hoped that Vincent had also risen early that morning, so he too would see the beauty. I imagined him capturing it with his brushes and paint, like a child seizing a handful of fireflies.

SEVENTEEN

Like a Sister

VINCENT wasted no time in beginning his portrait of Father. He arrived the following morning full of energy and excitement.

"Good morning, mademoiselle," he said when I opened the door. "Your father is expecting me."

He was smiling in a way that I had not seen before and his pupils were widely dilated. I wondered if it was a result of the digitalis.

"Please, come in." I motioned. I took his hat from him and hung it on one of the pegs on our wall.

I had dressed differently that afternoon, as I knew that Vincent would be visiting us. The memory of having been caught unexpectedly in an old cotton dress—and being painted in it, no less—was still fresh in my mind, and I desperately wanted to make a more stylish appearance.

I had sewn a new yellow dress from a pattern I had seen in one of the monthly fashion magazines. The neckline exposed a little more décolletage than I normally revealed, but I sewed it anyway, thinking it might be a nice change from the high collar I typically wore.

That morning, I looked in the mirror and hardly recognized myself. The deep square neckline exposed an area of flesh that had rarely been exposed. My bosom peeked out from the trim like two ripe apples, and my neck seemed longer and leaner than before.

I hesitated, worried that this change of dress might appear immodest, but as I smoothed down the front plackets of the skirt, Louise-Josephine passed by my door and told me otherwise.

"You look so beautiful today, Marguerite," she said sweetly. She came in and stood by me.

Both of our reflections were now cast in the mirror: she small and petite with her black hair and dark eyes, and me tall and fair.

She took her hand and swept it across the box pleat. "It's a gorgeous dress. Is this the one you've been working on all week?"

"Yes," I replied. "I'm afraid it might be a bit too immodest to wear."

Louise-Josephine giggled. "Absolutely not! It's lovely and it suits your figure perfectly. You shouldn't be ashamed. There's nothing inappropriate about it."

I twirled around and the hem of my skirt lifted like a bell.

"He won't be able to keep his eyes off of you." She giggled again. "I bet he'll change his mind as soon as he sees you and decide he wants to do that second portrait of you instead of painting your father!"

"Oh, God, I hope not!" I shook my head and covered my mouth to hide my smile. "That would only make Papa angry!"

She shook her head. "You shouldn't worry so much. When I lived in Paris with my grandmother I spent the first three years living in fear of her. But when I was eleven years old I began to realize that there was little she could do to punish me. If I were to be banished to my room all day, how was that different from any other day? I was a bastard child with few prospects in life, so why not enjoy a certain amount of freedom? Those who might have a more secure station in life have more to lose." She looked at me and shrugged. "I have little."

I turned around and looked at her. I was shocked by her frankness.

"Don't look so surprised, Marguerite," she said. "I was eight years old when my mother left me to go live with your family. She packed up her small leather suitcase and kissed me on the forehead, telling me she'd be back within the year. She wasn't, as you know. . . ."

Louise-Josephine continued to stare ahead. "Luckily Mother had taught me to read when I was six years old, so I could find some sort of solace in the books she left behind. But otherwise I lived in a small, dank apartment with an old woman who thought very little of me. She constantly reminded me that I was the product of my mother's indiscretion. My grandfather had been a glassblower from Biot and had lofty dreams of creating glass chandeliers for the rich in Paris. He ended up dying a few years later from heart failure, leaving my grandmother in the capital with enormous debts and no source of income. Mother had little choice but to find some employment. Your father was a young medical student at the time and hired her to keep his apartment tidy. Before his engagement to your mother, she helped him maintain his office—she did menial housework; she assisted him with his files."

I'd always wondered how Papa came to find Madame Chevalier as our governess. Now I knew.

"I was born the year your parents married, and my mother stopped working for your father a month before their betrothal. I know few other details. I only know that your father has continued to be generous and supportive of us both. He sent my mother's salary from governing you and Paul directly to my grandmother so she never had to worry about rent or food. Sometimes he visited us when he was on business in Paris."

I raised an eyebrow. It seemed unlikely for Papa to make such a social call for people clearly beneath his social station and without any ties to the artistic world.

Was this the confirmation for what I had always suspected? Was Louise-Josephine my half sister, born before Papa and Mother married?

Secretly, I had always wondered about the coincidence of Louise-Josephine's name. Papa's father's name was Louis and his mother, Clementine-Josephine.

Louise-Josephine cleared her throat. She now had the ribbon around my waist and was in the process of retying the bow tighter.

"I am not telling you all of this so that you will pity me, Marguerite. I am telling you so you know why I believe in seizing adventure when it presents itself. You see, I have little to lose. I don't have a proper birth certificate and without the proper documentation, I will never be able to marry. It is Napoleonic law."

I had no idea about her predicament.

"I am sorry, Louise-Josephine," I said, gently reaching for her hand. "I have been selfishly complaining about myself when your life has been so hard."

She smiled and shook her head. "Your father has been generous with me, Marguerite, even if he prevents me from showing my face in public. I cannot deny that he has always in a strange way looked out for me."

I remained quiet as she continued.

"Just before I arrived here, your father arranged for me to assist a young doctor and his family on the Côte d'Azur. He paid for my train passage and even gave me a few extra francs for a new dress.

"Dr. and Madame Lenoir had two small girls and I helped mind them during the afternoon. They rented a small villa on the cliffs overlooking the sea and every room smelled delicious, like jasmine and tuberoses with a hint of the ocean just behind.

"This family was kind to me. They spoke to me as if I were their third daughter, including me in conversations about art and music. The husband gave me books from his own library to read; his wife always complimented me about my easy way with her children. I had never sat at a table with real silver and elaborate place settings and the wife gently instructed me so that my manners could improve.

"I was heartsick when it came time for me to leave and I secretly hoped that they would ask me to come and live with them back in Paris. But they didn't. When we parted, they kissed me gently on each cheek and wished me well. I can't tell you how heartsick I was when I left them and learned that I would have to come live here."

"How heartbreaking. You must have found your situation here absolutely unbearable."

"Yes and no, Marguerite. Here, your father has been generous in giving me a roof over my head, yet he keeps me away from the public eye in order to preserve his privacy. It is unfair and even cruel but, still, even with these restrictions, I have found Théophile. Life, you see, is not that bad." She placed her hands on my shoulders and smiled. "If a woman is truly clever, she can find freedom even in the most restrictive circumstances." She tapped the side of her head. "One just needs a little imagination and a little fortitude."

"I envy your creativity," I sighed—and I wasn't just speaking about the small knickknacks in her room. She had succeeded in duping Papa. And no one knew more than I that this was no small feat.

"Somehow you've maintained your optimism while living here. It's remarkable."

She let out a small laugh. "Never mind about me, Marguerite. Go now and prepare the downstairs, he'll be here any moment!" She took out a small coin-sized tin from her pocket and undid the lid. Inside was a pale pink wax.

"Here," she said. "One last thing . . ." She dipped her finger into the salve and rubbed a little into my lips and cheeks. "You look a little brighter now."

I took one last glance in the mirror and straightened the pins that held up my hair.

"You've been like a sister to me these past two days," I whispered and took her hand in my mine. "Thank you."

She said nothing, but she squeezed my hand tightly in hers. And, in my heart, I knew what she was trying to say.

EIGHTEEN

A Symbol of Modern Man

THE dress clearly had the desired effect on Vincent. As I showed him into the garden, I could see that he could not take his eyes off of me.

"You look different this afternoon, mademoiselle," he said as we walked down the hall. "Even more radiant than before."

I smiled back at him and smoothed out my bodice-hugging dress with my palms.

Vincent appeared at ease. He spoke of eating an almond pastry with great relish earlier that morning. "We Dutch don't have pastries like you French!" he laughed and flicked a finger in his beard as if to ensure there weren't any embarrassing crumbs lurking in his patch of red whiskers. "I should have saved my sous for a tube of malachite green, but one must succumb to the seduction of the bakery shop every now and then, *non*?"

I giggled. "Monsieur Cretelle has the best in town. We would be lost without his croissants."

Vincent smiled. Our exchange was light and cheerful and it filled me with such temporary happiness, I would have done anything to prolong it. But the distance from the house to the garden was a short one. I slowed down as we approached the entrance. It was not I who pushed open the gate. It was Vincent. I did not want to leave him.

FATHER had been waiting in the garden for Vincent to arrive, and he sat at our red picnic table with one hand forlornly placed on his cheek, the other resting at his side. He was brightly dressed in a cobalt blue smock and a voluminous scarlet bow. His strawberry hair was covered by a cotton-white cap.

I could tell by the slow, nearly silent way Vincent approached Father that he had already found the pose he wanted. There, sitting before him, was Papa, looking sad, melancholy, and preoccupied with his thoughts.

When Father finally heard the rustle of Vincent and my footsteps, he looked up half-startled and rearranged himself.

"I didn't hear you arrive!" he said, and one could detect that he was taking special pains to make his voice sound in high spirits. "You surprised me, Vincent! I was just dozing off."

Vincent took his rucksack off his shoulder and placed his paint box on the grass.

"I'm happy I did. I was able to catch you in a natural setting . . . see you lost in thought. I think I'd like to paint you in that same pose."

Father's brow wrinkled. "I'm not sure I want to be portrayed napping, Vincent!"

Vincent combed his fingers through his hair and squinted into the sun. "This will not just be a painting, Doctor. It will be a symbol . . . a commentary on the modern man and the conflicts that plague him."

Father seemed impressed. "Me as a symbol, eh? Your brother sent me a copy of Monsieur Aurier's article on you. If I am to be one of your symbols, you're bestowing on me a great honor!"

I could see Vincent felt uncomfortable lavishing any unnecessary flatteries onto Papa. He mumbled something about not choosing his symbols but them finding their way to him.

"We'll need to get to work now." His voice suddenly became loud as if he were barking an order at Papa. "The sunlight's perfect. I want to move quickly before I lose my train of thought."

Papa agreed.

I could see how excited Father was to begin. He smoothed out his smock and ran his hands over his cheeks. "This will be an important day!" he told Vincent as he watched him set up his easel and paints.

"Will you need anything before I return to the house?" I asked both of them. Father shook his head but Vincent turned toward me and asked me to come closer.

Father had already sat himself down again at the red picnic table. So I now stood a few meters away from him, next to Vincent, who was adjusting his canvas on the lip of his easel.

"Mademoiselle," he said softly, and I could see that his gaze did not rest entirely on my eyes as it had in recent encounters. Now it seemed to travel from my collarbone to my breasts, just as it had in the hallway. "If it's no trouble to you, I will need you to bring two books from your father's library. Look and see if he has copies of *Manette Salomon* and *Germinie Lacerteux*. But if you can't find the novels on his shelf, bring him any by the de Goncourts." He folded his hands behind his back and looked around. "Also, Marguerite, might I have a small drinking glass filled with water?"

I nodded my head to show him I understood his instructions.

"You are a big help to me," he said, to which I lifted my chin and looked directly at him. This time, however, I was certain I was not imagining the connection between us.

"I will be back in a few minutes, monsieur," I replied, and as I turned, I saw Father give me a disapproving glance.

"Don't keep us waiting! Vincent and I have a lot of work to do!"

I RETURNED quickly with what he had requested. I knew Papa's library like the back of my hand, having dusted those shelves one too many times. The ocher spines of the two novels were split from countless readings during Papa's bachelor days. I myself had read both of them. *Manette Salomon* was one of Father's favorite novels, as he likened the story, which revolved around a group of artists living in midcentury Paris, to be similar to his *vie bohème* days. His love of *Germinie Lacerteux* was also evident by the subject matter. The novel traced the fatal decline of a working-class woman through her trials with alcoholism, tuberculosis, madness, and eventually death. In general, any novel where one of the characters suffered from melancholy fascinated Papa. Germinie, like Flaubert's Emma Bovary, was the embodiment of this affliction. It was no wonder the cover of this novel was worn thin.

After obtaining the novels and fetching the glass of water for him, I brought everything out to Vincent.

"Thank you, Marguerite," he said as soon as he saw me.

"I found the novels you requested," I said.

His face was flushed with excitement. "Excellent. Excellent. Art and neurosis!" he said, referring to the books. "The two things your father knows best!" He let out a small laugh. "Would you be kind enough to put them down next to your father?"

I quietly walked over to Papa, who continued to stare at me with fixed eyes, and placed both the water glass and the books down.

"Now, if I could trouble you with finding me one more thing . . . could you pick me two stems of foxglove?"

I knew Father would not be happy if I went into his medicinal garden without his permission, so I looked over in Papa's direction and asked him if it would be alright.

I could tell by the strained way in which he answered me that he was less than pleased that I would be entering his private garden, but he did not want to appear rude in front of Vincent. So he reluctantly agreed.

It was only a few meters away from the picnic table, fenced off by a small border of white posts. The foxgloves, being among Papa's most frequently used herbs, grew abundantly in the left corner. I lifted the hem of my dress and knelt down, careful to pick two stems with several lavender bellflowers.

"I will come and see if you would like lunch in a few hours," I told them as I placed the foxgloves on the table next to the glass and stack of books.

They each nodded to me and I smiled a little as I left, leaving Papa to be immortalized, just as he had always dreamed, in a canvas full of creamy paint. Finally, the symbol of all great men—his conscience weighted, his spirit full of melancholy. He was no longer just Gachet the doctor, the collector—he was now included in an exalted circle: a temperamental artist and a deep thinker. Papa beamed.

VINCENT spent several hours on the portrait, painting at his usual lightning speed. He had Papa lean his head on one hand and rest his other palm on the table. Eventually Father's face softened from the energetic mask he wore when guests arrived to the one he wore in private. It was a tired, sadder expression and that made him appear lost in thought.

Only after Vincent had finished could I detect the rapid, intense brushstrokes that ran across the painting. My first impression upon looking at the painting was that it seemed as if Vincent had taken a scalpel with paint on the end and carved the frustration that emanated from Papa into every one of his features: his hands, his long face, his mournful eyes.

Papa's skin was layered in yellow and taupe, and accented in puce. He looked unhealthy; the sockets of his eyes were hollow and underscored in green. Vincent had used a palette that was full of different shades of ultramarine. Papa's dark blue smock was executed in a repetition of deep indigo and gray. One lapel curled into the other; the three round buttons popped out in apple green.

The flame of Father's hair peeked out from underneath his white cap. His nearly white hands rested like a monk's on a burning red table. And his eyes looked out into a corner of nothingness, while the two de Goncourt novels shone in bright yellow and the blooming foxgloves twisted in a glass jar in the foreground. Years later when I looked at the painting I wondered if the placement of the herbs—an allusion that a tincture was imminent—was meant for Father or for Vincent. I was never sure.

NINETEEN

The Isolated Ones

VINCENT stayed for dinner that evening. The wet canvas was taken upstairs to Father's studio to dry. Papa showed Vincent some more of his prints while I prepared supper.

Madame Chevalier and Louise-Josephine remained, as per Father's orders, behind the closed doors of their bedrooms and Paul was in the parlor with his sketch pad and paints. Like me, he had dressed up for Vincent's arrival, though I knew that Vincent had said nothing to him since he arrived that morning. Nonetheless, Paul waited patiently on the couch near the fireplace, his black hair and goatee shiny from pomade, his exuberant bow of red silk tied underneath his chin.

He had been fussing over his sketches far longer than it had taken me to prepare our meal. When I went into the parlor to escape from the heat of the stove, I found him with his face scrunched up and his fingers nearly breaking the vine of charcoal.

"You've been quite industrious today, Paul." I sat down beside him and placed my feet on the small cushioned stool.

He looked up and, still, his face did not soften.

"I've been trying to do an interior scene all afternoon, but I've had no luck with the perspective." He took the pad and turned it to me. "I will have to leave it for the moment and get back to studying for my exams."

"At least you're starting to realize what you need to work on," I said, trying to sound positive, though I could clearly see that the lack of perspective was not the only problem with the sketch.

He seemed to grunt when I said that, as if I had just made him feel worse. He took the pad and leafed three or four pages back and lifted the corner. "Look, I have done several other sketches of the same scene, but each one is as bad as the one before!"

"Oh, Paul . . ." I sighed. "You shouldn't make yourself feel bad about this. Look at Papa. He always wanted to be a painter, and although he wasn't talented enough to become a professional, he's still having quite a run at being a dilettante."

"I'm not like Papa. I will not be satisfied just with being a dabbler!"

There was something noble in how Paul desperately wanted to push himself. But he lacked practicality.

"Have you seen Vincent's painting of Papa?" he asked.

"Yes, it is not like anything I've ever seen before," I told him. "He uses color almost as metaphor, and everything from the objects in the foreground to the expression on Papa's face is symbolic of something. I am not even sure I understand it all."

"I found this over there." Paul pointed to a small table next to the upholstered chair. He handed me a torn-out magazine article entitled "The Isolated Ones: Vincent van Gogh" written by the critic Aurier.

"Have you read it?" I asked quietly.

"Yes." Paul made no attempt to lower his voice. "It praises him. It says he belongs to a new movement of symbolists."

I held the article in my hands and tried to read it quickly. I knew I would have to return to the kitchen shortly.

"Papa will be angry if he sees it's missing. You should put it back where you found it."

Paul shrugged his shoulders. "I'm not sure what all the fuss is about." He placed his pad down beside him and took the article from me, placing it on the table next to the chair.

"So you never answered me. Did you like the painting of Papa?"

I stood up, anxious to get back to my cooking. "Like it?" I repeated his question. "I think he captured a side few people have seen of Papa."

"Really?" he said, seeming intrigued. "I want to see it!"

"Perhaps you should wait until after dinner," I tried to caution him. "It's probably better to wait to be invited, rather than to barge in when he and Papa are discussing things."

"Papa won't mind," he snapped. "What's wrong with a son visiting his father unannounced?"

"It is not Papa who might mind," I said softly. "I was thinking about Vincent."

TWENTY

Permission

I'M not sure what happened when Paul went upstairs to Papa's studio. I only know he returned quickly and with an even more sour look on his face than before. I, however, had little time to talk to him. I was finished with the cooking and had just rung the small bell we kept outside the dining area to signal dinner was served.

I was placing a bowl on the table when Vincent and Father appeared. Paul had come a few seconds earlier and was already standing by a chair.

"Sit here," Papa said to Vincent, pointing between him and Paul. I returned and took the only remaining seat, which, although it was not next to Vincent, was directly facing him.

I had not changed out of the yellow dress I had worn all afternoon, and my skin was now damp from having been next to a hot stove for so many hours.

I tried not to appear self-conscious, but with Vincent sitting across from me, it was hard to escape his eyes. He ate sparingly, seeming to spend more time looking up from his plate than putting a morsel of food on his fork.

It was difficult for me to raise my head and meet his gaze because I felt Papa's eyes equally heavy on me. I am not sure if he noticed that I was acting differently or if he noticed that Vincent seemed unable to stop looking at me. All I know is he tried his best to distract his patient with endless conversation.

For nearly a half hour, Papa asked him questions about his time and his paintings in Saint-Rémy, especially one called *L'Arlésienne*. He wanted to know about what inspired him there, and whether he wanted to paint similar subjects while he was in Auvers.

"My friend Paul Gaugin," he said after swallowing a glass of wine, "did a painting while we were in Arles called *Christ in the Garden of Olives*. I did not understand it at first, but it haunted me all the same. Now, today, when I painted you, I did not draw upon that which I already knew when I painted my Arlésienne." Vincent paused to take another sip and made a quick glance at me. "Instead, I sought to answer the questions I had about my friend's painting of Christ. How does one paint beauty, using color and creating an aesthetically satisfying painting, while also alluding to despair?"

Papa nodded his head and chuckled. "You're both a psychologist and a painter. You've succeeded in making every impressionist painter look lazy!"

"I cannot succeed in what I've set out to do without looking into the soul of the person I paint. I would rather paint a landscape than a person who doesn't interest me psychologically."

I could have anticipated Paul's interrupting Vincent even before he opened his mouth.

"How can you tell who's interesting and who's not?"

Vincent spoke without turning to him. "I can tell by looking behind the eyes," he replied. "Far too often, there's nothing there."

"But that can't be your only criterion, Monsieur Van Gogh. . . ."

Vincent still did not turn to him.

I did not want to look at Paul. I knew he was trying to formulate why Vincent had not yet asked to do a portrait of him. He was now grasping at straws, trying desperately to unlock what it took to be painted by Vincent.

"Sometimes people are shy. Sometimes they just hide behind awkward masks. . . ." He was using everything he could to engage Vincent.

"That may very well be true," he finally replied to Paul, with little compassion in his voice. "But an artist knows almost instantly what will inspire him and what won't. I would never even begin to paint something that did not immediately excite me. To tell you the truth, I prefer to paint that which doesn't naturally draw attention to itself. I would prefer to paint a farmer, an average postman, or a common barmaid than paint a beautiful aristocrat. I would like to think of myself as seeing what eludes the average eye—to show that there is great beauty in what is normally overlooked."

When Vincent said this, I could not stop the smile from crossing my lips, even though I knew I should be more sensitive to my brother's feelings. Vincent thought *I* possessed something special! It was the first time I felt a form of self-satisfaction and I nearly burst out giggling from the sheer joy of it. If neither Papa nor Paul had ever seen that I had something unique, Vincent at least had!

My brother was not used to me receiving any attention, and it clearly disturbed him. For Vincent to have painted our father was one thing, but for me to be among his chosen subjects was a huge needle in Paul's side.

Already his annoyance was visible. His face appeared to swell like a chestnut soufflé, accentuated by the billowing silk of his scarlet foulard. Things were only made worse when Vincent mentioned he wanted to do a second portrait of me.

"I have been meaning to ask you, Doctor," he began politely, "if I might not return and do that second portrait of Marguerite."

Father looked up from the table, clearly surprised that Vincent had been sincere when he had first mentioned it. I too could hardly believe my ears and as Vincent continued, my heart began racing and my face grew hot and red.

"She was such a moving subject, and I have already written my brother that I imagine painting her sitting at the piano."

Papa did not answer him at first. I could see him moving his vegetables across his plate with a fork, contemplating how he was going to reply.

"Our Marguerite is so busy these days with the garden and with her chores around the house," he said dryly. "Since her mother died, we've always relied on her to manage the house while I attend to my patients and my clinic in Paris. There is little time for her to do anything else." Papa cleared his throat but continued: "By late next week, Paul will be done with his studies and home full time; you might want to consider painting him."

I looked over at Vincent and at my brother Paul. Both were staring blankly at our father. He had already suggested Paul once before and had been rebuked.

"Forgive me, Doctor. I would like permission to paint your daughter at her piano. I mean no disrespect to you or your son. It is only that I have already envisioned the painting of Marguerite at the piano and will have little rest until I complete it." He paused. "As fellow artists, I'm sure both you gentlemen can understand what that's like."

Father let out a small sigh and placed his hands on his lap. "Very well, Vincent, in a few days' time you can paint Marguerite. But in the meantime, I urge you to paint some more of our beautiful surroundings."

"I will," he answered Father quickly. "Tonight I'm planning to paint your local church." He turned and took a glance outside the window. "The moonlight should be perfect in a few hours."

"Vincent's father was a minister," Papa said, addressing Paul and me. "His brother told me Vincent nearly became a man of the cloth at one point."

"Now I am just a man that uses cloth," he said with a chuckle.

I covered my mouth and giggled. Paul and my father remained unamused.

"I look forward to seeing how your painting turns out, Vincent," Papa answered. "I'm glad that you've been so prolific since you've come to Auvers."

Vincent smiled. "I had no idea I would find the north so inspiring." He exhaled. "As long as I have something to paint, my attacks will hopefully be kept at bay."

"That's what I've said all along!" Papa agreed excitedly. He tapped Vincent on the shoulder. "Just remember before you leave tonight, I have your weekly vial of medicine." He lowered his voice slightly. "I certainly wouldn't want you to leave here without that."

TWENTY-ONE

An Adventurous Spirit

THAT night I could hardly contain my excitement to tell Louise-Josephine what had happened. I had barely finished explaining what had transpired over dinner when she suddenly perked up.

"If you know that he will be painting the village church this evening, then you must sneak out and visit him there."

Her eyes were bright with a sudden devilishness and I could see how her mind was spinning just trying to plot the logistics.

"It will be too difficult," I whispered. "And anyway, he hates to be disturbed when he is painting. I wouldn't want to distract him."

"No, no," she agreed with me. "Go a little later when you suspect he will be finishing. You can wait in the bushes until you see him begin to pack his things up!"

It was a masterly plan and it made me reaffirm, again, what an invaluable ally she was to me.

"You really think I should go?" My voice was shivering from the thought of doing something so secretive, so romantic.

"Absolutely," she said without hesitation. "You have to! It will be the only time you'll have the opportunity to see him alone."

I was filled with excitement at the prospect of sneaking out the window just as Louise-Josephine had and meeting Vincent underneath the stars. I only wondered if it would be unwise to surprise him.

"He'll think you have an adventurous spirit."

She took hold of my brush and gently pushed me toward the bed and sat me down. With her small nimble hands she quickly unpinned my hair and began brushing it furiously.

"I think you should wear your hair down," she said as she held a thick chunk of it between her fingers.

Indeed, it did feel luxurious on my shoulders, and the mere weight of it forced me to hold my head straighter.

I took one of the ash-blonde locks and twirled it around my finger.

"You look beautiful, Marguerite," she said and she handed me a mirror. I held it close, barely recognizing myself in its reflection.

She took a pot of lip rouge from her pocket and undid the lid.

I was so excited about the nascent possibilities of that evening. I did not know if I would be successful in sneaking out of our house, and if I was, whether I would be able to see Vincent at all. But without Louise-Josephine's encouragement, I would have never had the courage to try either.

So much adrenaline rushed through my veins that evening. Louise-Josephine stayed with me as we waited to hear Father and Madame Chevalier go to sleep and, finally, to hear the end of Paul's footsteps pattering around his room below.

"We must wait to make absolutely sure everyone's asleep before you sneak out," she warned.

We waited, speaking in hushed voices and keeping our ears attuned to every sound that echoed through the house.

Finally, when nearly a full hour of complete silence had passed, Louise-Josephine whispered to me her secret for scaling down the trellis.

"You mustn't wear shoes," she said solemnly, holding one finger to her mouth. "They will only increase the noise and inhibit your flexibility." She looked down at my feet, which were in tightly fitted ankle boots.

"Go barefoot and then slip into your garden shoes by the gate."

I knelt down to untie my boots as she continued on with more important details of my imminent escape. Over the past few months she had become masterful at sneaking out of our house. She knew which rail squeaked and which stone made a sound when you walked on it. She even knew how to turn the latch of our gate without making a noise.

"There is an extra key in the flowerpot by the door," she told me carefully, drawing a diagram of our front lawn with her finger. "Use that to get in when you return and drop it back in the morning after breakfast."

I nodded my head, but felt that my head might explode from all the information she wanted me to command to memory. I could feel myself starting to panic, and when I pushed the hair away from my face, I'm sure Louise could see I was terrified.

"I'm not sure I'm capable of doing this," I muttered. "What if Papa discovers me?"

"He won't," she said reassuringly. "He and Mother sleep soundly. You must trust me, I've done this at least a dozen times. . . ."

I nodded my head in assent. My shoulders were trembling underneath my gown and my heart was racing.

"Don't worry so much, Marguerite," she said, placing her hand over mine. "The first time it's petrifying, but you'll soon find it's not so hard!"

I shook my head in disbelief. "I wish I had your courage," I whispered.

She tossed back her long black hair and smiled. "Marguerite, you've already proven that you do."

TWENTY-TWO

Rendezvous

It was eleven o'clock when I began my descent from Louise-Josephine's window. I wore a simple blue cotton dress and my hair swept loose.

I stood there barefoot, waiting as she quietly undid the latch and opened the window.

"Hold on to the ledge when you first secure your footing," she warned as she helped lower me down. I held on to the stone lip with one hand and to her tiny fingers with the other, watching her face without blinking as I lowered myself to the garden below.

She was right about the added agility from going barefoot. I was able to lock my toes around the wooden slats and claw my way down. Louise-Josephine continued to watch me as I made my way through the garden, and did not close the window until I slipped safely through the front gate.

With my garden shoes inelegantly cloaking my feet, I lumbered down the rue Vessenots. I had never been outside our house at such a late hour, and I reveled in the silence of our village. The moon illuminated the limestone farmhouses, and the daylilies that grew by the cobblestone streets were as tight as fists.

The warm balmy breeze penetrated the cotton weave of my dress, and my breasts revealed my excitement. There was something so liberating about having my hair loose and my bare feet slipping against the soles of my woven garden sandals. The air was heavy with the perfume of jasmine and roses as I headed down the street. I could see the stone bell tower of the church and wondered if he would still be there working under the white globe of moonlight, his canvas already heavy with paint.

It took me nearly twenty minutes to reach the center of town, and I tried to catch my breath before making the final ascent to the church. I smoothed down my hair with my palms and patted my neck with my handkerchief. I could see the faint outline of his body as I began walking up the hill to the church's entrance. He was hunched over his easel, the cuffs of his smock cloaking his hands.

I dared not approach him as he labored furiously over the stretchers. I took a step backward and camouflaged myself among the poplar trees.

It was such a joy to watch him work. He mixed his pigments expertly, squeezing his bladders of paint onto his palette with deliberation and care. He took not only brushes to his canvas, but also alternated between sweeping the canvas with a thin piece of willow and at other times cutting through the paint with a blade.

I waited, watching him for nearly an hour as he painted the ominous spire of the church, its dark, hollow windows, and the crouching gargoyles from above. Only when he had stepped back from the canvas and begun packing up his satchel did I finally approach him. And even then, I trembled with fear.

"Vincent," I said with a hushed voice.

He looked up from his canvas, alarmed that someone was whispering his name.

"I hope you're not angry that I came." I stepped out from behind the trees.

To say he was surprised was an understatement. He could barely speak when he saw me there, standing in front of him like an unkempt mermaid with my downswept hair.

"I nearly did not recognize you," he said, stuttering to overcome his shock. "I was not expecting visitors this time of night." He wiped his palette knife with a rag and placed it on the lip of his easel and smiled.

I took one step closer and stood there looking first at him, then at his painting.

It was darker than I expected. Most of his other paintings had been full of high tones of bright yellow, green, and white. But this one, with an opaque whale-blue sky and violet stones, sent chills down my spine.

I stepped another foot closer to him; the edge of my arm grazed his as I moved closer to see the painting. There was something skeletal about the bones of the church, the sharp jagged outlines, and the tower that nearly pierced the cobalt sky. He seemed to capture the church as if it were frozen. Blue-white, dove-gray—it was completely devoid of light except for the patch of flame that rose from the roofline.

There was a curious forked path in the front that was accented by quick staccatos of brown and yellow. To the left, he had drawn the figure of a Dutchwoman with a pointed white hat, gathering her skirts and hurrying past darkened windows.

"Who is she?" I asked, pointing to the figure. "I've lived here all my life and have never seen a Dutchwoman scampering around our church in the middle of the night."

He seemed to be taken aback by my question, as if it made him uncomfortable.

"There's no need to tell me, " I said softly. I was sure he now thought me rude.

"No, that isn't it," he answered. "I suppose I'm just pleasantly surprised that such insight could come from a girl who, as you say, has lived in Auvers her whole life."

He looked at me and smiled.

"You are right to suspect the figure is a symbol," he said. "I once considered a life in the clergy but was rejected by the Church."

He said no more but it was obvious whom it really was passing to one side of the road, the one that led away from the church's entrance.

"I read the Aurier article, and they're saying in Paris you're one of the great symbolists."

"You read that article?" He seemed surprised yet visibly pleased. "Well, then, you already know I often place symbols in my paintings."

"Like literature!" I said enthusiastically.

"Yes, just like literature, Marguerite." He paused.

"Then there was a specific reason you placed the foxgloves and those two books in Father's portrait. . . ."

"Yes. There was," he answered but he did not elaborate any further, as I hoped he would.

There was silence between us. I became concerned that I had begun a conversation I was not intellectually prepared for. I understood the notion of symbols and metaphor but anything beyond that was treading foreign ground for me.

I stood there shivering as the night grew colder. Staring at the dark, swirling canvas before me, I clasped my fingers around my arms and pulled them close to my chest.

"Does your father know you are out this late?" Vincent asked as he unbuttoned his smock and handed it to me. He was looking at me intensely, his eyes steadfast on mine.

I slipped my shoulders into his smock and inhaled the heady smell of turpentine and perspiration.

"No," I said, shaking my head. "I snuck down the trellis to come see you."

"To see me?" He chuckled. I could see he was delighted with my response.

"Yes," I replied. "I wanted to see you paint."

"You placed yourself in such great risk just to see me paint, Marguerite?" he raised his eyebrows. "That's quite brave of you."

"Well . . . I . . . ," I stammered. "I also wanted to see . . ."

"Yes?" he asked, stepping closer to me. I could smell the scent of his skin. It reminded me of the forest, high and green. Pine and juniper wood combined.

Suddenly I felt dizzy. He was no more than five inches away from me, and the air that separated us seemed laced with tiny magnets that forced us closer.

"You've got your hair undone," he said. His soft breath seemed to caress my cheeks.

I looked up and smiled at him. He took his finger and rested it beneath my chin, lifting up my head to meet his.

His hand rested underneath my chin for several seconds, and the soft fingertips of his other one stretched toward my neck.

My eyes must have been closed when he kissed me because I have no memory of his eyes, only his lips placed on mine. It was soft and gentle at first, a peck that one might give a small, fragile child. But soon his mouth enveloped mine more passionately and I found myself echoing his movement, my own fingers reaching into his back and clawing up the sides until I reached the top of his shoulders. He returned my kiss more powerfully. His hands, no longer cradling my chin and ears, now slipped over my shoulders. He unbuttoned the top of the cloak, kissing the top of my breasts with a gentle press of his lips.

His hands began to search through the fabric of my skirt, rustling through my petticoat. I felt the warm sensation of his hand on my leg, the grasping of the flesh between his calloused fingers. I could barely stand when he touched me there. I could feel myself collapsing into him. But a voice in my head warned me to stop.

"Vincent," I said, leaning slightly away from him. His hands immediately dropped from where they were, and cool air suddenly seemed to billow up my skirts where his palms had been moments before.

He pulled away from me and pushed his hands through his red hair, which was now standing in all directions from where my fingers had just run through it.

"I—I'm sorry," he said.

I was once again shivering from the cold air snaking across my skin. "There is no need to apologize," I said. "It's only I have so little experience in these sorts of things." I paused. "Well, none, actually."

I had been raised not only to be chaste but to be completely unavailable to the opposite sex. Now I had betrayed not only Father's wishes but also what I thought was expected of girls of my social background. Yet, if I were to be honest, I was secretly thrilled that I had the capacity for such adventure.

"It was wrong of me. You're so much younger than I, and I should know better than to jeopardize things with your father, when he's been so kind to me."

I nodded my head.

I could feel my embarrassment creeping up my neck in long, red strokes. My face, too, reddened from the uncertainty I felt in my actions.

"I see," I said, smoothing out my skirt. "Perhaps it was a mistake then."

"No. I wouldn't call it a mistake, Marguerite."

Again I looked at him for clarity.

"It's just there is truth to what you said. We should take this more slowly. In light of my . . . past . . . I will need to gain your father's confidence if there's to be a more permanent relationship between us."

I smiled again in understanding.

"Look here," he said, suddenly taking out his sketchbook from his rucksack. He shuffled through the pages until he found a sketch of me, one where he imagined me sitting at my piano.

"I want to paint you seated at your piano. Then perhaps a third portrait of you . . . maybe illuminated as Saint Cecilia, at the organ with stephanotis in your hair. You are so much like her—so musical, so pure." He brushed his finger again against my cheek. "Maybe I will do a whole series, like I did of my friend the postman back in Arles."

My heart was thumping hard in my chest. He had sketched me

from memory. Surely that meant he had been thinking of me when he was alone in his rented room in the Ravoux Inn.

"Of course you're much prettier than he is, and I don't recall ever kissing him like that." Vincent smiled playfully. "He was a married man, after all."

I giggled.

"I only need your father's permission," he continued. "Let's not risk getting him cross." He stroked my cheek with his hand. "Hurry home," he whispered. "It's far too late for you to be out."

And so I did. I rushed through the streets with my heart nearly bursting through my chest. My clothes felt weightless, my feet hardly felt the bulk of the cobblestones.

Only when I had managed to creep up the stairs and enter my room did I notice a smudge of yellow paint streaked like fireworks across my cheek. How I wished I could keep it there and never wash it off! But that would be foolhardy. Rather than risk being discovered, I dipped my washcloth in the water basin. And slowly, mournfully, I erased the evidence of our kiss.

TWENTY-THREE

The Yellow Fingerprint

My encounter with Vincent had left me breathless, and I was thankful that Father did not catch me stealthily tiptoeing back to my room. Had he seen me there in the stairwell, in my bare feet and smiling from ear to ear, Papa would have known I had just returned from something scandalous.

The first person I wanted to see was Louise-Josephine. Though I did not find her asleep in my bed as I had anticipated, there was a note on my pillowcase.

We'll speak tomorrow. I don't want Mother to awaken to our whispering . . .
Always,
L-Josephine

I folded her letter and placed it in my desk drawer. I stood by my mirror and looked at myself. The streak of yellow was still wet on my cheek, a faint fingerprint swirled into the pigment. When I cupped my hands to my face, I could still detect the scent of turpentine on my skin. It had permeated the places where Vincent's palms had pressed against me, and I greedily inhaled these last traces of our encounter.

I WAS late to the kitchen that next morning, but fortunately, Louise-Josephine had risen early. When I came down the stairway, I noticed she had already set the breakfast table.

I walked into the kitchen and greeted her. She held a blue glass pitcher in her hand and a lock of her chestnut hair fell over the left side of her face. She reminded me of a kitten, incapable of hiding the mischief in her eyes.

"So . . . ," she said, smiling, "what happened? I've been counting the minutes until I saw you!"

I closed the curtain and ran up to her. "He kissed me!" I blurted out. I covered my mouth with my hand to stifle my giggle. Still, it was difficult to contain myself.

I had practiced how I was going to tell Louise-Josephine what had happened. How Vincent and I had started talking about his paintings and his ideas, and how he had mentioned that he wished to paint me again. But now as I stood there within the cloistered walls of my kitchen, I could not be bothered with those details. The only thing I could concentrate on was that one fantastic moment when his lips touched mine.

Louise-Josephine beamed. "I knew he would! I just knew it!"

she said as she clapped her hands together. "And how was it?" She cocked her head a little and raised an eyebrow.

I giggled again.

"Tell me!" she pressed.

"It was wonderful. . . . I met him just as he was finishing his painting. It was beautiful, a haunting one of the village church—"

Louise-Josephine cut me short. "I don't care about the painting! What did he say when he first saw you there?"

"He was surprised, of course," I said, tripping slightly over my words. "But very pleasantly so, it would seem."

"And did you arrange for a next meeting?"

She was already quite ahead of me, as I hadn't even thought that far in advance. I was still relishing my triumph of sneaking successfully out of the house and meeting Vincent in the middle of the night.

"No, I haven't."

She shook her head. "Did he give any clue when he intended to see you next?"

"He only said he doesn't want to upset Papa," I said, reaching for a few of the pears that needed to be peeled. I set one in front of me and held the other with my hand.

"Eventually your father will find out and he will become upset." She took the pear from me. "You realize that, don't you?"

Louise-Josephine's voice was confident, as if she recognized what a naïf I was.

"If Vincent's intentions are serious and he shows Papa the respect and attention he requires, I don't see how Papa could object," I insisted.

Louise-Josephine shook her head again. "You remember what

I said about my grandmother? How I stopped fearing her when I realized that even if she did punish me, my life couldn't change for the worse. You need to realize that your father will never be your ally in finding you a husband."

I shook my head. "I don't understand what you're trying to say."

"I don't think your father wants to see you married."

I looked up at her, and my eyes must have revealed my disbelief.

"Why do you keep telling me that?" I said, annoyed. "Papa's had so much on his mind, he just hasn't been able to give it much thought."

"You're going to be twenty-one in a few days. How could he not have given it any thought? Most girls in your situation have fathers eager to make marital introductions for them." She took a deep breath and reached for another pear. "Your father has done nothing except instruct you on what he wants for dinner each night."

"I don't see why he wouldn't want me married," I protested. "It just doesn't make sense."

"Yes, it does," she said. "It makes perfect sense. Don't you see how he treats my mother? From what my grandmother told me, when Mother was younger, she used to wait on him hand and foot. She cooked for him when he would come home late from the salons of his artist friends. She swept his floors. She did his laundry. Now that she's older, he doesn't want my mother to have to lift a finger. And I'm sure you've noticed, he feels awkward asking anything of me. You, Marguerite, are a far cheaper servant than anyone else he might employ."

"Servant?" I furrowed my brow. "He doesn't think of me like that. . . ."

Then, from a few meters beyond the kitchen, I heard Papa calling.

"Marguerite, where's my coffee?" he hollered. His timing couldn't have been more perfect.

Louise-Josephine lowered her eyes. We both realized there was no need to state the obvious. Once again, she was exactly right.

TWENTY-FOUR

Plume of Gray

THE following morning, I awoke full of energy. I had slept well, and in my slumber, I had forgotten Louise-Josephine's cautionary words, and dreamed only of Vincent. It was a wonderful feeling to be a young woman, my entire being filled with the heady sensation of falling in love. I felt like a crocus bursting through the cold winter soil, my leaves thirsty for some sun.

I walked over to my window and opened the shutters. A few meters beyond, the meadows were alight with rows of poppies. All I could see was crimson, miles of red flowers intensified by threads of tall, green grass.

It was Sunday, and the church bells were beginning to sound. I quickly splashed some cold water on my face and rebraided my hair in a tight chignon.

I couldn't expect Louise-Josephine to make another breakfast in my absence, so I quickly put on a simple gray dress and ran down the stairwell to prepare Papa's meal.

"YOU'RE going to church this morning?" Papa asked, as I brought him a tray of croissants and coffee in the garden.

"Yes. I don't suppose you'd like to join me?" I said, knowing all too well what his response would be.

He let out a small laugh. "You can stop asking me that, Marguerite. I will go when I'm dead."

I shook my head. Father hadn't been to church for years. Once, over dinner, he blurted out: "Medical school taught me that the only God is science." He was vehemently opposed to organized religion and favored the teachings of Darwin as his personal philosophy. His attitude had obviously worn off on Paul, who had stopped attending church several years before.

That morning, Paul sat a few meters away from Papa, with a sketch pad on his lap. Both of them were busy trying to copy one of Cézanne's still lifes, a small painting with flowers and fruit.

"You're not going either?" I asked playfully.

Paul nodded. "Father and I prefer to spend our Sundays painting," he mumbled as he continued to sketch. His head was bent over the drawing, but I could see the scratches from his pencil and the faint smudges from where his hand dragged across the page. "But perhaps you should pray that I pass my last history exam this Wednesday!" He tapped at his textbook on the little stool and laughed.

"I'll put in a good word for you," I said in jest. Papa looked up and smiled.

I waved good-bye to them and hurried down the stairs,

knocking over the garden shoes that I had slipped on the night before last.

I RELISHED going to mass not because I was a particularly spiritual person, but because it gave me the opportunity to spend a few hours away from our house and my chores. Underneath the weighty ribs of the vaulted ceiling of the church, it was easy to let my mind wander freely.

I had done this since I was a child. Dressed in ribbons and lace, sitting next to a mother who used Sunday services as an excuse to wear all her finery, I learned to pass the hours by creating stories with the multicolored figures of saints and bishops that were frozen in stained glass. We must have looked so out of place then, ridiculous in our dresses compared to the villagers in their simple cotton clothes. Now when I went to church I always dressed in muted colors so as to blend in with the others in the congregation, though still the community never embraced me as one of their own.

I was shy and my family was different. This combination would always keep me at a distance. Just as the villagers preferred the local Dr. Mazery to my father (he could be seen in the front pew with his lovely wife and angelic daughter sitting next to him), they left me to sit alone in the church with no one making any attempt to have simple conversation with me. No one except Edmund Clavel.

Short, with a round, pasty face that reminded me of a brioche, Edmund was the owner of a small trading store in town. He only exchanged pleasantries with me once, an awkward stumbling of words that I made out to be a comment about the weather. For the most part, he preferred to sneak glances in my direction. The first time I found him staring at me, I thought it was my imagination.

This was several months before Vincent arrived. Edmund was sitting three pews ahead of me, the slope of his gray jacket facing the altar. Slowly, however, as the sermon progressed, I could see his chin turn over his shoulder.

It was not a face that anyone would find handsome. His skin was the color of custard and his eyes were a dull pewter. Even his smile—which he revealed to me like a winning hand of cards—was crooked.

Had he shown some sort of magnetism or originality, I'm sure I would not have found his physical flaws so bothersome. But he appeared expressionless, as if he were a marionette whose painter had forgotten to draw in his eyes.

And although his interest in me was obvious, I never once imagined myself as his wife, as I had already begun to do with Vincent. Vincent was infinitely more attractive to me. His eccentricities, his unlikely dress, his abandonment of social conventions for the pursuit of art and beauty were things that intrigued me. I closed my eyes and imagined him at his easel again—his smock unbuttoned, a smear of pigment on the edge of his sleeves—and could not help but feel enchanted by the vision. If I was considered an oddity, a curiosity for gossip in the village, then the two of us were destined to be kindred spirits.

I dreamed about my rendezvous with Vincent while the organ sounded high into the rafters and the stained-glass windows pulled long fingers of blue and red onto the stone floor.

I thought of Vincent's painting with the midnight blue palette and the ribs of the church. He had painted it as dark and foreboding as an impenetrable fortress, gloomy and alone. Now I was sitting within the walls of what he had painted so opaquely. And I was seeing in my mind's eye the church as he had seen it. The windows that had no reflection. A clock tower that had neither numbers nor hands.

The choir sang, the organ sounded, and our village priest droned on about Christ's sacrifices and our shortcomings in a sinful world.

I debated whether I should make confession and ask for forgiveness for my sins of the night I snuck out. *Surely a kiss as passionate as the one I shared with Vincent was a sin!* I thought to myself. *Shouldn't I ask for forgiveness?*

But I did not want to go into that rosewood closet and seek forgiveness for something that made me feel more alive than I ever had before. I did not want to hear that it was wrong, or ask for penance, and I certainly didn't want the memory of it to be washed away. To ask for it to be cleansed was the cruelest thing I could imagine.

So after the service, and after taking communion, I forwent confession. I walked out to the front of the church, where Vincent had painted that night, and remembered how we two stood there heading toward our first embrace. If I could have replayed it in my mind a thousand times, I would have. But the bell tower was sounding the end of the service, and Papa and Paul would be waiting for their lunch.

I gathered the folds of my skirt and began to make my way around the circular path that Vincent had painted so symbolically. I took one last look at the church's spire, the peaked roof that he had depicted partially aflame. It now looked charcoal against the noon sky.

I walked to the left side, the direction his little Dutch figure had taken as she hurried away. With the billow of my gray skirt whipping behind me, it amused me to think how much I now resembled her.

TWENTY-FIVE

Gifts and Warnings

OVER the next few days, he painted in our garden as well as in the neighboring fields. Every morning when I woke up and began my way toward the village, I looked for him. Sometimes there would be traces of him. A paint-spotted oil rag left behind, or a canvas stretcher that had fallen out of his rucksack. Each time I spotted a sign that he had been in a certain place, I stood there for a moment and looked out into the landscape and inhaled what he had thought beautiful enough to paint.

I had begun to take Louise-Josephine's words to heart. If she were right, as I now began to suspect, Papa had little expectation for me other than to maintain his household. I would not let myself end up unhappy and disillusioned, as Mother had been in her last months. I wanted to love.

* * *

I REJOICED when, earlier in the week, Father mentioned that he had invited Vincent's family for lunch.

"Perhaps the Van Goghs can help us lift Vincent's spirits a bit," he told Madame Chevalier over dinner.

I bit my lip to hide my excitement, not wanting to give myself away and let Papa know how happy I was. I was anxious, after all, to meet Vincent's family.

"I sent Theo an invitation in Paris," Papa told Madame Chevalier. "His wife can bring the baby, and Marguerite can prepare lunch. I'll entertain them all in the garden."

"You're so thoughtful, Paul-Ferdinand," she said. I thought her comment ironic, as I knew she would not be invited to this luncheon. She turned her face toward Papa and smiled at him. She was wearing makeup. Her face, dotted with circles of rouge, stood out against the black collar of her dress. I could see a dusting of powder caught in the tendrils near her ears.

"I'll help with the cooking," Louise-Josephine piped in suddenly. Her voice startled me, as I was not used to hearing her speak at the dining table. It was clear and strong. She was obviously determined to make a lovely gesture for me in honor of the occasion.

"Oh, no . . . don't be silly," Papa said. "Marguerite will have no difficulty preparing something for the afternoon. She can easily handle it by herself."

"Yes, I know she *can* do it," Louise-Josephine answered. She was looking Papa straight in the eyes. "But two sets of hands are better than one. And after all, *I* need to get better in the kitchen."

Papa raised an eyebrow and looked at me. He was suspicious

of Louise-Josephine's gesture. He knew we had never been close in the past, barely exchanging words in his presence.

"Well, the two of you can work out the details by yourselves. In the meantime, I'll send an invitation to Vincent."

ALL week I waited for his visit. I had so much energy, but my only outlet was throwing myself into my chores. I took out my metal pail and scrub brush and scoured the floors. I washed the curtains even though I had washed them the first week in April. I weeded my garden with extra tenacity, pulling out the tall green stalks—sometimes three at a time. I dusted Father's bookshelves and took out one of the de Goncourt novels that Vincent had painted, lightly touching the leather binding with my fingers.

I thrust open all the windows to force the light into the parlor. I filled several of Mother's Dresden vases with fistfuls of gardenias and peonies so the house had pockets of pink and white blooms. The air, no longer stale from the faint medicinal smells of Father's tinctures, was now filled with the light fragrance of flowers.

Papa also seemed to take extra measures to prepare for the arrival of Vincent's family. He brought extra canvases down from the attic and hung them along the hallway of the house, making the entire first floor more crowded than ever. He filled the cave behind the picnic table with a case of wine he'd ordered from Paris, and brought home a basket of fresh cheeses and cured meats from his favorite stores. On Friday, when I returned home from my errands, I found Papa sitting in the garden with Madame Chevalier behind him. She was busy massaging a henna shampoo into his hair. She had tied a thin strip of cotton around his scalpline so the orange color wouldn't tint his skin.

"Marguerite," he said as I walked closer. The olive green mixture had a strong smell and it looked as though his entire head was caked in mud. Madame Chevalier hadn't applied the shampoo in months, and I knew Papa had been anxious to hide the white in his hair.

"Did you decide on the menu for Sunday?"

"Yes, Papa," I replied. Madame Chevalier did not look up. She was busy scraping some of the dried mixture at the nape of Papa's neck.

"Good." He cleared his throat. "We have everything in order then."

I nodded my head. "The sun is quite strong today, Papa. Don't stay out too long or your hair will look like a tube of crimson madder."

He chuckled. "Well, I just might. After all, Vincent might want to do a second portrait of me then. We know how he likes vibrant colors!"

THE next day he arrived just before noon with Theo and Jo and their little son. Louise-Josephine had spent much of the morning helping me, and I felt awful when the bell sounded and she was forced to scurry back to her room.

Her assistance had been invaluable. Not only had she helped me with all the baking and preparations, she had also given me more advice on what dress to wear and how I should plait my hair.

"Wear blue," she told me that morning. "It will offset your eyes. And let's weave a ribbon through your braids before we twist and pin them back." She picked a lovely cornflower blue one from my dresser and started braiding it right away.

She was right as usual. The color did make my eyes seem bigger. She took a step backward and pinched my cheeks. "And the final touch," she said with a flourish. She reached into her apron and handed me some lipstick that she had stolen from her mother's drawer.

"Thank you," I gushed.

It was so refreshing to have Louise-Josephine close by and I felt an outpouring of love toward her, as if I suddenly understood the blessing of having a sister. It was her sophistication and her reassuring nature that gave me a rush of confidence before seeing Vincent.

Papa greeted Vincent and his family as soon as they arrived, showing them directly into the garden where the red picnic table was crowded with food. The baby, who had been named for his uncle Vincent, was resting in Jo's arms, and was immediately amused by all of Father's animals.

Later on, just before we all settled down to eat, Jo came over to me and thanked me for making such a lovely luncheon.

"Theo and I wanted to give you and your brother a little something for being so kind to Vincent," she said. She reached into her basket and handed me a small flat package neatly wrapped in festive paper. "I'm afraid Theo's already given your brother his. . . ."

I looked over and saw Paul laughing heartily with Theo. He was holding a book in one hand and the wrapping paper in another. Paul had finished his last exam just the day before, and had arrived home in Auvers only one train earlier than Vincent's family.

"Thank you," I said appreciatively. "It wasn't necessary at all. Vincent is more like a friend of the family now than a patient . . . and I know how happy Papa is—all of us are—to have him here in Auvers."

Jo smiled at me and urged me to open the present.

I carefully fingered the edges of wrapping paper so I wouldn't tear it. Inside I found a book on the art of Japanese woodblock prints.

"Vincent is a tremendous admirer of these plates," she said softly, "and we thought you and your brother might enjoy them too. We bought the books at an exhibition on Japanese art in Paris a few weeks ago. We actually went there with Vincent just before he left for Auvers."

"Oh, they're lovely," I said, as I turned the pages and saw the beautiful scenes of women in kimonos, bridges at sunset, and branches of plum blossoms.

"It makes Theo and me so happy to see how well Vincent is doing here," she said to me, again touching my arm. "We were terribly afraid before he came north, but it seems your father's been a positive influence on him."

I tried to muster a smile but it was difficult. Obviously, Vincent had not written to Theo about Father forcing him to take his homeopathic tonics.

"Well, the good thing is," I said, trying to sound positive, "that he's painting a great deal. It seems he does at least one painting a day . . . sometimes more."

Jo smiled at me. "He *is* prolific," she said with a warm smile. "And Theo's certain of his genius. It's a shame he wasted his early years at Goupil's." She let out an exhaustive sigh. "Then there were those years as an evangelist . . ." She shook her head. "He's spent most of his adulthood searching for himself, searching for something greater. Theo is just so happy that Vincent has finally found something that gives him some peace."

"Yes," I said. "I know Papa said it is imperative that Vincent continue to paint."

Jo sighed again. "It's been trying," she said, shaking her head once more. "We have been through a lot with him. The attacks, the bills . . . It has been a difficult road getting him on his feet." She looked at me and smiled, and gently reached toward my wrist in a gesture of affection. "My husband and I are obviously most concerned about his health, of course. I don't know what Theo would do without Vincent . . . they're like twins . . . the two of them so close."

I nodded my head. It pained me to think of Vincent so unhappy in the past.

"I love his paintings so much," I said softly.

Jo chuckled. "Yes, they're lovely. But now we must all wait for the collectors to come and buy." She emphasized the last word ever so slightly and then smiled at me again.

I nodded back and the two of us looked over to Vincent, who was now deeply engaged in making faces at his young nephew.

"He's certainly good with children," I said, more to myself than to Jo, but she obviously heard.

"In short spurts, I suppose," she said as she crossed her arms. "But he certainly wouldn't make a very fine husband. His last love affair proved that much." She turned to me and smiled. Perhaps it was a warning for me. For she clearly knew what was on my mind.

TWENTY-SIX

Bridges in the Garden

THEY left our house a little after three o'clock. Vincent wanted to take Theo to the Ravoux Inn to show him some paintings before they returned to Paris. It had been a festive afternoon, and the picnic table showed how heartily we had all eaten. Only the bones from the chicken remained on our plates, and a pile of olive pits was left in a small ceramic bowl. In the middle of the table, the cake stand held but a single slice of butter cake, with a few strawberries submerged in a melted puddle of whipped cream.

Papa was lying down in one of the lawn chairs, his waistcoat half unbuttoned and his swelling belly eager to find release from his leather belt. His shirtsleeves were rolled high above his elbows, exposing a smattering of pale freckles, like tiny constellations, on his long, wiry arms.

As I collected the plates for washing, I could hear the sound of the birds chirping and Papa snoring in the garden. The animals were nestled on the grass, and Paul was hosing down some of the furniture so the bugs wouldn't feast on any of the leftover food.

Jo's cautionary words were still echoing in my head. I had never thought of Vincent with another woman, though now I realized that it was naïve of me. Perhaps she had been one of his models; the idea crept into my mind like ants feasting on crumbs. I imagined her dark and experienced, with the black eyes of an Arlésienne, her brightly colored dress and apron discarded carelessly over one of the chairs in his studio. I could never imagine myself casting off my clothes so effortlessly. I had cultivated my modesty to a high art over the years. Madame Chevalier's penchant for rouge and lipstick, her garish boudoir, and her midnight tiptoeing to Papa had inspired me to be the opposite of her. But now all I could do was think of ways to capture Vincent's attention. My skin—which knew no other hand than my own—my body—which had never been caressed by anything but a washcloth and a bar of soap—now yearned for that hand that I had pushed away that night in front of the church.

I scraped the last of the plates furiously. I wanted to rush to Louise-Josephine's room as quickly as possible and tell her about the conversation with Jo, admit to her that the news of Vincent's past experience with love made me even more insecure about my lack of it.

But, just as I was finishing, Paul came shuffling up to the table. For the first time in months he was smiling. School was over for him and the party had been a success. It was such a rare and refreshing sight for me that I momentarily forgot about my plight with Vincent and welcomed Paul's conversation.

"I think today's party went well, don't you?" he asked.

He came closer. I noticed he was no longer wearing his foulard, but had instead tucked it in his breast pocket. His naked throat revealed a patch of pale, pink skin. It made him look younger and sweeter to me. The way I remembered him as a little boy.

"It was so nice of them to give us a present," he said. I could tell he had been as touched as I had by the gesture.

"Yes," I said. "The prints look quite interesting." I had already placed my copy of the book in my bedroom for safekeeping, but Paul had his in a satchel by the table. He knelt down and retrieved it.

"They're wonderful," he said as he flipped through the pages. "The bridges by Hiroshige are so calming. I wish we could construct one in our garden . . . we could put a small pond with carp underneath!"

I laughed. "I think that would be a bit ambitious, Paul."

"I'm going to do some sketches and show Papa," he said. My skepticism obviously made him more determined. "I'm sure he'll love the idea!"

It was true that Father was fascinated by the Far East. He had painted those Chinese characters on one of the doors upstairs by copying them out of a book. He had several catalogs of Japanese and Chinese paintings in his library. He also had a few blue and white ceramics from the Orient as well, the one from Cézanne being the obvious favorite in his collection.

When I was just a little girl, shortly after my mother died, I remember Papa coming home with a suitcase full of Japanese woodblock prints. There were so many to look at: ones of crooked plum trees, others with kimono-clad women preparing for their bath, and ones with footpaths and spindly wooden bridges.

So, like Paul, I was eager to look through the book that Theo and Jo had brought for me. Not only did their strong, black outlines and delicate washings of color intrigue me, but, according to Jo, they fascinated Vincent as well.

After Paul retreated back to the garden to work on some sketches, I rushed inside the house and bounded up the stairs to show Louise-Josephine the gift. Though perhaps I was more eager to tell her what Jo had said.

I found her lying in bed, the Prussian blue coverlet offsetting the waves of her chestnut hair. With the afternoon sun streaming through the glass, Louise-Josephine looked majestic. Like a peacock painted in Chinese blue and white. Even when she was wearing an unembellished cotton dress, she had an uncannily regal appearance. I stood there in the doorway staring at her, wondering, if Vincent stood where I was now, would he fall in love with her?

Her face was turned toward the window. The long stretch of her neck reached across her pillow; the high blades of her collarbone protruded through her almond-colored skin.

She was looking past the glass, toward the distant rooftops of Auvers just ahead. I didn't want to speak as I stood there watching her. I wondered if she was thinking the same thoughts I had when I was alone in my room, looking past the garden toward the horizon streaked in blue and gold.

There was a world outside of this small village that I hardly knew. I was not only inexperienced in love, I was also severely deficient in the ways of the world. My twenty-one years had been spent wrapped up like a gumdrop in a glass bowl and now I desperately wanted to discard the packaging and have all that had remained dormant finally come alive.

At least Louise-Josephine had experienced life in Paris. She had told me of the smell of dark, gritty alleys, the carved splendor of the Louvre. She could describe the way the windows of Notre-Dame were illuminated at sunset, the sparkle of boats riding the Seine at dusk. I had visited Paris only on a few brief occasions. Papa had taken Paul and me to his office on a few rare trips. But I had seen the capital only through the glimpse of a carriage window.

I wondered if it was worse to have known the freedom of life in the city, only to then be forced to spend one's days in a crowded, narrow house in the country. I couldn't believe Louise-Josephine had spent nearly a decade with us and not had her own nocturnal adventures sooner. Perhaps she had disobeyed Papa's orders for years, leaping from the window while we all slept, secretly roaming the streets with the moonlight bathing her long, amber limbs.

I continued to stare at her unnoticed. "Marguerite?" she eventually whispered as she roused herself from her daydream. "I didn't see you standing there." She sat up on the bed. "Come here," she said, patting the bed.

I walked toward her and sat down. I placed the book of Japanese prints between us.

"How did the luncheon go?"

"It went well. They all enjoyed the food, and Vincent's nephew was adorable." I paused. "I met Vincent's sister-in-law, too."

Louise-Josephine raised one of her eyebrows. "And how was she?"

"She was nice, very intelligent." I fumbled with my fingers. "She told me Vincent had had a failed love affair. I felt as though she were warning me not to get too attached."

Louise-Josephine listened carefully then nodded her head. "This is no surprise, Marguerite. After all, he is a grown man." She laughed to herself. "He's an artist. He's probably had several love affairs. This shouldn't affect your attitude toward him. When I lived in the Cote d'Azur with the Lenoirs, Madame would always say with a wink: 'Every heart has its secrets.'"

"Yes," I sighed. "I suppose that's true."

Louise-Josephine came closer. "Is anything *else* the matter?"

"Well, perhaps I'm just being foolish with this fantasy that I have the talents and the beauty to sustain Vincent's interest."

Louise-Josephine touched my wrist. "It's not a fantasy, Marguerite. You *are* beautiful." She said it softly and with such reassurance I almost believed her. "Had your mother lived, I'm sure she would have stood behind you and gazed at both your reflections in the mirror and told you just how lovely you are." She shook her head and straightened her back, as if determined to banish my insecurities. "And what about your talent at the piano! You've already impressed Vincent with that—he's already mentioned wanting to paint you with your elegant fingers at the keys!"

Her confidence in me was flattering and it temporarily abated my fears.

I smiled up at her and told her how her words comforted me. I opened up the book of Hiroshige prints. It was a rare thing, being able to share something foreign with Louise-Josephine, and I relished the chance to show her something new.

TWENTY-SEVEN

Impatience

HE arrived at our house unannounced the next morning, clutching his hat to his breast. He looked handsome in his white smock; a red patch of skin revealed itself just beneath his neckline. He had forgotten to wear his scarf.

"I wanted to thank you for such a lovely afternoon yesterday," he said sweetly. "I was distracted by seeing my nephew and I fear I haven't shown you the appreciation you deserve, for all the trouble you took in having us all feel so welcome."

He appeared so relaxed, so sure of himself, and it helped give me confidence. Perhaps he really didn't resent my ineptitude back at the church, I thought to myself. I tried to remember all the nice things that Louise-Josephine had said the night before, so I wouldn't reveal just how insecure I was in his company.

"I suppose you've come to see Papa," I said and ushered him

into the hallway. "He's resting in the garden. Would you like me to tell him you're here?"

"Eventually," he said deliberately. "There's no rush."

He had no idea how my pulse began to quicken when I was alone with him. All sense of control vanished and my head felt light from just the mere proximity of him.

I stood motionless in the hallway for several seconds.

"I am glad your father is in the garden." He bit his lip nervously and for the first time his French seemed to falter. "I wanted to say that I am glad to have a moment alone with you. Your father keeps a very close eye on you, *non*? I suspect you're the prized piece in his collection."

"Oh, no," I blurted out. "That would be his Renoir!"

Vincent shook his head and smiled. "Then he's not the collector I suspected he was. Only a fool would choose a Renoir over you."

What color was my face at that point? Carnelian red? Mallow pink with a touch of Indian yellow? How must I have seemed, blushing there in front of him?

He was undeterred. His face came closer to me and he tilted his head as if studying me. "You're like a piece of sculpture in the different hours of light." His fingers were now pulling me toward him. "One moment, you're behind a shadow. The next, you're illuminating an entire room."

There was a part of me that wanted to release his hand from the fabric of my sleeve and thread it through my own. I wanted to feel the sensation of his skin against mine. I wanted to trace the lines of his palm, touch the tiny pads of his calluses. I wanted to feel like the stem of his brush, my fingers held firmly against his own. I stood there trembling against him, my body teetering to stay erect.

He did not move his hand. And with his body so close to mine,

I felt his heat so intensely that it was as if I had been standing too close to a fire.

I was trembling. My hands, my shoulders, even my jaw was shaking.

I stepped away from him. "It's just someone might see us. . . . There are more eyes in this house than you know. I wouldn't want someone to stumble upon us."

He shook his head. "You don't need to explain. But there are places one can go to be alone, Marguerite . . ."

"But my father . . ."

"Shhhh . . . ," he said as he placed a finger on my lips. "This village is full of little hiding places, caves covered in leaves . . . a cushion to lay your head on."

I smiled. It was not difficult to imagine. The grotto that Paul and I had played king and queen in so many years ago came to mind.

"One night you'll come to me as you did that night when I painted the church. Then we will speak freely between ourselves."

I smiled, as though listening to a dream. His words were like honey in my ears. I could not have scripted it better myself.

TWENTY-EIGHT

Downpour

ON Wednesday he painted a view of the vineyards, looking east toward the hills of Montmorency. Papa said he saw Vincent standing knee-deep in the grass, as he walked down one of the winding roads near our house with Henrietta.

"It was such a beautiful canvas," Papa told us over lunch. "Every day his paintings become stronger, more ambitious. Today he painted one of the vineyards, and he executed the slope of the hill, the low angled walls merging with rambling fences, as if the entire meadow was adrift at sea." Papa took a sip of wine and leaned in toward the table. "If only you two could have seen those brushstrokes! He painted the vines as if they were bunches of mermaid's hair—cornflower blue and bottle green bordered by roundels of red poppies. I felt as though I could reach in and grab them by the fistful."

Even then, Paul was curious—if not bordering on obsessive—about every painting Vincent was working on. Once he learned a new canvas was in the making, he would ask Father numerous questions about the palette Vincent chose and the way he constructed the painting's composition. I was far more intrigued by the fact that Vincent seemed to be choosing his landscapes closer and closer to our house. As I knew he placed symbols in his paintings, I hoped he was trying to say something to me through his proximity.

The next afternoon I saw him standing in another field near the rue Vessenots. It had begun to rain, and I pulled my scarf over my head and trudged closer to where he was painting.

By the time I reached where he stood, my hem was covered in mud and the cotton of my dress clung to my chest.

He didn't seem to notice me as I came closer to him, his eyes planted on his painting. He looked the same way he did that evening I saw him painting the church: his back bent over his canvas, the handle of one brush between his teeth, the other clasped tightly in his hand.

I was now only steps away from him, and my breast was heaving from walking through the thicket of plantings and dragging my skirt.

"Vincent," I said, somehow finding the courage to interrupt him in his work. "I saw you painting here from the road!"

He looked up and his skin was moist from the onset of rain.

"Marguerite," he said before taking the brush from his mouth. "You should get home before the rain gets any heavier. You'll catch your death out here!"

"I wanted to see you paint again," I said. My breathing was short. I knew I sounded flustered. "I know this isn't a cave or the most clandestine of places, but . . ." I was nearly yelling over the wind, which was whipping my hair over my face.

"The storm is growing heavier, Marguerite. I'll need to wrap this up in a tarp or it'll be ruined." He extended his hand and I saw pellets of rain hit his palm.

The canvas rested on the lip of his easel—a field of blossoming pea sprouts set against rows of pink alfalfa. His brushstrokes were like tiny stitches in some places and long, lacy ribbons in others. Long blue-white plumes of smoke billowed from a locomotive set against a robin's-egg sky. A slash of white road sliced the canvas in two, and a tiny black carriage trotted through a drizzle of blue and gray lines.

"Let me help you," I said as I knelt down beside his rucksack and unrolled the tarp.

"I've been here for several hours, but the painting is still damp in places. We'll need to wrap it loosely to prevent it from smudging."

I nodded my head and helped him swaddle his canvas.

"You've been doing nearly a painting a day," I said, awestruck.

He smiled as he loaded his rucksack on his back. "I still need to paint you a couple more times before I even near a sense of accomplishment."

"You have my permission to do that," I teased.

"I fear I'll need more than that."

With his rucksack strapped to his back, he knelt down on the ground and began to work with the tarp.

I tried to assist him. "No," he said, correcting me. "We cannot put the tarp directly on the painting. It's still wet. It will smudge."

I watched as he created a protective bridge with some extra canvas stretchers.

It was a marvel to watch him, so calm and in control, and I

found myself admiring him even more. With his damp hair pushed back one could see every angle of his face; his skin glistening from the rain looked like wet stone.

The water began to beat down harder on us and I feared my dress would soon become transparent. "Vincent," I shouted, "I think I had better head home!"

He stood up and hoisted the wrapped painting underneath his arm. "Yes, you had better, my little piano player . . ." I caught him looking at my breasts, every bit of them accentuated by the wet cloth. "Or your father will send out the gendarmes . . ."

IT was true, I needed to hurry back to the house or else Father would notice that I was away far too long. I had not been able to stay dry; my dress was completely soaked and my boots were ruined with mud.

I hurried up the narrow stairs and hid my boots under a garden pail. I would clean them after the rain stopped and, hopefully, with the proper polishing, Father wouldn't notice how stretched the leather had become.

But when I entered the house it wasn't Papa who reproached me, it was Paul.

"Where have you been, Marguerite?" he asked. He stood there at the doorway, his face drawn and unhappy. His arms were crossed over his chest, and his face, long and disapproving, looked like Papa's when he was in one of his foul moods.

I was shivering in the hallway now, my wet clothes hanging on my bones like soggy drapes.

I tried to move past him. I wanted to change my clothes and dry off my hair.

"Paul," I said, nudging him slightly with my shoulder, "I was only out for an hour! I saw Vincent painting in one of the potato fields and I went over to say hello."

I had my hand on the banister when he took hold of my arm.

"You shouldn't be carrying on like this . . . with one of Papa's patients; it's just not right."

I wiggled out from his grip. I could see a red welt spreading underneath the material in the place where Paul's hand had just been.

"Paul, let go of me!" I said. "I need to change before Papa arrives home!"

"If he saw you returning home like this, he would never let you out!"

"I don't know why you're carrying on like this, Paul. It had begun to rain, and I thought Vincent might need some help wrapping up his canvas."

"He is a grown man, what good would your help do him? I'm sure he knows how to wrap up his own canvases."

I shook my head at him. The house, dark from the rain outside, cast long shadows across Paul's face. The length of his nose, the heavy draping of his hooded eyes, all seemed more unattractive in unflattering, gray-blue light.

"I don't know why my helping Vincent with his painting bothers you so much."

He didn't answer me, as I walked up the stairs to my bedroom. But I knew all too well why it bothered him. He was jealous.

I FOUND myself in the kitchen more out of comfort than out of necessity. I took down a stack of dishes and set about rearranging the cupboard in order to calm my nerves. A few minutes later, Louise-Josephine joined me. She had a novel under her arm and she placed it down on the butcher's block.

"I heard what Paul said to you," she said sympathetically. "He is struggling so much these days, and I've tried to be kind to him."

It was true. Whereas my relationship with Louise-Josephine was new and fresh, Paul and Louise-Josephine had been quite close before. After all, she was the one who had assisted her mother in his care when he was young.

"Perhaps he is feeling threatened. . . . You and I are friends now, and also he sees Vincent developing a fondness for you. He can't help but be a bit jealous."

I shook my head. I knew Louise-Josephine was right. Paul was observant and I'm sure he noticed the strengthening bond between Louise-Josephine and me. And, to make matters worse, Vincent still hadn't asked him to pose for him.

"Do you think he will tell my father?"

Louise-Josephine looked pensive for a moment. "I'm not sure, Marguerite. I would hope not, but he's always been eager to gain your father's favor."

I nodded. She was right. And one could only imagine what Paul might do to gain Papa's approval.

TWENTY-NINE

Tinctures and Portraits

Papa told me on Friday that he had invited Vincent for Sunday lunch. I breathed a sigh of relief. Paul had obviously not said anything to Papa. At least, not yet.

"Can you make a quiche and a salad? Vincent has complained of a delicate digestion," he asked.

"Of course."

"Good, then. I need to make more tinctures for him, so please try not to disturb me this afternoon."

I nodded my head and went downstairs to get his glass jars and the press. I brought them out to the outdoor stove we had in the garden and hurried back inside to let him be alone.

Around three o'clock, I went outside to water the garden and noticed Papa was still there, snipping stems and flowers off his plants. He held a basket in one fist and scissors in the other. The wicker basket was overflowing with hyssop and foxtail.

I walked past Father and went straight to my roses, pouring water over their hearty pink and white blooms. It bothered me to think of Papa medicating Vincent and it was a struggle to clear my mind of the image of Father pressing that tincture so forcefully into Vincent's hand.

I wanted to believe Papa's homeopathic remedies were actually working. After all, Vincent didn't seem to be complaining of any of the maladies that had plagued him back in Arles. I had never seen him act weak or vulnerable, but I had overheard his conversations with Papa where he described these awful periods of his life where he could do nothing—not even paint.

I didn't want to believe that Papa's remedies might be flawed. I wanted to have confidence in his curative powers not just because he was my father, but also because I so desperately wanted Vincent to be well. But still, something was gnawing inside me—signaling that something wasn't right about Vincent's seemingly endless productivity since he came to our village. A painting a day seemed exhausting. I remembered how in summers past, Cézanne and Pissarro worked furiously in the beginning of a painting in order to capture the immediacy of a landscape, but how they then took the canvas back to their studio and worked at it for weeks.

Certainly, Father behaved differently after he had ingested one of his own homemade remedies. After one dosage, he could hardly sit still, and he suddenly had limitless energy. I wondered if he was giving Vincent a similar dosage.

I had only touched upon Vincent's medication once with him. It was the afternoon he came to the house to thank me for the party I had hosted for Theo and Jo. As we walked toward the garden,

Vincent mentioned how he had previously relied too much on absinthe to soothe his nerves. The doctor in Saint-Rémy had warned him that his condition—particularly the seizures—were worsened by his weakness for it.

"Can you not take wormwood?" I had asked, concerned. I knew that Papa had often prescribed this to his patients in the past. Because absinthe was derived from wormwood oil, I feared Papa might rekindle Vincent's addiction.

"Your father is aware that I am trying to curb my addiction, Marguerite. He knows one of the main reasons I came to Auvers was to ensure that the seizures and depression don't return."

"Oh, how you've suffered . . . it's terrible." I could see Papa in the distance and I made sure my voice was almost a whisper.

Vincent's face changed. "It was terrible. Those months in Saint-Rémy were some of the worst in my life, but I must continue to be positive if I am to remain well. I have confidence in your father's expertise." He waved to Papa in greeting. "If he has treated Master Pissarro and his family with his medicines, then I am in capable hands."

I could feel my conscience begging me to correct him. Papa hadn't treated Monsieur Pissarro or his family for depression. He had treated his son once for a broken wrist and the rest of the family for their occasional aches and pains.

AT noon, he showed up at our door, bringing with him his most recent painting. He had only finished it the night before.

"I'm calling it *Ears of Wheat*," he told Father as he set it against one of the benches. He took a few steps back to give Papa space to look at it.

It was a beautiful painting, done in a magnified composition so that one could see the detail of the sheaves of wheat. Tiny braids of gold spearheaded the tall yellow shafts. Pale yellow ocher and sea-foam green highlighted the leaves. The canvas seemed to have captured the movement of the wind. Both the grass and the wheat were intertwined, each one swaying into the other.

"It's exquisite," Papa told him as I carried their lunch outside. "You've made the sheaves look like delicate ribbons."

"It was good for me to do a study up close. It forces me to examine every detail." Vincent took a deep breath. "Still, I've been anxious to begin working on some more portraits."

Immediately my ears perked up, as I was hoping Vincent was trying to lay the foundation to ask Papa for me to sit for him again.

"Well, that's a good idea," Papa responded rather absently. He was still studying Vincent's painting.

"I am expecting some more supplies from Paris, so I should have more pigment in a few days. I'm hoping to do a portrait of the innkeeper's daughter, Adeline. And of course, I would still like to do another one of Marguerite."

"Adeline?" Papa asked; now his interest was finally piqued.

"Yes," Vincent replied. "Monsieur Ravoux's girl."

Father let out a small laugh. "She's very pretty, isn't she? Bright eyes and a lovely profile."

I could tell by the clarity of Papa's voice that he was trying his best to ensure I heard the contents of their conversation. It was obvious that he wanted me to realize I was not as unique as I might have thought. Clearly, Vincent had other girls that he wanted to paint. But Papa needn't have tried so hard. I was close enough that I could hear every word.

I was now clutching the pitcher of water so tightly in my hand that I thought the tiny veins in my palm might burst.

I knew Adeline was only thirteen. But she did look mature for her age and, had Monsieur Ravoux not informed Vincent of Adeline's age, one could easily mistake her for a girl of at least sixteen.

And she was beautiful. With large saucer-shaped eyes and a long mouth that turned up at each corner like a cat's tail, it was no wonder Vincent had asked her to pose. Still, I was angry at my father for making it seem like Vincent had eyes for every young girl in the village. And I was upset with Vincent for even wanting to paint another girl's portrait before he had completed a second one of me.

My mind began to flood with doubts. Had his kiss meant nothing? Had I naïvely believed he had no feelings for any of the other girls in the village?

Yet just when I thought I might faint from the humiliation, Vincent changed the direction of the conversation.

"So I only need your permission now for a second portrait of Marguerite." Vincent sounded eager and not at all aware of the fact that he might upset me by painting Adeline. "Perhaps Wednesday would be good?"

Father looked as shocked as I felt. I was trembling so, my pitcher began to leak water down my wrist. I saw Papa nod reluctantly and look up at me. "Very well. Not this week, but next." I had been trying to busy myself around the table, but it was obvious that I was eavesdropping just as Father suspected.

"Will the two of you need anything else before I return to the house?" I stammered.

Vincent looked up at me, but I quickly turned away. I wanted him to know I was still smarting over the fact that he wanted to paint Adeline.

But neither Vincent nor Papa seemed to notice my displeasure. Probably because it seemed only natural that Vincent would want to vary his subjects as much as possible. Perhaps that was why Papa didn't understand why Vincent would want to paint me more than once.

As I went back to the house, I overheard the last remnants of their conversation.

"Vincent, remind me to give you your next batch of tinctures," Papa said as he reached to dish himself out some salad. "I wouldn't want you to be painting—and painting my only daughter, no less—without your latest dosage."

THIRTY

A Crane and a Plum Blossom

He did paint her. I heard it from Papa, who heard it from Monsieur Ravoux. Vincent created Adeline's portrait in a symphony of blue, a thousand tiny brushstrokes in cobalt. Like the palette he used for Papa but without the darker accents, and without the putrid green and firebrick eyes tinged with melancholy and regret. Adeline was depicted as an innocent angel. Cast under a blue background composed of countless sapphire stitches. Little lapis lazuli bricks stacked between strokes of indigo and sky.

He carved her out in yellow. The blond of her golden upswept hair in a perfect powder blue ribbon; her cheeks in swirls of peach and saffron; her lemon-colored hands resting delicately in her lap.

I did not want Papa or Paul to know how much it upset me that Vincent had painted Adeline. After all, I didn't want to appear selfish. He was going to paint me a second time, and he had yet to ask to make even a single portrait of Paul. But I was still jealous. Unlike the image of Adeline, he had not painted my features with any great clarity in my last portrait, and I wondered how he would portray me this second time.

My birthday—which I shared with Paul—arrived that weekend, and Papa surprised us both by arranging a small impromptu party in our honor. We never formally celebrated it so this was wholly out of the ordinary.

He decided to invite Vincent, scripting an invitation on a piece of stationery that depicted a beautiful Japanese woman dressed in a kimono standing beside a crane and a plum blossom.

Paul looked just as perplexed as me when Papa informed us of his plans. The only sort of festivities we had on previous birthdays was Father giving us each a book.

"Perhaps this is a good sign," I said to Louise-Josephine. "He's both allowing Vincent to paint me and inviting him over for my birthday celebration." I fidgeted. "He's obviously not preventing me from seeing Vincent, so I don't think Paul said anything to him about that day in the rain."

She shrugged her shoulders. "Paul hasn't said anything to me either way. He seems busier than ever with his paintings. He spent nearly three hours in your father's studio yesterday."

I nodded my head. "Yes, I noticed two completed canvases and one new one stretched and primed. Hopefully, he'll be too exhausted to interfere."

Louise-Josephine let out a small laugh.

"And your mother?" I asked. "Do you think she has any idea?"

"My mother has her own secrets. She'd be a hypocrite if she warned you against it."

I smiled. All of us were navigating Father's rules and manipulating them so there would be punctures of freedom where he least expected them.

"I just never thought it would be possible to defy Papa. I guess I was wrong."

"You still must be wary of him, Marguerite. He has a vested interest in you. You run his household and he's not about to give that title to my mother. That would only give the villagers fodder for gossip."

"But if something comes of Vincent and me, Papa will eventually have to know."

Louise-Josephine nodded. "Yes, he will."

"Perhaps Father thinks I'm a good influence on Vincent." I took a deep breath. "Or now that Vincent's been taking the medicine Papa's been preparing for him, maybe Papa feels more at ease about a possible courtship between us."

Louise-Josephine shook her head. "I don't think either of us knows exactly what your father is thinking."

But she had that look in her eyes and I suspected she knew indeed.

FOR the party, I wore my yellow dress again, the one with the deep neckline, and Louise-Josephine helped me with my hair.

"Let's make you look even more beautiful than before," she whispered that morning as I stood in front of the mirror. She pulled up one of the rush chairs and sat me down, placing her hands on my shoulders.

She brushed my hair with vigorous strokes and then parted it down the middle. Smiling the whole time and humming softly, she braided each side and then pulled and pinned each section on top of my head.

"Now you look like a queen." She looked at her reflection and mine in the mirror and winked.

"I made an orange cake this morning," she said. "This way you'll have a little extra time to gather yourself."

I turned around and hugged her—my hands bringing her tiny frame close to my chest.

"Happy birthday," she whispered.

"I wish you could join us," I said as I released her.

She smiled and shook her head. "How would your father explain us at this point?"

She was right. If Papa were to introduce Louise-Josephine and her mother now, it would seem odd. He couldn't very well introduce them as servants, as Vincent should then have already seen them serving and clearing the many lunches he'd already had with Papa. And he could not introduce them as family, because he had never introduced them that way to even Paul or myself.

For a home that had so many colors and vibrant paintings on its walls, there were still so many shades of gray between us.

VINCENT arrived around noon carrying not his usual rucksack and paint box but two small gifts for Paul and me.

"Happy birthday!" he chimed as I opened the door.

"Thank you," I said as I ushered him in.

"These are for you and your brother." He pushed the two flat packages into my arms. "I hope you enjoy them."

"You needn't have brought anything."

He laughed. "My sister Willemina taught me better than that."

I giggled back and thanked him for his thoughtfulness. My anger at him for painting Adeline the week before had vanished.

I HAD tried to make the garden look festive for the occasion. I strung little Chinese paper lanterns over the two lime trees. I also put a pretty red cloth with tiny yellow flowers on the picnic table and filled a vase with fistfuls of champagne-colored roses.

When Vincent followed me into the garden, both Paul and Papa jumped up from their lawn chairs to greet him.

"We're so happy you could make it," Papa said as he approached Vincent and patted him on the back. A peacock and one of our many cats followed at Papa's heels.

I stood there with the two packages in my hand. "Vincent gave us these in honor of our birthdays." I looked at Vincent. "Which one is for me and which one is for Paul?"

I looked down and saw that on one of the brown packages there was a small illustration of a butterfly done in bright yellow paint. Otherwise the two packages seemed identical. Each one was wrapped in brown paper and tied with coarse butcher's string.

"Yours is the one with the yellow butterfly on it."

Paul took the other gift from me and thanked Vincent.

Then when Paul wasn't looking, Vincent reached into his pocket and retrieved a small box wrapped in blue rice paper. Nestled under the ribbon was a small folded crane.

"Open it later," he mouthed. I nodded, and placed it in one of the front pockets of my dress.

As my brother and I began to open our seemingly identical presents, Papa smiled. "They both loved the Japanese catalogs that your sister-in-law brought from Paris. Every time I catch one of them in the parlor, they're poring over those pages."

Vincent seemed pleased. "Then I think they'll like these very much."

He was right. He had given Paul and me each a small framed woodblock print. Mine was of a beautiful woman in a kimono kneeling over a tub of bathwater. Her yellow robe was patterned with tiny black circles, and her long white neck arched over the reflection of glistening water.

"How beautiful . . ." I covered my mouth with my hand. I was so overcome by such a lovely and generous gift, I had to control my urge to rush over and embrace him.

My brother seemed equally pleased with his print of a Japanese actor. The large nose and vulpine eyes of the man seemed to amuse Paul. "What a face!" he said, holding it afar.

"He's a Kabuki actor, or at least that is what the dealer in Paris told me." Vincent wiggled his foot a little in the garden's soil. "I hope you both enjoy them."

"Oh, yes," I said enthusiastically. "It's the nicest birthday present I've ever received!"

"Yes, thank you so much, Monsieur Van Gogh," Paul said and he shook Vincent's hand. I knew he would take this opportunity to try to talk with Vincent about painting.

I offered to take Paul's print and place it inside since I needed to go back and retrieve our lunch. But, even more important, I wanted to go inside quickly so I could peek at the secret gift Vincent had brought for me.

Paul handed his print over to me and I hurried back to the house. Instead of going straight to the kitchen, I bounded up the stairs and closed the door to my room.

I could hardly contain myself as I carefully detached the crane and removed the rice paper. Inside, tied with a piece of satin ribbon, was a lock of red hair.

It was more the color of apricots than the fiery red of strawberry. He had tied the strands together with a twist of blue ribbon, the pin-straight ends sticking out like straw.

I could hardly believe that I was holding a lock of Vincent's hair between my fingers. As I twisted and turned it, I could see threads of gold and chestnut. Copper iridescence reflecting in the light.

I imagined Vincent clipping the lock of hair then tying the strip of cobalt blue ribbon around its center. Even I, with my lack of experience, knew that this was a sign. It was as if he had extended his hand in a dance and was waiting to see if I would accept his invitation. Such a romantic gesture was not lost on me. On the contrary, it filled me with confidence and thoughts of how to arrange our next meeting.

How I wanted to rush in to Louise-Josephine's room and tell her everything at once. But I had already stepped away from our lunch for too long and I feared Papa would be coming up the stairs to retrieve me. I quickly folded the paper and precious bit of Vincent's hair and placed it for safekeeping in my drawer. I would show her my most treasured keepsake, all by the day's end.

SHE came to my room later that evening. It had taken me some time to clean the dishes and put away the leftover food. I was lying on my bed with my feet resting on a pillow, my journal open on my lap.

"I have a birthday present for you." She sat down beside me and handed me a large, flat package.

"I've already received so much today," I said, placing my journal to the side. I was anxious to show her both the woodblock print and the lock of hair from Vincent. But I didn't want to appear rude.

"Open it, Marguerite."

I placed the package in my lap and carefully untied the string.

"You shouldn't have gotten me anything," I said. "You've already given me the most extraordinary present." I took hold of Louise-Josephine's hand. "You've become my friend."

She smiled back at me. "I feel the same way, Marguerite. But still I wanted to get you something special." She pushed herself back on my bed. "Without being able to go into town, it was difficult . . . I hope you don't mind that I made one of the gifts myself."

I gently opened the package and found a copy of Bernardin's *Paul et Virginie* and a beautiful paper portfolio underneath. The cover of the portfolio was full of cabbage roses and yellow jonquils that Louise-Josephine had pasted in découpage. There was a pink ribbon through two holes in the center so I could tie the folder shut.

"I am not sure if you have the novel already. It's one of my favorites. Madame Lenoir lent me her copy during that time I spent with her family." She paused. "I often imagine what it would be like if the two of us lived on the island of Mauritius, like the two main characters. Before one of them is coerced back to Europe, the two of them live idyllically on the island. They sleep under palm trees and climb the rocky cliffs overlooking the sea. How wonderful it would be to live like that and be able to wander freely in the wild and not care what one's neighbors think!"

Touched by her thoughtfulness, I reached out and clasped her hand.

She smiled. "As for the portfolio, I thought you could put your sheet music in it," she said sweetly. "Or perhaps love letters . . ."

"It's so beautiful." I took her hand in mine and squeezed it again. "I will think of you every time I use it. I already have something I can put inside."

"What?" Her voice was now full of mischief. She could barely contain her excitement.

I went to my drawer and took out the lock of hair.

"He gave it to me this afternoon along with a woodblock print." I pointed to the drawing on my desk.

She took it from me and examined it carefully. Like me, she took it and coiled it around her finger.

"It's a sign, don't you think?" I giggled excitedly.

"Oh, certainly!" she agreed. "I think we should cut a lock of yours and send it off to him. It's only fair."

"Really?" The thought of it delighted me. "You really think we should?"

"Absolutely. He'd be insulted if you didn't."

After a few seconds of pondering, I agreed. I stood up and walked to the mirror above my fireplace.

"Take a small piece in the back," I suggested. "The color is more golden there. Plus it will be harder to notice it's gone."

She went over and opened the top drawer of my desk and withdrew a pair of cutting shears.

When she was done, there was a small lock of blonde hair between her fingers. "Use a lavender ribbon," she suggested. "It will offset the color best." She smiled. "As a painter, he'll appreciate that."

THIRTY-ONE

Lit from Within

I PLACED my lock of hair in a plain white envelope and dropped it in the postbox near the train station on my way to do my errands the next day.

Then I waited three days for him to come. During that time, I spent much of my time either in the garden or in my room wrapped up in the saga of Paul and Virginie.

The story consumed me. I closed my eyes and saw the rocky shore; the bending palm trees; the sun descending into the horizon, like a ball of oozing marmalade. I could almost taste the ocean water on my tongue. I looked at my hair after it had been washed and was still in tangles. I imagined wearing it uncombed, the long tresses saturated with salt.

I imagined climbing trees and collecting coconuts for soup, instead of potatoes and leeks. I began walking barefoot in my bedroom after my bath and imagined my toes naked and brown. I opened my window and stuck my head out between the shutters and imagined the smell of tropical flowers. Wild orchids replacing my rosebushes, fig and mango trees replacing the oaks and poplars.

It was easy to envision Vincent there with me, along with Louise-Josephine and Théophile, our children growing up together as close as kin. It would be our own utopia. I could see Vincent there with his large sun hat, his white linen shirt, his pale skin red from the sun. He would paint the sunsets, the stretches of dunes and patches of tall, wild grasses where I would run barefoot every day. Just as I had, that evening, when I sought Vincent out by the church.

After I was done reading the story, I would pass Louise-Josephine in the hall and all she had to say was "Mauritius" and I could not help but smile. It became a sort of secret code between us. At night, if either one of us had trouble sleeping, all we had to do was sneak into the other's bed and whisper the word and we'd both fall into a deep and peaceful sleep.

PAPA had scheduled Vincent to come paint my portrait on Wednesday, June 24. That morning Louise-Josephine helped me get dressed and, as always, helped to calm my nerves.

"You're not wearing lavender," he said when I opened the door for him. He clutched his soft hat to his chest and winked at me.

"Papa told me to wear white." I blushed. The gown was a stiff white taffeta, with a pink ribbon sash that cinched at the waist.

"Never mind. It is a fine choice."

I took a few steps and motioned for him to come into the parlor. "The piano is here, as you know. Do you still wish to paint me at the piano?"

Papa came into the room.

"Ahh! You're here right on time!" he said, clutching his pocket watch. "I'm afraid my daughter's stomach has been in knots all morning!"

"There is no need for her to be nervous. . . ." His voice was soft now as he glanced around the room. It was obvious he was surveying the light to see where it would be best to assemble the large easel he had under his arm. "She is a natural at this."

"Well, I don't know about that," Papa chuckled. "Perhaps a natural gardener or pianist, like her late mother. But her brother Paul seems more inclined to the artist's world."

Vincent didn't respond to Papa. He squinted at the window. "I want the light to come in from an angle." His voice was exuberant, almost ecstatic, as if he were now in the mind of his painting. "We'll need to pull out the piano and rearrange some of the furniture. I want to paint the mademoiselle from her right side."

"Oh, yes," Papa said agreeably. "Whatever you want, Vincent. I'll ask Paul to come down so we can turn around the piano for you. Just tell us where to put it."

Papa withdrew from the parlor and called for Paul to come downstairs. Within a few seconds, Paul was in the living room with us, dragging the piano so that it stood perpendicular to the wall.

"Ah, that's perfect now," Vincent said, obviously pleased. He was pacing around the room, kneading his fingers before him. "Now, Marguerite, if you could just sit down and place your fingers on the keys, I'll do the rest."

I walked quietly past my father and brother, their eyes watching me as closely as Vincent's, and sat down at the piano.

From that moment on, I heard very little. Vincent began to assemble his large easel. He placed a long, narrow canvas on its wooden lip and opened up his paint box.

Both Paul and Father watched transfixed as Vincent squeezed out his paints onto his palette board. Their eyes did not waver as he blended the pigments with the back of his palette knife.

I remained sitting at the keyboard, my eyes glancing outward only occasionally in order to observe everyone in the room.

Vincent, however, did not look up at me those first few minutes he spent organizing his paints and brushes. Only after he had set at least six colors on the wooden board did he begin to tilt his head and study me more closely.

"Lift your chin a little, mademoiselle . . . yes, now rest your fingers on the keys," he instructed. I obliged. I swiveled to face the piano and delicately placed my hands on the ivory keys.

Louise-Josephine had suggested that I wear my hair in a chignon that afternoon. As I bowed my head slightly to pretend I was reading the sheet music in front of me, I could feel some of the pins unpopping, a few tendrils slowly unfurling behind my ears.

THE sound of his brush moving across his canvas sent shivers up my spine. I could smell the intense odor of the turpentine and heard him opening and closing the bottle of linseed oil. Although my eyes were firmly placed on the keys, I could not help but imagine him as I had seen him painting that night at the church. Hunched over his canvas, his eyes darting over his subject, the indistinguishable extension between his brush and his hand.

I wondered exactly how he was painting me, and whether this time he would delineate my features: the sharp triangle of my nostrils, the low ebbing of my eyelashes, the thin ripple of my tightly pursed mouth.

My skin felt both hot and damp underneath the crisp white taffeta. My legs were sealed together like two wet leaves. As he painted me, I imagined he was kissing me just as he had that evening in front of the church, all his fingers and eyes wrapping around me like large loops of ivy.

For the several hours that I remained in pose, I became hypnotized by the sounds of wet pigment being applied to the canvas. The dragging of his horsetail brushes, the rake of his palette knife, and the brief sweeping of a dried reed.

I didn't hear a peep from Father or Paul. Both of them were so mesmerized by watching him work that they didn't dare disturb him.

As the third hour passed, my neck began to ache and my back felt so sore I thought I might fall from the stool. Then, just as I was about to ask if it might be possible to stop for a few minutes, Vincent announced that he was nearly finished.

"We can take a break now, Marguerite," he said. "Why don't you stand up and stretch your legs?"

I could barely feel my calves as I stood up. My legs were so tired that I feared they might buckle from the shock of my weight. But as I gathered my skirt and lifted myself up, I felt the tension in my back and shoulders finally release.

"Your daughter's a natural," Vincent told Papa. "She's gone three hours without a break. I have painted other women before, but your daughter is different. Even her silence inspires me. It is like there is music under her skin. I hear it as strong as church bells."

Papa tried to smile back at Vincent but it was obvious he was deeply troubled.

"My Marguerite has always been a natural at the piano," Papa said diplomatically, clearly ignoring what Vincent was really saying. "Is the painting almost finished?"

Vincent nodded and put down his brush. "I can finish the rest at home."

I smiled and walked over to the canvas. Papa was commenting to Paul that he found it remarkable how quickly Vincent painted. Paul was nodding his head, staring at Vincent intently. He had not taken his eyes off of Vincent for the entire sitting.

It was a beautiful portrait of me, and I made no attempt to mask my great pleasure.

"It's wonderful," I said, touching one of my hands to my breast.

He had painted me in swirls of pink and white. My blonde hair piled high above my head, a delicate and flattering profile of me as I concentrated on the keys. He had painted the wall behind me in a mossy green with vibrant orange spots. The contrasting carpet in ox-blood red with verdant strokes resembled thick blades of grass. The rich wood of the piano was painted in a dark violet. The long, saturated strokes, glossy like candy.

And he had made me look beautiful—the swirls of pink and red mingling with the white of my dress made me appear as if I were glowing brightly, lit from within.

THIRTY-TWO

The Final Touches

He came back the following day to make a few adjustments to the painting. Paul was home that afternoon and fetched me in the garden.

"He's here," he said tersely. "He asked if you'd sit by the piano one more time so he can make some final touches to the canvas."

I moved my hands over my hair and smoothed out my bun.

"He's waiting, Marguerite . . . I left him alone in the vestibule." There was a tinge of impatience in Paul's voice. "I'll go upstairs and tell Papa he's here."

Our father had been in the attic all day tinkering with his print-making machine.

"Yes," I said. "I'll go at once."

I went into the house to find him. I was surprised my brother had left Vincent in the hallway and not shown him into the parlor. It was very poor manners on his part.

I found Vincent standing in the corridor looking at the stained-glass window. His straw hat was by his feet, next to the canvas of me at the piano.

"Good morning," I greeted him warmly. "I'm sorry my brother didn't show you in. He should have offered you a cold drink, at least!"

Vincent smiled. "Don't worry. I haven't come for your brother's hospitality. I just need to make a few adjustments before I can consider your portrait finished."

"Of course," I said, somewhat surprised by the businesslike nature of his tone.

"Also," he said as he stepped closer, "I couldn't wait to see you again."

I smiled and my cheeks began to warm.

"I, too, am happy to see you again."

But I could not help but feel nervous. I knew we were not alone. "Papa is finishing up in his studio; he'll be down any minute," I said. I felt the need to warn him that we needed to be careful.

"In that case, I must tell you now just how much I enjoyed receiving your gift."

Again, I blushed. He reached out and touched the back of my head. "So no one knows about the missing tresses but me?"

"No," I whispered. His hand dropped from the nape of my neck to my cheek. I felt his cupped hand against my jawline and the pressure felt strong, the calluses strangely comforting.

"When will you meet me again?"

There was a greediness to his voice, an impatience that I now understood to be that of hunger and desire. It was no longer something foreign to me. It was in my voice too.

"I promise I will. . . ."

"There's a cave not far behind the Château Léry . . . come tomorrow night."

I nodded, but it was not a confident nod. I was distracted by some noise I heard upstairs. Papa's footsteps were easily recognizable and I stiffened.

"Come, Monsieur Van Gogh, let's set your easel up in the parlor." I spoke loudly so Papa would hear me. This was a signal to Vincent that our privacy was threatening to be compromised.

In this case, Vincent's ability to abandon his intimate charms so easily when work was suggested worked in my favor. Perhaps his eagerness to get back to painting was greater than his inclination for romance, for the mere suggestion of setting up his easel energized him instantly.

Within seconds, his hands had abandoned the soft flesh of my cheeks for his sturdier companion, his easel.

He brought with him his lighter one, the one he was able to strap onto his back. And with the efficiency of a soldier, he picked up my portrait and slid his hand through the handle of his paint box, bringing all his equipment inside.

"We'll need to move the piano again," I said. "I'm sorry, Papa moved it back last night."

"Not to worry." Vincent walked across the room and began to move the piano so it was situated at the same angle it had been the day before.

He was just about to retrieve his paint box when Papa walked into the room.

"Good afternoon, Vincent!" Father had on a bright green smock and his hair, having been recently rinsed with his special henna shampoo, seemed even brighter against it. "How good of you to stop by!" Papa went over and shook Vincent's hand.

"I hope you don't mind, Doctor, I thought the painting needed a little tweaking. I wrote to Theo about it last night and I want it to be perfect."

"Yes, of course. Don't worry at all, my son."

"I just need to arrange my palette and then I'll get started. Marguerite has been kind enough to oblige me."

Papa gave him a weak smile. "Yes, she is a good girl, our Marguerite."

Out of the corner of my eye, I could see Vincent rummaging through his box. Suddenly, his face seemed worried.

"Is there anything the matter, Vincent?" Papa, too, sensed Vincent's agitation.

"I think I've forgotten my palette. I'll have to go home and fetch it! How could I have done that?"

Unable to believe he had left behind one of his essential instruments, Vincent began throwing all the contents out of his rucksack. Out tumbled his spare brushes, the dirty rags, and extra palette knives. Within seconds, the room was a mess.

"How could I have forgotten it?" His voice was beginning to escalate and Papa went over to him and tried to calm him down.

"It's all right, Vincent." He put his arm over his back and I could see the skin peeking from Vincent's collar was aflame. "I'll lend you one of mine. I have a spare palette upstairs."

Vincent put his hand to his eyes. "I am sorry to have this outburst. I'm just furious at myself."

I shook my head. To me Vincent's agitation was a sign of his perfectionism, the passion he held for his work. All I wanted to do was soothe him.

"It's not a problem. Papa says he has a spare."

"Yes, absolutely, Vincent. I'll run upstairs and get it! Don't worry. I'll relish telling everyone that you used my palette to paint my daughter's portrait!"

Papa rushed out of the room and bounded up the stairs. Minutes later, he was in the parlor again, with a palette in hand.

After that, Papa did not leave us alone. He watched as intently as he had the day before. I knew he was anxious to see if Vincent would sign the painting after he was finished. He had heard from Monsieur Ravoux that Vincent had signed the portrait he had done of his daughter, Adeline. I knew this irritated Papa. Being the collector that he was, Papa knew that the artist's signature would only increase the value of Ravoux's painting, if Vincent became famous one day.

Vincent, however, seemed to take little notice of Papa's presence. From the moment he began to set up his easel, nothing else seemed to matter. His bad mood about having forgotten his palette seemed to have vanished, and his eyes now focused on the painting in front of him.

"If you would be kind enough to sit by the piano, mademoiselle," Vincent asked me, signaling that he was ready to begin. He was now back to his old self and the shadow of his outburst seemed to be fading, forgotten by all of us.

I did as I was told. I sat down on the stool and tried to focus on something unremarkable, like the vase of peonies in the foyer. But it was of little use. I couldn't help thinking of the novel Louise-Josephine had given me. I closed my eyes and dreamed of the two of us marooned on Mauritius. I imagined jasmine-scented breezes and warm turquoise waters.

This time it was effortless to pretend I was somewhere else. I had to concentrate on suppressing my urge to smile.

He painted for nearly a half hour without uttering another word. Then, just as the silence began to worry me, I heard him ask me to pull away my hem.

"Can you move your skirt a little, Marguerite? I want to be able to paint the tip of your shoe."

I could feel Papa's eyes watching me carefully, when he said that.

Ever so slowly, I pulled the material toward my ankle. My petticoat brushed against my shins as I lifted the toe of my boot and placed it gently on the brass pedal.

Vincent, however, did not notice any of this. His eyes remained firmly glued to his canvas. He hummed softly to himself as he dabbed his brush in the corner. His face was now so close to the canvas that all I could see was the tuft of his red hair sprouting between the wooden stretchers of his easel.

There was the occasional clank of his brush hitting the sides of his can of paint thinner, and the sporadic cough from Papa. But other than that, the room, just like it had been the day before, remained painfully still.

HE was finished in less than two hours. He brushed off his knees and announced that the painting was now finally complete.

"With your father's permission, I want to give this one to you." He looked up at Papa to see if he would have any objection to his gift. The paint was still shiny and wet in places.

"It needs to dry, and I need to have it in front of me when I write to Theo about it. But after that, I would be honored if Mademoiselle Gachet would have it."

"That is most generous of you, Vincent," Papa said. I could see his eyes spinning, trying to think of a polite way to request that Vincent sign the portrait.

"It would be lovely if there was some way to show that it was a gift from you."

"Well, there it is, then. . . ." Vincent seemed genuinely pleased and Father's oblique way of requesting a signature seemed to have gone over Vincent's head.

Vincent began to rattle his brushes in a jar of turpentine, wiping them clean on a spotted, oily rag.

After stretching my legs, I returned to the piano and replaced the cover over the keys. I stood up and came closer to him. I could see the pale freckling on the nape of his neck, the thin protrusion of spine rising in the middle of his blue smock. I wanted to take my finger and trace the lithe ribbon of bone and feel the interlocking knots of vertebrae, the tiny pieces that, like a puzzle, made his body whole. But I needn't remind myself that we were no longer alone. Papa was standing there looking intently at the finished painting.

"It's a beauty, Vincent. You are a genius at portraiture."

"*She* is a beauty," he responded. "It was difficult to do her justice. There is so much she keeps hidden." Vincent cleared his throat and looked directly at Papa. "That is why I enjoy the challenge of painting your daughter. . . . That is the painter's job, after all, isn't it, Doctor? Revealing what others fail to see . . ." Vincent raised his eyebrow as he looked at Papa for a reaction.

Papa, however, gave none. He ignored Vincent's flattering comments about me and concentrated solely on the painting.

"I know you need to bring the painting back to the inn this evening, but when you return with it, we'll hang it up in Marguerite's bedroom," he said as he clasped his hands. "I'm sure it will serve as a very happy memory for Marguerite over the years. Something to break up her solitude."

THIRTY-THREE

The Beautiful Canvas

I WAS not able to sleep that night. I continued to replay our brief encounter, my promise to him that I would meet him in the cave behind the Château Léry. Strangely, I told none of this to Louise-Josephine. Not because I didn't want to—for it took all my strength to hold it in—but because I wanted to come to the decision by myself. If I were to give myself to Vincent without a marriage proposal, I wanted to do so without having been influenced by anyone else.

Thoughts of my mother kept creeping back into my mind. If only I could have replaced the image of her near her death, angry and ashen, with one of her triumphant and without remorse. She was a woman who mourned every crack, every fissure that appeared in her precious china. Only now did I wonder if she saw those painted dishes as a metaphor for her life.

But in some way her tragedy motivated me. I did not want to end up like Mother or even like Virginie in Bernardin's love story, stoically sacrificing my passion only to end up dying with regrets. It was easy to imagine myself with a similar fate, and I found myself yearning to create a more satisfying ending with Vincent.

By the time he arrived to drop off the painting, I had made up my mind. I would agree to meet him that evening.

He was wearing a new blue smock when I opened the door. The color offset his eyes and intensified the red in his hair. It reminded me of the effect that he had achieved when he painted the portrait of Papa.

"Vincent . . . ," I gushed. Surprised by my temporary lack of propriety, I tried to gather myself. His arrival had taken me off guard. I was already so far ahead of myself in imagining our imminent rendezvous that I momentarily lost my manners.

"I've brought you your painting," he said as he stepped inside. "I have done a small copy for my brother, so this one is all yours."

He handed me the beautiful canvas, my image in profile amid swirls of green and violet paint.

Although I was secretly imagining what it would be like if he swept me into his arms and kissed me right in the hallway, I could see how anxious he was to see my reaction to the painting.

I held the canvas to the light—stretching it before me as though I were grasping something that was a combination of us both. He had delineated all my features, the soft contours of my body—I inhabited the canvas because of his brush and his vision. It was exhilarating.

"Have you thought about my proposal?" he asked softly. He stepped closer. I could feel the heat rising from his body. I opened my eyes and saw the rake of red eyelashes, the tiny pores of his skin, the thin lips of his mouth protruding through his whiskers.

"Yes."

"And will you come?"

I waited several seconds. Every inch of me was trembling.

"Yes." The word almost caught in my throat. But, somehow, it got out.

THAT evening, I burned my first chicken. My nerves were on edge; my heartbeat was racing. I pulled out the charred bird and threw it into the garbage. Papa would disapprove if he discovered the carcass, but he would also be suspicious if he saw that my kitchen skills were not up to par. Without much time to prepare something new, I quickly began peeling some potatoes and washing leeks for a soup. Then I set about making a batter for Papa's favorite savory crêpes.

Louise-Josephine could read the distraction on my face. Throughout the meal, I pushed my food around and could not help glancing at the clock on the mantel.

We were in the kitchen hardly seconds when she took one of the dirty plates from me and thrust it into the sink.

"What's the matter?" she whispered. "You're acting strange."

"I know . . . I'm sorry."

Her eyes were pleading with me to give her more information. That was typical of Louise-Josephine. She was always so impatient.

"I'm going to see Vincent tonight." I was speaking as quietly as I could manage. I was so fearful that others might be listening.

I was nervous she'd be angry with me for not telling her earlier, but there was no disappointment on her face, only excitement about the latest development.

"That's wonderful!" She pinched my arm. "I'll meet you in your bedroom at nine o'clock. Everyone will be in bed by then."

I agreed.

At nine o'clock, she was there.

THIRTY-FOUR

Shattered Marble

SHE was dressed for bed when she came into my room. Her long white nightgown flowed like a bellflower. Her brown hair was swept underneath a cotton cap.

I was so determined that evening. My long blonde hair was down, and covered my shoulders. My breastbone shone like an arrow through my skin. I turned to face Louise-Josephine.

"I should be nervous, shouldn't I?"

"Not if you've already come to a decision." She came closer. Her nightgown rustled against her ankles.

The painting Vincent had done of me was already hanging on the wall. It was the first time she had seen it up close. For several seconds she was quiet, her face studying the canvas. I had never seen her scrutinize something so carefully.

"It's wonderful, Marguerite. He sees you. That much is clear."

I knew she was referring to the underpaint of pink and red madder beneath the swirls of white taffeta. It couldn't have been more accurate. I was fire encased in a tomb of white marble.

"I don't want to end up like *Maman*," I said almost defiantly. "I have these images of her so angry with Papa. She knew of his liaisons, I'm sure of it. And she hated Auvers. . . ."

Louise-Josephine took me in her arms. The smell of tea roses permeated her skin and it comforted me. When I thought about it, she had met Théophile by chance. She had been out for a brief errand in the hope of buying a simple box of soap and her life had been changed by that unexpected meeting.

Just weeks before, I had been shocked to see a girl I had lived with for years sneaking out her bedroom window while her mother cavorted in my father's bed and Paul slept soundly downstairs. The façade of Papa's propriety was shattered that evening. Now I realized that every one of us was plotting to get what we wanted under the smoke screen of night.

Louise-Josephine sat with me for nearly two hours, before I finally opened up the window and slithered down the side of the house.

I felt a moment of déjà vu as I ran down the road toward the caves behind the Château Léry. Perhaps it was the sound of my dress whipping against my heels or the sensation of my unpinned hair flowing over my shoulders. I felt just as I imagined Louise-Josephine must have felt that evening I first saw her running down the road in front of our house, her entire body racing like a thoroughbred escaped from its paddock. With that rush of temporary emancipation, I couldn't move my body fast enough to get to the cave where Vincent was waiting.

I found it without much difficulty. There were tracks in the grass, as if he had come here when it had rained. Large necklaces of leafy vines dangled over the mouth of the cave. I pushed them back and dipped my head inside.

"Vincent?" I spoke quietly but my voice still echoed down the limestone channel.

I could see a circle of candles farther in and I followed them.

He stood there in his white hemp shirt. The flicker of the candles cast an orange glow to his skin.

"I wasn't sure you'd come." He came out of the light. The cave was cold and damp and I was shivering in my flimsy gown.

He didn't speak, as I had imagined he would. Instead, he took hold of me with a strength that I was quite unused to. My body shuddered in its offering. I did not resist him. I embraced him without protest and he brought his lips to mine.

I must confess that his kiss emboldened me. I suddenly imagined myself as one of his former mistresses, someone with far more experience than I truly had. When Vincent lifted his hands, I lifted mine. As if pressing against our own reflection, our palms pushed against each other until I finally let go. With my arms at my sides, he pulled down my sleeves, revealing my naked shoulders, and planted his mouth on my bare skin.

Had he sliced through my dress with his palette knife, he would have found every inch of my body the color of cadmium red. I could feel his excitement escalating, my own rising in a rhythm that matched his. His body became tense as his hands moved my gown farther and farther downward until it fell to my knees. Naked in front of him, he felt every inch of my body. The narrow of my waist. The length of my thighbone. All the areas that had never felt another hand against them but my own. He lifted me so that my back was pressed against the limestone wall. Cool, damp powder pressed into my back along with the impression of rock. There was a sensation of pain that washed over my body. The arrow of the stone's jagged edges knifing into my skin. I gasped for breath as Vincent took hold of me. A thousand red strokes of crimson flashed before my eyes. I bit my lip. I had never felt more alive.

I HAD not expected the cool air to chill me as it did when we separated. I noticed it almost immediately as he untangled his limbs from my own. I went to put on my dress, but the neckline was ripped. Although the fabric covered most of my body, I was still left feeling terribly cold.

He was busy dressing himself before he noticed me shivering. He seemed smaller to me somehow in the candlelight now.

I accepted his coat and slid my arms into the big sleeves. It was the same one that I had noticed was threadbare that first Sunday afternoon he came to lunch with us. And it didn't keep me warm.

THIRTY-FIVE

Boatside

I DID not see Vincent again for four days. Every morning I would wake up and be certain of his arrival. I would spend extra effort on my hair; I'd bake something special: an almond cake infused with orange blossom water or a plum tart whose center looked like a wheel made from dark lavender glass.

As busy as I tried to be, I could not stop thinking of our last encounter. My brain dissected each detail, the way I imagined an artist composing the paint on his palette. There was me in my cotton nightgown. The soft halo of candlelight. Vincent in his white hemp shirt. As I fell deeper into the memory, the details became even clearer. I could feel the almost rough gestures of his hands; taste the lacing of salt on his skin, the pressure of his torso against mine. These thoughts were in my head when I was in the garden, when I sat down to do my needlepoint, even when I was answering one of Papa's questions. But as the days passed, it no longer took on the seamless perfection of a romance novel. Vincent's absence seemed to echo the coldness I had felt at the evening's end. And I began to fear the worst—that I had been made a fool.

Still, I continued to look for him when I went out to do my errands. But my time in the village was brief, and I could not spend hours searching for him in the fields without inciting suspicion within the household. I would return with my basket full of bread and cheese, eggs, and some milk, but I would feel emptier than when I had left the house in the morning.

I tried to put on a brave face, but inside I was crumbling. I yearned to see Vincent's face. I needed confirmation that his feelings for me were genuine. I had interpreted the energy with which he made love to me to be reminiscent of the way he seized painting. But now, I began to wonder if I was wrong. As I tried to make sense of his absence, I had no other choice but to wait.

On the first day of July, the boaters were out on the banks of the Oise, and I decided to ask my father if I might be able to go out for a few hours.

Papa had been sitting in the garden with his feet propped up on one of the lawn chairs. He was wearing a pair of darkened spectacles to protect his eyes from the sun and a large floppy hat I had never seen before. From a distance, he could have been Vincent, and I wondered if he had purchased the hat because he thought it would make him appear more artistic.

"Papa," I asked as I set down a small tray with some sandwiches and a pitcher of iced tea beside him, "might I spend a few hours reading by the river?"

He placed his papers down on his lap and removed his glasses. His eyes looked glazed and tired.

"By yourself?" He raised an eyebrow and I felt my skin grow cold even though the summer was hot upon us.

"Yes, of course, Papa," I replied. "Unless you count Flaubert." I withdrew the novel from my apron pocket. I had finished reading *Paul and Virginie* a few days earlier and was now on to another novel.

Papa reached over and poured himself a glass of tea. One of the lemon wedges fell into the cup and caused a slight splash to fall on the tray.

"I'm not feeling so well today," he said as he took a sip of tea. "You can go, but before you leave can you bring me a vial of my foxglove tincture? I left it on my desk."

"Of course," I said and patted his knee. It wasn't a gesture I often did, but he looked unusually vulnerable sitting in the chair. Even when he lifted his eyebrows in suspicion at my request, he didn't appear threatening. Perhaps it was the heaviness in his lids, the thin papery webbing that made him suddenly appear older than before.

I went upstairs to his study. The green and red wallpaper shone between patches of oil paintings from his collection. Tacked against his desk was the etching Vincent had done as a preliminary sketch for his portrait of Papa. Vincent had made a copy of the oil painting of Father sitting at the picnic table; this one was loose and rested against the wooden side of his desk. The copy did not include the two Goncourt novels, and the foxgloves in this version rested on the table, not in a water glass. Father had yet to have it framed.

I hadn't been in this room for several days, and the veil of dust on the windowsill was a blatant reminder that I needed to be more on top of my chores on the house's higher floors. I went over to his desk and straightened some of his piles of papers and found the vial of his medicine near his pen and ink set.

The silver flask felt nearly empty. I had seen him refill it only days before with a larger pitcher that he stored near the icehouse. Obviously Papa had not been feeling well for some time, and his self-medication had not yet remedied his ailments. He claimed he took foxglove to cure a slowness that often overcame him, a sort of melancholy and a weakness of the heart combined. But there were always periods of highs and lows with him. Much like Vincent, I thought, and my skin grew cold.

I tapped the tiny flask through the cloth of my apron and hurried down the stairs and into the garden.

I gave Papa his tincture and gathered my things. I took with me a small woolen blanket, my novel, and a small kerchief that I filled with some rounds of bread and a napkin knotted with some cheese. I was eager to have a few moments outside the house, for I was secretly hoping that I might see Vincent.

It was a bright, clear day and the water of the river rippled in small green waves.

Past the bridge near the village church, I found a grassy area where I could see the boats launch. The punters had lined their boats against the shoreline. Women in crisp linen dresses and straw hats sat at the bows holding parasols the color of meringue.

I couldn't help but smile, as there was something so refreshing in seeing the boats bobbing against the tide. One of the boatmen called to me and asked if I might like a ride.

"Come with me, mademoiselle!" he cried. "Don't hide your

face in a book when the river begs your reflection!" He motioned with his hand for me to come over.

I laughed and buried my head in my book.

Again he tried to persuade me, as he stood balancing himself on the ribs of his boat.

"Oh, I couldn't, monsieur, but thank you. . . ." I waved my hand to indicate he should go ahead without me.

Just then I heard a rustle in the trees.

"Why didn't you go off with him?"

Vincent's voice took me by surprise. He was standing before me carrying a wet canvas and his box of paints. His face was streaked with red and blue pigment. Absentminded fingerprints intermingled with the stubble on his cheeks.

"I was saving myself for Flaubert," I replied sarcastically and buried my face in the book. Seeing him act so flippantly after four days had passed since our liaison angered me.

"What's the matter, my little piano player?" he asked.

"It's been nearly a week since I last saw you." I felt my face grow hot and I was fighting back tears. "I feared you had forgotten about me."

"I've been painting," he said, his voice strangely unapologetic. He turned and motioned toward a canvas he had rested against a tree.

It was a beautiful painting filled with colorful boats moored against the river. He had painted the water in a series of emerald and blue strokes, with two white figures between a bright red dinghy.

"I didn't forget about you, Marguerite," he said, his voice softening this time. He took my book and moved it out of the way so he could sit down beside me. "How could I forget that slender white neck of yours, that skin as supple as a camellia blossom? You should not worry yourself unnecessarily."

I managed a weak smile.

"My absence had nothing to do with how I felt about our last evening together. This week has been a very difficult one for me . . . one full of trials." He looked away from me and took one of the pebbles by the blanket's edge, throwing it into the river. "Theo wrote that little Vincent has been sick, and Theo has been having problems with his employers. I'm planning to go for a visit because I worry Theo is holding back from me in his letters."

I looked down and saw Vincent's hand now on the grass, the long white fingers nestled against the green, silvery blades. The cuff of his sleeve had a smudge of red paint on its edge. Against the white cloth, it looked like a smear of lipstick on a husband's collar. Even as I heard him talk about his troubles, I could not help but feel a silent jealousy against it.

But the allure of his genius was intoxicating. The sight of his painting nestled against the tree, beautiful in its waves of color and crosshatch of sea-foam and malachite green, took my breath away. It was impossible for me to maintain my resentment.

So with the brilliance of his work before me, I tried to soften my tone toward him. "You needn't take everything so much to heart, Vincent," I counseled. "I'm sure Theo is just preoccupied now that the child is sick."

Vincent rubbed his face with his palm.

"I came to Auvers to escape worrying about such things so I could paint, but it seems I can't avoid it. Life, with all its aches and pains, still follows me." He let out a small cough. "But the sight of you, Marguerite, is a welcome relief."

He moved closer to me, the bottom of his trousers sliding over the wet grass. His mouth was now only inches away from mine, and I could feel the heat of his skin hovering close to me.

I didn't feel as sure of myself as on that night in the cave. There was no blanket of darkness to mask my clumsiness or to hide us from the eyes of gossip. But I was weak in his presence. The image of him small, with his threadbare coat on my shoulders, was a distant memory. Once again I was that young lover who ventured into the night, greedy to be close to someone who made everyday things beautiful. After all, he had made me feel that way, and I could not help but feel grateful.

THIRTY-SIX

A Conflict of Passions

"PERHAPS you should consider running away with Théophile and me," Louise-Josephine suggested one afternoon while we were sewing alone in the parlor. Vincent had left to see his brother in Paris and Papa and Paul had gone to Chaponval for the afternoon to pick up some more canvas stretchers.

There was great excitement in her voice as if the possibilities of adventure were at our fingertips.

"Oh, Louise-Josephine," I said. I was always the sensible one in her company and the dreamer when I was alone. "We can't possibly do that. . . ."

"And why not?" she asked. "What's left for us if we are to remain here? I will continue to be kept upstairs and you will continue to remain a servant or, worse"—she placed her fingers over her mouth and whispered comically—"an unmarried spinster, serving your father and brother for the rest of your life."

I shuddered. The thought was truly terrifying to me.

"Does Théophile know that you cannot get married without this certificate that you speak of?" I asked.

"Yes," she said. "He tells me it's no matter to him."

"And his family?" I asked tentatively. "Will they object to the relationship?"

Louise-Josephine shook her head. "Although his family lives locally, he's been living in a small boardinghouse in Pontoise for the past several months. He tells me he is able to support himself independently of his family."

"Then he's better off than Vincent," I sighed.

"He was just promoted to senior conductor," she beamed. "And he suspects he'll have enough money saved to buy us an apartment in Paris by next year!"

"This is wonderful news," I said as I forced a smile. I could not help but feel a little jealous.

"I know he realizes that I have no father to speak of, but he assures me that his parents will accept me. His sister married an Italian man three years ago."

"Then it seems like it will all work out for you." Again, there was tinge of regret in my voice. Not because I didn't want Louise-Josephine to be married, but because, in my heart, I wanted the same thing, too.

"Do you think Papa will object?"

"What—to me marrying Théophile?" She shook her head, scoffing at my suggestion. "Why would he object? As long as we do it quietly outside of Auvers, it will only be good news to him. He won't need to go to such lengths to keep me hidden!"

It was bittersweet for me to hear her speaking. I was happy that finally things would be in Louise-Josephine's favor after a lifetime of having little opportunity. But I knew Papa would be harder on me. He had more to lose if I were to leave. There would be no one to help him with his tinctures, Madame Chevalier was not much of a cook, and I knew how to make everything run smoothly for him.

Louise-Josephine pulled another length of thread through her needle.

"I would love to see you leave this place, Marguerite. You really could come and live with Théophile and me."

"But what about Vincent?"

Lousie-Josephine shook her head. "You must remember, Marguerite, Vincent came to Auvers because he wasn't well. Will he be willing to fight with his own doctor? The man who is supposed to oversee his care?"

I looked over at her with disbelief and paused. The dress I was working on remained forgotten on my lap. "What are you saying?"

"I just worry that Vincent might feel conflicted . . . that his passion to get well might supersede all other desires."

"Why should one mutually exclude the other?" I asked, clearly puzzled.

"He might feel that your father will no longer provide him his tinctures, if he is cross with him."

I remained quiet and tried to concentrate on my stitching, but my mind was now racing. I knew how Vincent had become used to Papa's remedies over the past few weeks. He had started out quite skeptical of them, but now I saw him swigging regularly from the little glass flask Papa prepared weekly for him. I no longer knew what Papa was mixing, as he began to get up earlier and earlier, making them before I was even down to fix breakfast.

"He has to stand up to Papa at some point if we are to have a future together. . . ."

She shook out the skirt she was hemming. "No matter what happens, Marguerite, you must have some satisfaction in your experiences with Vincent. . . . Even if you and Vincent don't end up together, you've still had an adventure!"

I put down my sewing again. "I could not think like that!" I blurted out at her. "I am not like you! I did not embark on all this just for silly amusement!" I shook my head. "I have a proper family name and I'm entitled to a marriage of my own—a family of my own!" I was crying now. My face was red. I had believed that night I snuck out the window that I had no other expectations except to be with Vincent for as long as he'd have me, but now the bourgeois little girl in me was returning. If Louise-Josephine could muse on her future life in Paris, I, too, wanted all of the things that were promised in storybooks.

But my words had been cruel to Louise-Josephine and as soon as they flew out of my mouth, I regretted saying them. To this day, I can't believe I lashed out at her with such venom.

She sat there staring at the skirt that now took over the entire breadth of her lap. Her face was without expression; her eyes were downcast.

"I'm so sorry," I said. I put my sewing completely aside and went to take her hand. "It's just that I want to have a life outside this place and sometimes I fear that will not be possible."

Louise-Josephine remained stiff. I had wounded her. I could sense it even though her face revealed little reaction. This was the other side of Louise-Josephine, the one that I had known in the past. It was the harder side, the one she had cultivated all those years she lived with her grandmother in Paris.

Now she lifted her chin and straightened her shoulders: she would not tell me just how deeply I had hurt her.

"I'm sorry," I whispered again.

She shook her head. She was gathering herself before she finally spoke.

"I want the same thing for you, Marguerite. But you need to talk to Vincent. You need to find out if he even wants a wife or family. He might not want all the responsibilities that being a husband entails. He sees what Theo goes through and he might feel he can only be an artist."

I took her arm and brought it to my chest. The warmth comforted me and I held on to her tightly. "I will talk to him when he returns," I promised.

There could be no other way to put it all to rest. Even I knew that.

And so I waited until he arrived back in Auvers. This time there was no need to search for him. He came to our front door straight from the train, although when he arrived, I hardly recognized him.

THIRTY-SEVEN

Relapse

He stood there in his blue smock and felt hat. Haggard and withdrawn, he looked as though the sea had brought him to our door.

He was carrying a small valise with him and no canvas or paints.

"I've come directly from the station," he said. He looked at me with blank, dusty eyes. "Is your father at home, Marguerite?" He rubbed his forehead. "I need to see him at once."

Papa was in fact home, and I told Vincent to wait in the parlor while I went to get him.

I had been so shocked at Vincent's appearance that I hadn't had any time to be upset that he had seemed uninterested in seeing me.

"Papa," I cried when I went into the garden, "Vincent is here. He's come straight from the station. . . ." I was having trouble breathing, having run from the back door to the far end of our backyard.

"Take it easy, child," Father said as he rose from his lawn chair. "What's the matter?"

"Vincent . . . ," I said in between deep breaths. "He's returned from his visit with Theo, and he looks terrible!"

"Where is he?" Father asked. He looked almost as alarmed as I felt.

"He's sitting in the parlor. I told him I would get you at once."

Father rubbed his eyes with his thumb and forefinger. "I just need to get a few things from my office. Go tell Vincent I'll be there soon."

When I returned to the parlor he was wringing his hands together and sweating tiny droplets down his neck.

"Father will be with you shortly," I told him. "Would you like some tea? Perhaps a slice of cake?"

"No. No, thank you," he answered and his voice was clipped and anxious. "I just need to speak to your father. I had unexpected news during my trip to Paris, and I'm a bit agitated over it."

I nodded. My hand was still on the doorjamb when Papa arrived. He had his stethoscope around his neck and carried his black medicine bag. He went quickly to Vincent and sat down beside him.

"Vincent," Papa said gently, "tell me what has happened."

I STOOD there behind the curtain to the parlor, listening as Vincent explained to Father what had happened in Paris with Theo. I heard Papa quiet him for a moment so he could check his pulse and hear his heartbeat. Then, after Papa's medicine bag was snapped shut, Vincent began telling his story.

"The baby was still sick when I arrived," he said. His voice was shaking. "I tried not to be a nuisance, but I also needed to clarify my financial situation with Theo."

He fell back into the sofa.

"Theo's been saying for some time that he might leave Goupil's, and I hoped for some reassurance that he could still continue to support me."

"Yes, of course," Father said. "That is a reasonable concern."

"I did not expect Jo to interrupt our conversation, but it seems she has come to resent me, or at least resent Theo's supporting me. I was so shocked when she showed her displeasure."

"Well, with the baby being sick, perhaps she was just exhausted and overwhelmed," Father suggested sympathetically. "Surely, you can understand the stress she's under now. . . ."

I did not recognize the compassion in Father's voice. It sounded strange and foreign to me.

"She said some awful things to me, and my brother looked so helpless. He didn't defend me. He just said nothing." Vincent put his face into his palms. I had never seen him look so weary.

Vincent continued, "An artist should be free to paint and not have to worry about money or where he will find his next set of paints or bolt of canvas. My brother is not only kin but also my dealer . . . I pay him in my work. I don't just take from him like some leech and not compensate him."

"I know how talented Theo thinks you are. But he has a family now, and it's difficult to feed a wife and child on paintings alone."

Vincent's voice was cracking now. "But what will I do now?

This stress is not good for me . . . it's not good for my health, it's not good for my painting."

"You need to calm down, Vincent," Papa said. He reached for Vincent's pulse. "Your blood pressure is high and this could bring on another attack. Let me go get you another type of tincture . . . it will help you relax."

I quickly darted back to the kitchen as Father got up from his chair. I stood there silently by the heat of the warm stove as Father opened the door to the cellar. I heard the heavy sound of his feet lumbering down the concrete stairs. He returned clutching one of his glass vials. Though I was always skeptical of Father's homeopathic remedies, I prayed that—especially this time—one of his tinctures would work.

THIRTY-EIGHT

A Premonition

I COULD think of nothing else but Vincent, frail, helpless, and alone in his room at Ravoux's. I wanted to nurse him. I wanted to hold him. I wanted to wipe his brow and feed him warm potato soup with a silver spoon. I stopped thinking about how Father would react to a courtship between us or how it would be to be Vincent's muse. Now all I could focus on was ensuring that his health didn't take a turn for the worse.

After he left our house, I remained in the kitchen, fearful that Papa would realize that I had been eavesdropping on their private conversation. I could hardly maintain my balance, however. I dropped two pot lids in a period of minutes and sliced the tip of my finger with the vegetable knife. Paul, who came into the kitchen looking for a snack, saw me wrapping myself in a bandage.

"What have you done to yourself, Marguerite?" He leaned down and picked one of the lids up off the floor.

He was staring at my hand now. Tiny droplets of blood were now beading through the white cloth I had tied around my finger.

"I had an accident," I replied, trying to appear nonchalant.

"You had an accident? You were probably thinking of things you shouldn't be."

"I don't have time for your snide comments, Paul," I retorted.

"Here, take this," he said. He gave me an additional towel to wrap around my hand, as I had already soaked through the first one.

I sat down on a stool and lifted my finger over my head in an attempt to further stop the bleeding.

"We should forget about our argument," Paul said, referring to the afternoon I had come in from the rain. "Anyway, it seems Vincent's had another relapse. We shouldn't let this get the better of us."

I didn't even register the second part of my brother's sentence. "What do you mean Vincent's had another relapse?"

"You know as well as I how he looked when he came here this afternoon. He was a gibbering mess of nerves. He was wringing his hands; his brow was beaded with sweat. Papa had to actually give him some valerian root as a sedative."

I felt the color drain from my face and it wasn't the cut in my finger that made me grow pale.

"I know, it's a shame," Paul continued as if he was rather put out by it all. "I was upstairs in Papa's studio all morning doing a self-portrait and I was rather anxious to show it to him. I think it's my best work yet."

"Oh, Paul," I said, shaking my head. I could not believe he could be speaking about himself during a time like this.

"Well, I guess it's unfortunate for you, too. I suspect he will not be doing any more painting of you for some time, Marguerite."

"You are more tragic than I suspected, Paul, if you think that is the reason for my concern."

He did not answer me at first. He turned to walk out of the kitchen but just before he did, he looked back and said to me: "You and I will be living here long after Vincent has gone. It would be a shame to have him come between us."

THIRTY-NINE

Weakness

THE self-portrait Paul had done that afternoon was hideous, a mess done in thick impasto. Aside from the dark palette of aubergine and black—a choice that didn't appeal to me at all—he had also painted himself in quick, overlapping strokes as if he thought he was successfully imitating Vincent.

"What do you think?" he asked as I walked into his room to deliver his laundry. I put down my basket. It was obvious that he wanted to hear something positive about his work.

"It's very dark, Paul," I said. I was grasping for the right words that would not offend him.

"Exactly," he said. "I wanted to experiment with symbolism, like Vincent does."

I wrinkled my brow. Aside from the opaque color, I couldn't see any use of symbolism. Still, I chose not to tell my brother that I found his painting confusing and awkward. I didn't want to appear cruel.

"Have you shown Papa?" I knelt closer to the painting to see his brushstrokes.

"No, not yet. But I will soon."

"Well, hopefully he'll support the idea of art school," I said. "You'll be lucky if he lets you go."

I doubted Father would support such a venture, but I didn't want to burst Paul's hope for it.

"I need to go finish the laundry," I told him. I was desperate to come up with an excuse to leave his room. I needed some time to conceive of a plan to see Vincent again.

My mind kept returning to the sight of him in our living room—weak and in need of comfort—perhaps taking too much of one of Papa's tinctures alone in his room at Ravoux's. The memories of the weeks before, ones that shone in my mind like golden halos lifted from one of Vincent's canvases, were quickly becoming dark and muddied. I needed to find Louise-Josephine. No one else would be honest with me and no one else could give me better advice.

SHE was busy studying railroad timetables when I found her in her room. Théophile had been circling the trains he would later be assigned. He'd roll them into the pocket of her dress so that she knew when their next meeting would occur. Louise-Josephine would go over his black circles with a red crayon. She looked up from the papers that were fanned across her bed and smiled.

"I need to talk to you," I said as I dragged a chair up to her side. "It's about Vincent."

"Oh?" she said. Immediately her eyebrows peaked.

"He came by today and visited Papa. I overheard their conversation, and he seems to have had a relapse."

Her eyes fell slightly. "About what?"

"His trip to Paris left him feeling unsettled. His nephew is ill and his brother is under financial pressure at home and at work. He fears his brother will no longer support him."

Louise-Josephine shook her head. "I'm sure his feelings about you have not helped either situation."

I looked at her blankly.

"Well, he's probably trying to come to terms with whether he should pursue something with you or not. We know he's attracted to you, his actions have already proven that. . . ."

I remained silent.

"But before things get any more serious between you two, Vincent will have to decide if he is prepared for the responsibilities of a wife. Now that it seems his brother might not be able to support him, there's extra pressure on him."

"But we've never even mentioned marriage," I said. My voice was now straining to remain low. I did not want to let my emotions overcome me as they did in our last conversation, when I had ended up hurting Louise-Josephine by citing the differences between our two situations. But in a way my trepidation was unnecessary. Louise-Josephine was not shy in pointing it out.

"Yes, I know . . . but Vincent has to realize you're the daughter of a physician—*his* physician, no less—you're not a scullery maid or a poor girl that he can have his way with and leave without any repercussions. He knows he has to act appropriately with you."

She cleared her throat and continued.

"We don't know the details of what happened back in Paris

that threw him into this state. Perhaps he confessed to Theo that he was interested in marrying you. Perhaps Jo questioned whether you had a dowry because they could no longer support Vincent's expenses and maybe this angered Vincent. Perhaps Theo was unsupportive because he feared Vincent's relationship with you might affect his productivity." Louise-Josephine's eyes were shining as if she had been a sparrow on their windowsill listening in on all the details. Her imagination was spinning. "We really don't know what happened between his brother and him. But what I am sure of is that he respects his brother greatly and doesn't want to be on ill terms with him, and *also*," she added, taking a deep breath, "that he does not want to intentionally hurt you."

Louise-Josephine's words brought a shred of comfort to me. At least it made Vincent's recent behavior make more sense.

"But how should I proceed now that he's in such a state?"

Louise-Josephine looked at the window for several minutes before responding. "Perhaps another outing is in order," she mused. "You should go tonight and visit him secretly at Ravoux's. Speak with him, Marguerite. It's the only way to know what he wants from you and it will be good for him to hear how much you care for him."

I felt faint at the prospect of another rendezvous. I wasn't sure I felt up to it. But Louise-Josephine was right. I had few other choices.

FORTY

A Certain Kind of Nobility

THIS time, I waited an extra hour just to make sure that everyone in the house was sound asleep. Everyone except Louise-Josephine, of course.

I had spent the past several hours alone in my room, lying on my bed with my eyes planted on the ceiling. There were several tiny fissures in the plaster and I helped pass the time by imagining them as a web of thin, black vines. In my mind, I created tiny flowers to accompany them—small pink and white blooms—so that soon there was an entire imaginary garden suspended over my head.

When it seemed as if the house had finally gone quiet, I got up from my bed and stood in front of my long dressing mirror. In the moonlight, I could see the faint outline of my body through the thin veil of my nightgown—the soft mounds of my breasts, the rose tip of each nipple. I pressed my hands flat against my abdomen and mimicked the effect of a tight corset—forcing my décolletage to pop up through the square neckline of my gown.

The girl who first snuck into the cave was slowly vanishing. I was far more nervous this time. It was as if I could feel his presence receding. What had once been an enormous force of energy, a tornado capable of capturing a landscape in a thousand tiny brushstrokes, was now fading. A formidable spirit now breaking into thin air. This feeling was palpable. I imagined him alone in his room, his paintbrushes thrown in a corner, his slender body becoming sunken and concave, and there was nothing I could do to pass the hours until I could get to his room and help him.

I tiptoed into Louise-Josephine's room nearly thirty minutes later, having changed into a simple cotton dress. She was awake and sitting up in bed, obviously waiting for me.

"You kept your hair up," she said.

I touched the braids on top of my head.

"I thought it best under the circumstances," I said.

She looked up at me and nodded her head. "It's good that you are going. If he is in as bad a state as you suspect, your presence can only be a comfort."

I smiled and took her hand. Then Louise-Josephine walked quietly to her window, slowly opening the latch and lifting the sash.

THERE was the faint sound of crickets chirping in the flowers beds as I walked up the rue de la Sansonne. I knew Vincent had painted this winding road a few weeks earlier.

The gate to the inn was on the right. From the street, I could see over the red wooden pickets and into a small courtyard, but I could not see directly into the building. There was an unexpected stillness to the air, as if the trees had ceased to rustle and the fireflies had hid behind bended boughs.

I had never been inside the Ravoux Inn, but I knew from Papa's description of Vincent's room that they often entered through the back courtyard. Unfortunately, I hadn't the faintest idea how I'd actually gain access to his room.

I threaded one hand through the latch and slowly used the other one to push open the gate. The hinge made only the faintest squeak as I walked into the garden.

The inn was completely dark except for a single room on the top floor. There, against the thick glass pane, I could see a faint flicker of a candle.

That must be either Vincent's room or Hirshig's, I thought to myself. I had heard Vincent speak of the only other boarder at Ravoux's—a Danish artist who boarded in the room adjacent to his. The Ravoux family, who resided below their tenants, were clearly sound asleep, as the ground floor was completely dark.

I stood there trembling in the courtyard and was suddenly overcome with a sense of ridiculousness. How could I have come out like this—in the middle of the night, no less—when I hadn't a clue about how to let Vincent know I was here? And even worse, I didn't have the faintest idea what I would say to him if I did get his attention.

I was just about to turn back when I noticed a small stairway on the outside of the inn. If I was correct, it seemed to lead directly to the attic where Hirshig and Vincent slept.

Still, there was a door at the top which I was sure would be locked. And even if it wasn't, I would still run the risk that Monsieur Ravoux might hear me creaking up the steps.

I had resigned myself to going home, when suddenly I saw a

shadow at the window. At first I thought it was my imagination but, sure enough, it was Vincent standing by the glass.

I heard the din of the window opening and then saw his face emerging.

I stood there, my flesh suddenly gone cold. Had I made a terrible mistake in coming out unannounced this evening? The last time, our meeting had been romantic, but this time his head was heavy with personal problems. I suddenly worried that he might consider me a nuisance, when he obviously had so many other things on his mind.

He looked down and saw me standing on the cold pavement. "Marguerite?" He mouthed my name, but did not utter a sound. He held his lantern out of the window, shining the glow on my face down below.

I lifted my arm and gave him a small wave.

He closed the window and snuffed the candle. Moments later, he appeared creeping down the outside stairs.

He looked haggard, as though he had been tossing in his bedclothes all night. His face was lined and his hair on end. I almost didn't recognize him, he looked so different from the wiry and energized man whom I had admired that day he first arrived at the station.

I walked over to him and, not knowing how to comfort him, could think of nothing else but to take him in my arms.

A few days of not eating had left him almost skeletal. The pointy blades of his scapula protruded like skate wings. His rib cage felt like an empty barrel. It was as though I were embracing a rag doll.

We stood there for several moments in silence before he moved away from me.

"It was so kind of you to come here. I know it's always a risk for you to be discovered by your father."

"Someday perhaps we will not need to meet on such clandestine terms. That is something I truly wish."

His face seemed to change when I said that. "Your father will never approve of me, Marguerite. No father would. I will only end up a burden to you. Just as I have for Theo and Jo."

"Oh, don't even say such nonsense!" I said. My heart was breaking that he would even think something so terrible.

"It's true, Marguerite. How could I ever support you? I've sold only one painting in my life. How could I keep you in the way you deserve, with fine dresses, a house with a garden, even a piano for your fine hands. Seeing Theo, seeing how hard he struggles to be both a dealer and a good husband and father, was humbling. I have been too selfish my whole life and now I regret it."

"You are a great artist!" I interjected. "Even Jo spoke of your genius when she was here. She does not resent you. She and Theo are confident that one day you will succeed."

"Things are different there now. My nephew's ill. They need to care for him and put his needs first. It is only right."

"Then let me take care of you. Let Papa! Together we will make sure that you are comfortable and that you always have a place to paint!"

The desperation in my voice was escalating. The feeling I had in my bedroom earlier that evening of Vincent physically shrinking from me was now becoming a reality. I could see him physically retreating from me, even when we were steps away from each other.

Vincent's voice, however, was clear and determined.

"Your father cannot help me, Marguerite. I just wrote to my

brother that when a blind man leads another blind man, don't they both fall into a ditch?"

I looked at him, puzzled.

"Your father's tinctures cannot help me!" He placed his hands over his eyes. "This is something that will not change within me."

After a moment he went on. "I do not have the stamina for both a woman and my art. My passion cannot support it. I have tried before and failed. I once had a relationship with a woman back in the Hague," he said beneath his breath.

"I don't want to hear this now!" I said, choking back tears.

"No, you must listen. Marguerite, in the end, I had to leave her. Not only because my brother could not support us both, but more because my art suffered." Vincent took another breath before continuing. "This woman . . . although my feelings for her could not compare to the ones I have for you . . . I did care for her . . . at least as much as I could at the time. But when I finally did leave, she tried to poison herself. I cannot do that again to another woman, especially you. Just the thought of the despair I caused her terrifies me. . . . I'm afraid I will only hurt you in the end."

Tears began to roll down my cheeks.

"I have often thought of how it might be to be your wife," I said. I hadn't thought I had the courage to say it but somehow the words flew out of my mouth. "I have spent nights imagining what it would be like to help you with your paints, to care for you when you are sick, to make sure that you have good meals and a tidy roof over your head."

"Marguerite." He pulled me closer so that now my face was in the crook of his neck. I felt the hard nob of his collarbone against my cheek and again, the pinelike scent of turpentine imbedded in his skin. "I, too, have thought that way. I have imagined you in a small yellow house, in the south, with me upstairs painting. I have imagined the smells of your cooking, coming not from your father's kitchen but one we share as our own."

His voice was soft now, cracking slightly over the words. "But then I worry. My brother can no longer support me . . . let alone my wife. And, even worse, what if I were to become sick again? I am no use to anyone when I am helpless and full of despair. That would be terribly unfair to you."

"I would not mind at all!" My voice leapt forth. "I am used to my father and his own mecurial nature, his fits of despair. I would not be frightened by it!" I took a deep breath. "Vincent, if you give me the opportunity, I will leave my father's home in a second. I would take only the clothes on my back . . . I wouldn't even return to retrieve my shoes that I left at the front gate. I would leave tonight with you and never return, not regretting it once, not even for a moment. I would work as a housekeeper . . . a cook . . . a charwoman even . . . so that you could paint. We needn't rely on your brother's kindness—I would work my fingers until they were as brittle as straw just so that your hands could bring beauty into this world!"

Vincent trembled as I stood there. He looked as fragile as glass.

"Marguerite. . . ." His voice was quiet at first but then gathered force. "I saw a special light in your eyes that afternoon I first came to your father's house. I gave you the poppy because I saw the life in you. You were bursting like a spring flower and I recognized that flame in your gaze. But I won't let myself drain the life from someone I love."

I was now crying and he took a small handkerchief from his pocket and wiped my eyes.

"You came to Auvers to paint, not to find a wife," I finally managed to say through my tears. "I realize that."

"But without even trying I found you, Marguerite," he said, again touching my cheek. "My little piano player. My Saint Cecilia."

He took my face between his hands and kissed me, not on the lips as I had hoped, but on the forehead.

He pulled away from me and said, quite softly, "I never wanted to hurt you. Sometimes I think the Japanese have it right. There's a certain nobility in death. There's no shame in it. Only honor." He took a deep breath. "I've shamed my family by having them think I'm a parasite. If only I were Japanese, I would take my own life and my honor would be restored."

FORTY-ONE

Two Things Revealed

It started to drizzle as I ran home that evening and my tears mirrored the rain. I had failed to comfort Vincent and I was now certain that my romance would not have the same ending as Louise-Josephine's. But what upset me more were his parting words. They worried me greatly. I was anxious to seek Louise-Josephine's counsel. She would tell me if I needed to tell Papa. I trusted her judgment to always be right.

Sadly, I did not get the chance. I was halfway up the stairs when I suddenly had the sneaking suspicion I was not alone.

He was standing there in his silk bathrobe, his face crooked and cross like a gargoyle.

"Papa," I whispered. But he did not hear me, or at least he chose not to. When I reached where he was standing, a cold slap found its way across my face.

"Where were you?" His voice was icy and harsh. I realized that he had no intention of keeping my excursion a secret from the rest of the household.

I did not answer him at first, and again his voice boomed, this time even louder. "Where were you, Marguerite?" he bellowed. "Answer me, now!" Again, he slapped me. The sheer force of his hand made me totter backward. Quickly, I grasped the banister so that I wouldn't fall down the stairs.

I looked up at him with tears filling my eyes. My cheek was stinging as if I had been hit with a mitt of hot needles. I sensed his hand had left a large print across my skin.

In the corner of the hallway, I saw Louise-Josephine stick her head out from her door. She had a terrible look on her face, half fright and half anger. I tried to tell her with my own expression: "Go back! Go back to your room and save yourself from Papa's anger," but she would not be deterred.

She walked over the floorboards to where Papa was standing and in her white nightdress tapped Papa on his shoulder.

"Please," she begged of him, "please stop! It's my fault she left this evening. It was all my doing!"

I was in a state of disbelief.

"No, Louise." I tried to stop her. But she would have none of it.

"It was me—all my fault," she repeated. I could see the outline of her spine through her white cotton gown. Her slender frame trembling through the cloth. Still, she continued to defend me.

"I told her to go. I told her that Monsieur Van Gogh might need comforting. It was me who put the idea in her head. It is me you should blame!"

Papa now seemed visibly confused.

"You? You? Why would you encourage her?"

Louise-Josephine was now standing in front of Papa. In contrast to her diminutive form, Papa appeared like a giant.

"Yes, I encouraged her! Why not? What does she have to live for here, in this house? Neither she nor I have any opportunity to marry. She, because you have never given her the opportunity. And I am denied it because I don't even have a birth certificate."

Her voice was as clear as a battle cry. I was kneeling on the flight of stairs, my crossed arms covering the neckline of my dress.

"I was the one who encouraged her because I thought we both had little to lose in our present situation!"

Louise-Josephine's face was now as red as a stick of rhubarb. I had never seen her so impassioned, and I stood there completely in awe of her.

Papa, however, was clearly not impressed with her behavior. He wrinkled his face with disgust. "You don't know what you speak of, Louise-Josephine. When you were two years old, I helped your mother secure the proper papers for you—the ones that verify that your birth was not through incest or an adulterous relationship. You are in fact free to marry. . . . My daughter's behavior, on the other hand, is unacceptable!"

Louise-Josephine took a step backward and I could see the shock register on her face. "What do you mean? Why have I never been told about this certificate?" She shook her head. "I can't believe my mother never mentioned it to me before!"

"It is true. But that is another matter." Papa turned to face me. "None of this, however, is any excuse for Marguerite's behavior."

Louise-Josephine began to stammer as if she wasn't sure she should thank Papa or continue to defend me.

"Please do not be cross with Marguerite, Pa—" She nearly said Papa. I heard it at the tip of her tongue, but she stopped short. "I was the one who put this fantasy into Marguerite's head. She was only trying to ensure that Vincent was feeling better."

"It's true . . . ," I managed to interject.

"It is very courageous of you to defend my daughter," he said to Louise-Josephine as he reknotted the sash of his silk robe. "But only she can be held responsible for her actions. Marguerite has insulted her upbringing, embarrassed me and our family name. Do I need to remind the two of you that Monsieur Van Gogh is a patient of mine? And a very troubled one at that, sadly. He is not a potential suitor for any young girl, especially my daughter. I have told her this before. Yet, still she went against my wishes. What sort of practice can I have if people hear that my children are cavorting with those entrusted to my care?"

I was now sobbing and my knees were rattling like two winter branches underneath my dress. Had I not had the support of the banister, I would have fallen to my knees.

Papa was still staring at me. Although his face had softened slightly, traces of his anger still remained. I noticed that he had bitten through the skin of his lip.

He now looked exhausted, as if he had used every ounce of his energy confronting me. "This is simply unacceptable behavior."

Louise-Josephine, realizing there was little further she could say to Papa, walked over and pulled me up from the stairwell.

Papa continued to stare at us both.

"We will speak of this tomorrow, Marguerite. I want you in my study after breakfast," he said sternly. His blue-gray eyes looked like sharp, broken pieces of china in the moonlight. He walked past me and said nothing as he solemnly returned to his bedroom.

FORTY-TWO

A Fitful Night

I EMBRACED her that night. We clung to each other, her arms wrapped around me as the tears fell down my cheeks and my half-braided hair fell in tangles around my ears.

"He will be less angry in the morning," she promised. But I could tell in her voice she didn't believe it. After so many weeks of secret meetings and whispering, Louise-Josephine and I could read each other too well.

"He will forbid me from ever seeing him again," I said, burying my face in the cloth of Louise-Josephine's nightdress. "Tonight was a mistake."

"Tell me," she said stroking my hair, "tell me what Vincent said. Were you able to see him?"

"I don't want to talk about it," I said through my tears. "But it is wonderful news that this certificate exists for you. You will be able to marry Théophile."

Louise-Josephine shook her head. "Yes, but let's not talk about that now. Your situation with Vincent is far more pressing. Tell me what happened."

I tried to gather myself and tell her what had transpired.

"I did see him," I said. "But his meeting with Theo has sent him into a deep depression." I took a deep breath. "I hardly recognized him."

Louise-Josephine threaded her hand into mine. Her fingers wrapped around my own, like a child holding on to something precious.

"He's depressed about Theo and worries about money. He says he's tempted to have a wife and speaks of yearning to have a courtship with me. . . ." I paused. "But he knows he's incapable of it. He believes it's impossible to have both love and art in the same life."

She said nothing but continued to hold my hand.

"You were right," I said. "You were right. It was just as you suspected."

"Marguerite," she said soothingly, "I will not let you waste away here. I promise you that."

"No, one day you will get married and you will forget about me."

"Never!" she said. "I would never do that to you, Marguerite."

I could read the sense of determination she had in her voice. "I have the railroad timetables, and you will join me and my fiancé. We will ride away on the train and never return to this place."

I closed my lids, imagining the three of us riding off as she described.

I wanted to call her "sister." But this time, I was so overcome in my own grief, the word only floated through my mind, unable to fall from my lips.

I SLEPT fitfully for those few hours before daybreak. As the roosters sounded in the morning, I rose slowly, unwrapping Louise-Josephine's tangled limbs from mine.

There was nothing I dreaded more than seeing Papa at breakfast. The image of him standing atop the staircase, his face swollen in anger and his hand swiping across my cheek, was now indelible in my mind.

In a desperate attempt to soften his mood, I decided to bake madeleines for him and prepare a pot of hot chocolate. I took out the heavy cast-iron mold from the cupboard and prepared the golden batter to ladle into the delicate shell formations.

At least he'll awaken to one of his favorite scents, I thought as I inhaled the sweet aroma of the madeleine mixture.

Paul came downstairs before Papa and came into the kitchen.

"What's this?" he said, opening up the door of my oven. "Madeleines for breakfast?"

I didn't answer him. I wiped my hands on the front of my apron and began to fill one of the work bowls with water.

I had made up my mind that I was not going to discuss the details with him, so I tried to busy myself with the cleaning of my pots. Paul, however, seemed determined to get the full story from me.

"So where were you last night?" He swiveled around on the heel of his shoe before nestling against the counter. "Madame Chevalier had to hold me back. We were both listening to you and Papa from the hallway."

I winced. If Madame Chevalier was on the second-floor landing when this all occurred, it meant she had spent the night with Papa. The hypocrisy of his anger infuriated me.

I tried to ignore my brother. "I'm not discussing this." I paused. "It was an unfortunate event."

"You had another secret meeting with Vincent, didn't you?" He had one finger idly hooked in his breast pocket, but his eyes were firmly planted on me.

I didn't answer him. I took out a saucepan and filled it with milk then lit the stove.

"There's no reason to be so coy, Marguerite," he said. "I'm your brother—you should be confiding in me."

I shook my head. "I'm not confiding in anyone."

He narrowed his eyes and looked deeper at me. "You're confiding in Louise-Josephine and she's not even blood!"

"Are you sure of that, Paul?" I stepped closer to him.

Paul's eyes now grew wide. He could not believe I would be so bold as to suggest we were related to Louise-Josephine. But I knew he, like me, had contemplated the possibility before. He just couldn't believe I would utter it aloud.

"Why do you think Papa has gone out of his way for Louise-Josephine all these years? Why do you think he went to all that trouble to secure that certificate he spoke of last night?"

Paul was shaking his head. He did not want to listen to what I was saying. "It is because he has deep affection for Madame Chevalier! That is why he has done so much for her daughter."

"Don't be so naïve, Paul."

"I am not naïve," he said. "You're the foolish one, Marguerite, if you think Papa will stand for your indiscretions."

I didn't answer him. He reached over to the fruit basket and took a pear before leaving.

"Good luck with Papa," he said as he left me. His voice was full of venom.

As I lay the cooling madeleines on the wire rack, I heard the sound of Father's footsteps treading slowly down the stairs. The garden door shut and he was suddenly in the garden talking to his animals.

I knew Papa would be waiting for me shortly to come out with his breakfast tray, so I quickly arranged everything—placing the soft yellow madeleine shells on a scalloped plate and pouring his hot cocoa into a ceramic bowl. For a finishing touch, I broke off one of the stems of roses from the arrangement in the hallway and placed it in a small vase on the side.

I walked down the hallway and opened the door to the garden. Papa was reclining on his lawn chair and I could tell from the way his eyelids fluttered, he was just as tired as I was.

"Good morning, Papa," I said as I placed the tray down beside him.

He didn't answer me but continued to stare at the animals pecking at the ground.

"I made you something different for breakfast today."

He peered down at the three madeleines and hot chocolate and nodded. "Thank you," he said.

I stood there for several seconds waiting for him to speak, but he uttered nothing. The broad, flat leaves of the lime tree had cast a large shadow across his face so that half his features seemed to be in darkness. He had not shaven and there were tiny strawberry and white whiskers where his cheeks were usually soft and clean.

"I don't know what to say about last night," he finally said to me.

I lowered my eyes.

"I cannot tell you how much you've disappointed me, Marguerite."

I looked up at him and saw that his gaze was still focused on something other than me. He couldn't bear to look at me when he spoke.

"Your behavior has left me speechless."

He reached over and took a small bite of one of the madeleines.

I felt a small noise come from my lips—a feeble protest—but he silenced me before I could articulate the right words.

"Vincent is a sick man, Marguerite. He may very well be a genius, but he *will* not be a potential suitor for you. Is that clear, Marguerite?"

I nodded my head.

"Furthermore," Papa added, "you are far too young to be considering marriage."

"I am twenty-one!" I cried. "I am not too young—I am actually close to being too old!" The words were now flying from my lips.

"Stop this!" He had no patience to listen to my protest. "You belong here taking care of me and Paul. We are alone here. Your mother died and left me with you and your brother. . . . I don't understand why you think a life helping out your family is shameful. Especially with all the good work we do here for my patients. I need you here with me if I'm to keep on helping them. We can't only be thinking of ourselves and our own needs!" He placed his head on the table as if in despair. "These are very important people, Marguerite . . . artists! And if I cure Vincent, more artists will come. . . ."

"Father, but you would not be alone here. Madame Chevalier could assist you. She's devoted—"

"Madame Chevalier has nothing to do with this conversation, Marguerite. Your responsibilities and hers are wholly different."

I could not respond to him as I wished. What I wanted to say would have resulted in another slap across my face. I didn't even risk raising an eyebrow in response.

"Yes, Papa," I said, instead.

It was just as Louise-Josephine had forecast. It wouldn't be Vincent or anyone else if Papa had his way. I belonged to him and this house, like a piece of furniture. I was to remain.

FORTY-THREE

A Suitable Punishment

THE next day when I asked permission to go to church, Papa shook his head no. Then Monday, when I needed to go into town to do my shopping, he told me he had already sent Madame Chevalier out to do the errands.

When Papa informed me that my brother would be keeping an eye on me when he was away on business, I was mad with fury. To be watched by my younger brother was the worst insult I could imagine. But Father would not tolerate my protests.

It was clear Papa was now limiting my movements, to prevent any future contact with Vincent.

"You have brought this upon yourself, Marguerite," he told me. "You have proven you cannot be trusted."

His words were chosen to inflict the maximum amount of cruelty.

"You will no longer be allowed to see Vincent at all. When he comes here to receive his tinctures or to paint in our garden, you will remain upstairs in your bedroom."

"Papa." I felt his name fall from my lips as if I were uttering a lamentation. "Please don't do this. . . ."

"Marguerite, there will be no further discussion." He cut me off before I could say anything more.

Henrietta was now nuzzling at the ankle of Father's boot. I watched as he dug his wrinkled white fingers into her fur. She looked up at him with those big, wet eyes of hers, the whiskers of her chin rubbing against his knee. He was so pleased to be in the company of his pets, and I wondered why he felt the only company worthy of his attention were animals and artists. There was obviously little room in his heart for me.

OUR tall, cluttered house now felt more like a prison than ever before. Even my garden gave me little comfort. I began to imagine escaping by climbing the vines in the backyard—the ones that led to the cemetery on the land above—and never returning to the place that I now despised so much.

I thought of my late mother with increasing frequency. That she, too, felt trapped within these very walls was not lost on me. I saw us as one and the same. Both of us held here against our will, oppressed and unloved by the same man. The only difference was that I had silently rebelled against Father. And although I desperately wished I could escape from my confinement, I played over the secret meetings I had had with Vincent like a hungry schoolgirl sucking on a honeycomb.

But I could not sustain the sweetness of the memories for very long. In the end, my mind returned to worrying about him. Had he been serious about contemplating suicide? When I asked Louise-Josephine she seemed skeptical.

"Do you think he was seriously considering ending his life?"

"I didn't get that impression," I said as I pondered it more. "It was in the context of Japanese culture. He spoke of it abstractly, as if it were a curious thing. . . ."

"I would not worry too much about it then," she said comfortingly. "He probably had just read something about it and was intrigued by their different attitude toward death."

"Yes," I said, shaking my head. "It is like the Japanese prints. He loves the style of their artwork but he doesn't adapt his own work to it completely. He just absorbs a little. I'm sure he was just intrigued by something he read. After all, he's anxious to have his brother and his wife not have any ill will toward him. That's where this is all coming from, really."

"Yes, of course," Louise-Josephine agreed. "That makes perfect sense."

I felt a little better having shared my concern. But at night, my worry for Vincent was hard to suppress.

FORTY-FOUR

Three under the Lime Tree

SEQUESTERED away in the house, I silently raged at my predicament. Both Papa and Vincent seemed to be placing their various artistic passions over my happiness. But still I could not help but worry about Vincent. I had no idea how Father would continue to minister to Vincent's health needs after what had transpired between us. He had stopped speaking about Vincent at the dinner table and did not mention when and if he would be having him over to our home.

Three days after my punishment began, however, I heard Vincent's heavy footsteps bounding up the stairs to our house.

I was upstairs in my bedroom trying to finish a piece of needlepoint. I cannot express how much I wanted to rush downstairs, open the door, and greet him. But now I was like Madame Chevalier and Louise-Josephine, kept hidden by Father on the topmost floor of his house.

I cracked open my window and stuck out my head to see him. He was wearing the same blue smock he had draped around my shoulders that night outside the church. His hat was clutched in his fingers and he had two paintings resting against his knees.

I wanted to whistle and get his attention, but within seconds he had already knocked at our door and was ushered inside by Paul.

"So very good to see you, Monsieur Van Gogh!" Paul's enthusiastic greeting echoed through the house. "I believe he's been expecting you . . . he's in the garden."

I was seething hearing this from my younger brother. It was clear that Father had decided to confide in Paul about his meetings with Vincent and had purposefully chosen to keep me in the dark, hidden away under lock and key.

Just as I felt my blood might boil over, I heard Paul answering a question Vincent had apparently put to him.

"Marguerite? No she's not here at the moment. . . ." Then the garden door shut behind them.

I was at a loss as to how I could follow them. If I were to run to the other side of the house and peer through one of the windows that looked out over the garden, I would no doubt run into Madame Chevalier. So instead, I quickly dropped my needlepoint and headed to Father's attic studio.

Up the winding staircase, I entered through the coarse wooden door. The place was cluttered but still filled with light. From the skylight high above, I looked around past the stacks of oil paintings and the etchings he had pinned to the walls. Papa's printing machine stood in the corner. Behind it I saw a ladder, which I quickly moved so I could stand at eye level to one of the high windows.

My breathing was heavy and my veins were filled with adrenaline. All I wanted to do was see the two of them in the garden—to see if Papa was actually speaking with Vincent or just lending him our backyard as a backdrop to another painting.

As I cranked open the window and peered down below, I saw something that infuriated me beyond words. There, the three of them—Papa, Paul, and Vincent—were sitting under the shade of the lime tree enjoying themselves while I remained trapped inside.

Had I been as resourceful as Louise-Josephine, I would surely have found a way to get Vincent's attention. There were tin cans brimming with brushes and glass bottles filled with gold and clear liquids that I could have tossed down below to cause a dramatic scene. But I lacked the courage.

So instead I continued to watch. Vincent stood up and propped his two paintings against the trunk of the tree. He was standing with his large straw hat over his eyes, his hands gesturing in gentle circles. I could see how both Paul and Papa sat there transfixed by him. Even from several meters above, I could see the bright colors of his paintings. The malachite green of the cypress trees, the deep azure of his cloudless sky. It appeared, from my vantage point, that he had fully recovered!

After staring at the three of them for several minutes, I lowered myself down from the ladder and sat on the filthy wooden floor. The planks were unfinished pine boards, now spotted with pigment and sawdust. There was a metal pail filled with rags that smelled of turpentine. I sat there for several minutes wiping away my tears.

Eventually footsteps could be heard coming up the stairwell.

"Marguerite?" I heard my name called in the faintest whisper.

"Yes?"

It was Louise-Josephine. She was wearing the skirt she had been hemming that day we sewed together in the parlor. It was very becoming on her, a print of small flowers on a pale background. It made her look very young.

"I've been looking for you," she said sweetly. "I couldn't find you anywhere."

"They're all out there without me!" I cried and I found myself rushing into her arms. I was sobbing now and Louise-Josephine could do nothing but hold me.

"I know, I know," she said, gently cradling the back of my head.

It was cruel for me to complain about being excluded this way, when I knew that Louise-Josephine had been kept hidden for as long as I could remember.

"It doesn't even matter," I said, my voice choking. "Papa will never let me see him."

"You will see him again," she said gently. "This cannot last."

I shook my head skeptically. "No," I protested. "I know Papa will make good on his word. He will never let me see Vincent again!"

"Vincent will continue to ask for you," she said confidently. "Your father will have to give in at some point. He'll eventually let you see him."

"I don't think so," I said, wiping my tears with my handkerchief.

She thought for a moment. "What about the third painting Vincent wanted to do of you?" she asked as she looked around the room and saw Paul's mediocre paintings. "Maybe Vincent will ask your father if you can sit for him again, claiming it's therapeutic for him. Maybe he can explain to your father that you have only shown him compassion and nothing more."

"I don't think Papa would believe that." I shook my head. "There will be no more portraits."

"You can't give up hope, Marguerite," she said as she gently took me by the arm. "Let's go back to your room. We wouldn't want my mother to catch us upstairs like this."

FORTY-FIVE

A Second Letter

He called me "Saint Cecilia" that night I stood with him outside the church and again the night outside the inn. Since then, I'd heard his voice whispering it to me time and time again.

"I will paint you at the church's organ with stephanotis in your hair."

I imagined myself sitting upright near the altar of our church, the gleaming brass organ pipes before me, my foot pumping the pedals into song.

I could do little but daydream during those first few days of my forced seclusion. Papa and Paul continued to enjoy their summer, while I remained inside doing needlepoint or baking. When my father or brother was upstairs in the studio or in town, I gardened or played my piano.

When I was alone in the garden, I thought of him. I saw him

taking out his easel, arranging his palette of paints, and squinting at the tile rooftops or the pink hydrangeas, whose edges were only beginning to turn blue. I thought of how we kissed that first night in front of the church, how weeks later I met him in the cave. I wanted nothing more than to feel that alive again. That initial rush of pain, that intoxicating sensation of another's skin over mine. The memory of our union made our separation feel even more intolerable and my body ached to see him again.

At my piano, my fingers stretched out to reach him. As if the ivory keys were ladders to his heart. I struck each note with the precision of a harpist, plucking out a melody that I imagined could reach only him.

I could barely sleep. My bedroom window beckoned me with the possibility of more adventures. How I wanted to cross over the sill and climb out! I took the combs out of my hair and let the evening wind whip through my bedroom and run through my nightdress.

I walked barefoot over the wooden floorboards and imagined the sensation of the trellis under my toes, and the damp garden stones between the house and the gate.

There was music in my head even though our house was perpetually silent. I heard the lonely music of Schubert, the mournful sonatas of Beethoven, and the hopeful, yearning notes of Chopin.

I wondered at every moment what Vincent was doing. Was he painting or was he brooding by himself? Had he mended things with his brother, and was his nephew's health restored? Had he made up his mind to stay in Auvers and paint, or was he headed down another path of darkness, with another attack imminent?

I thought I would go mad with all these questions in my head. I could not risk going to him, though I desperately wanted to. And even worse, I was unable to see him when he visited our home. They would all eat the cakes I baked in the mornings and drag their forks and knives across the plates I would later wash, but I would be pushed away like one of my mother's porcelain dishes, banished to a room upstairs.

IT was Louise-Josephine's idea to write him a letter. "If you can't come to him, perhaps he can make an effort to visit you."

It was a masterful plan. I would draft a short note and she would have Théophile deliver it to Vincent at the inn. That way, no one would suspect it was from me.

I took a piece of stationery from my desk and wrote his name at the top. *Vincent*—I wrote the first letter with a large, generous hand—*What about that third portrait? Perhaps Papa will give in for art's sake.*

I signed it with only my first initial.

It was delivered on Tuesday, and on Thursday I heard him at our front door.

"He's here!" Louise-Josephine rushed into my bedroom and closed the door.

"I know," I said, hushing her with my finger to my lips. My head was halfway out the window, and I strained to hear what he was saying to Father.

"Might I paint in your garden this afternoon?"

I could hear Papa greeting him in enthusiastic tones and ushering him inside.

"He will suggest another painting of you, I know it!" she gushed. "Just you wait!"

"But what will Papa say?" I sat down on my bed. "What if

Papa refuses him? After all, he was reluctant to have Vincent paint me the first two times."

"Vincent will persist."

I secretly hoped Louise-Josephine was right, but I remained skeptical.

"He's kept you and your mother a prisoner all these years," I said with my face in my hands. "If he wants to, he will do the same with me."

"I have learned to work around him, and so will you."

She took my hands away from me and held on to them. "I will make certain that you see Vincent. I promise you."

"You needn't stay here," I said as I embraced her. "You know that certificate exists now and you are free to marry Théophile."

"I have yet to discuss it with my mother," she said as she fingered the cloth of her skirt. "I have to have more details before I tell Théophile. It would be wrong to give him any false hope until I know more."

FORTY-SIX

Behind Closed Doors

DURING that second week in July, I could see that Louise-Josephine was becoming more anxious about her own situation. The heat and our seclusion seemed even more oppressive this year, perhaps because we both were yearning to be someplace other than our house. Still, she continued to slip out for her evening rendezvous with Théophile, taking extra precautions that neither her mother nor my father would hear her as she scurried down the front steps to the street.

She said he was growing more impatient with each passing day. "He changes our meeting place each time because he says he doesn't want to have only one memory of me. Sometimes we meet near Le Blanc's farm . . . just last night, we met by Père Pilon's."

"You must be careful, Louise-Josephine," I cautioned.

"I know . . . but I too am getting restless."

Every night I snuck into her bedroom to wait for her, and I could sense her before she had even slipped into bed. She would return just before dawn, carrying her own nocturnal perfume. The damp clung to her hair, the smell of the dew, and of wet grass on the hem of her housecoat.

One evening she chose not to go out. I listened for her footsteps leaving, but instead I heard her voice coming from her mother's room. The two of them were arguing and both sounded defiant.

"It is not as you think, Louise-Josephine. It's just not that simple!"

Louise-Josephine was angry, and I could hear the agitation in her voice. "What are the details then, *Maman*? He says there is a certificate. What are these complications you speak of, then? Why have you never mentioned this paper before?"

"Louise-Josephine, you have no idea what I went through when you were first born . . . your grandmother called me the vilest of names . . . I was nearly homeless, penniless. I went to Paul-Ferdinand, but he was in the middle of his wedding preparations. . . ."

I could hear Madame Chevalier sobbing. "It was your grandmother who insisted that he help me get this certificate for you. She said it would protect you . . . and so I went to him again and he finally agreed to help me."

"So why the secrecy all these years? Why did I never know it existed?"

"Because just having this paper does not mean you can get married at your will. There are still other requirements that need to be met. . . . I never thought you could obtain them, so I chose not to give you false hope."

I could hear Louise-Josephine beginning to cry. I waited to hear if there was any more of their conversation I could make out, but

Madame Chevalier's voice became muffled and I could hear nothing. So for nearly an hour I waited for Louise-Josephine to emerge. When she did, she did not come to my room as I expected; instead, she went directly to her own bedroom and quietly closed the door.

That following morning Papa returned home from Paris having no idea of the night's dramatic events. We all ate lunch together though no one except Papa uttered a word. He spoke of his day in Paris, the dinner he had eaten, and a few of the patients he had seen, never even once seeming to notice the tearstains around Louise-Josephine's eyes.

Later that afternoon, when we had a private moment between us, I asked her what happened with her mother.

"She told me the reason she didn't tell me about the certificate is that it's useless unless your father is present at the wedding. *Maman* says he will never do this. And she's right. Your father would never risk his reputation to attend my wedding ceremony."

"Well, maybe she could at least ask him . . . or—" I was about to suggest myself but Louise-Josephine cut me off.

"No, no, Marguerite, it's useless. And I was so rude to your father that night, he'll never do another thing for me again."

I shook my head. "I don't think that's true—he has such a soft spot in his heart for you."

"She said the only other way I can get married is if I produce two male witnesses at the ceremony who knew my family. Now who could do that for me? I cannot even have you do it and you're my only friend."

"Perhaps Papa will do it after he's relented a bit. Last week's episode is still fresh in his mind now."

Louise-Josephine nodded through her tears.

"The irony, Marguerite, is that my mother is angry at me that I encouraged you to sneak out and see Vincent. But the truth is, she has snuck around all these years with your father. Now she feigns surprise when her daughter acts as she does. It's ridiculous!"

"Papa is the same way."

"One day," she said, "we'll go. We'll go as far from this place as we can."

I smiled as I imagined us packing our bags and helping one another descend down the trellis to the garden stairs.

"And we won't go barefoot, either," she said, laughing. "We'll put on our noisiest shoes and clank all the way down the road!"

FORTY-SEVEN

Bastille Day

WITHOUT any contact with him, I had no idea how Vincent's health was faring during my seclusion.

Vincent had not visited the house for several days, and it began to worry me. Then, one evening, I overheard Father telling Paul about Vincent's latest painting.

"He's painting an expansive plain with sheaves of wheat against a violent sky. He's so intent on finishing it, he's refused several of my invitations for lunch."

Paul continued to ask Father questions about the painting. He was obviously curious about Vincent's technique.

"He's painting the wheat with staccato strokes. His palette is ocher and cadmium yellow. He's more interested in conveying the overwhelming enormity of the field than each blade of grass. It is difficult to tell where the hills and sky merge—both are painted in a murky sort of obscurity. Just layers of whale blue and indigo."

Papa paused. "It's all rather ominous, actually. Especially with the black crows flying into the dark sky."

THAT Monday was Bastille Day. Papa was in a good mood when I found him in the garden that morning.

"The town will be having a lot of festivities this afternoon," Papa mentioned as he nibbled on his breakfast. "Perhaps you and your brother should go."

I couldn't believe he was softening and allowing me to go into town.

"I trust your brother will keep a sharp eye on you."

My heart was racing. The center would be decorated all in red, blue, and white. I was confident Vincent would be in the town painting.

SHE didn't say anything as she watched me change my clothes that afternoon. She didn't have to. All those years when we hardly said a word to each other, Louise-Josephine must have secretly resented me every time I went out.

I took my yellow dress out of my wardrobe and she helped me—still silently—as I slid my arms into the sleeves and brought the skirt up to my waist. Her slender fingers felt like scampering mice's feet as she quickly fastened all the buttons. I felt her chin on my shoulder as she folded the two ends of the sash tightly around my waist.

She was trying to smile, but I could see there were tears in her eyes.

"I wish you could come with me. You'd be a far better companion than Paul!"

"Don't worry about me, Marguerite. I've gotten used to it all these years."

"One day soon I'll be the one helping you get into your wedding dress," I said affectionately. "It will only be a matter of time."

She smiled and clenched my hand affectionately.

"I hope you see him," she whispered. She reached into her pocket and took out a long swatch of lavender silk.

"It will be impossible to miss this," she said as she knotted the silk into a large voluminous bow at the base of my neck. "Now he'll be certain to see you."

THE town hall was adorned with flags. Around the circular entrance, tiny paper lanterns were strung from trees. Nearly everyone in the village was there. I spotted Adeline Ravoux chewing on a stick of hard candy, and Dr. Mazery promenading with his tall, willowy wife.

It felt so wonderful to be outside our home. I could smell the crêpes sizzling on the pan from one of the street vendors and the jasmine wafting from the trees. I looked up and saw the endless expanse of blue sky, the plumes of white clouds, and the horizon filled with the terra-cotta rooflines. It all felt glorious to me.

I did not want my brother to notice that I was secretly looking for Vincent, so I tried to keep my eyes focused on the mayor, who was now teetering onto the podium.

I searched the crowds for the top of his sun hat or the perch of his easel. If he was here amid the crowd, I was certain I could find him.

It took me nearly twenty minutes to discover him. He had cloaked himself behind a veil of manicured shrubs. But I could see the white of his hat and the familiar blue smock. As I suspected, he was working on a painting of the day's festivities.

Paul was cheering with the rest of the village as the band began to play. He clapped his hands and shouted in a way I had not seen since he was a small boy. Gone for a few moments were his self-conscious gestures, his careful mimicry of Papa's facial expressions. Beside me, if only for a few moments, was that happy innocent brother I had played with in the garden long ago.

There was no way I could have approached Vincent. Paul had certainly heard Father's orders and would never have allowed me to go to him unchaperoned. And so I stood there agonizing, watching him as he continued to paint, not knowing how close I was to where he stood.

The band was playing so loudly, though, that it gave me an excuse to move. "Can we go farther from the podium?" I pleaded with Paul. I touched my head. "I'm beginning to get a headache from all the noise."

He nodded and ushered me farther back, slightly to the side. Now, we were that much closer to Vincent.

I continued to look secretly in his direction, lightly touching my neck to calm my nerves. Then I saw him squinting out from behind his canvas, his eyes focusing on my profile. He had seen it—as Louise-Josephine predicted—the flag that confirmed it was me. The lavender ribbon.

FORTY-EIGHT

An Unframed Nude

It would have been impossible for us to meet that afternoon, but at least he had seen me in the crowd. I told Louise-Josephine that she had chosen well by selecting that strip of lilac silk. "I'm certain he saw it," I told her. "It reminded him that I am still here, waiting."

He came the next day. I could hear him quarreling with Papa downstairs. At first I heard him reprimanding Father for not having yet framed a particular painting he had, the Guillaumin nude.

"You promised me you'd frame it when I first arrived, and still you have not! Do you have such flagrant disregard for the work we painters do?"

"You are not well," I heard Father telling him. "Please try and calm down."

"You parade around like you're one of us . . . empathizing with our worries, our fears. But what worries do you have, Gachet?"

Vincent's voice was now shrill. "You are nothing but a bourgeois doctor, an amateur painter—a pathetic dilettante!"

Suddenly there was silence, a long, cold pause that seemed unending. Louise-Josephine and I held each other tight.

Finally, I heard Papa. I could hear the ache in his voice. Vincent had obviously wounded him deeply.

"Take this," he told Vincent. "It's my own tincture of foxglove."

"I don't want it."

"You will feel better, Vincent. Trust me."

"Trust you? You are a blind man leading the blind," he told Papa.

Again there was silence. Then the sound of the glass flask hitting the table.

"You know what I wrote Theo? I told him . . . you were not the man I first believed you to be! You've misled me!"

Vincent must have been moving wildly around the room. I could hear the erratic pattern of his footsteps, the sudden jostling of chairs.

"You ask me to trust you. But if you trust me, you'd let me see her."

"I cannot do that."

"I need to."

"What you need is to rest and then get back to painting. There are hundreds of vistas, dozen of people who would be willing to sit for you. I am simply telling you that you can no longer paint my daughter."

Again I heard the sound of shuffling chairs. Then, the noise of a book falling to the ground.

"It's in here . . . ," Vincent said. "I want to paint her as Saint Cecilia. I've done the drawing . . . see?"

There was the sound of ripped paper. A tear, and then a crackle. As if the sketch had been torn from a notebook and crumpled into a ball.

His voice was escalating. Louise-Josephine and I were now clutching each other's hands as we huddled by my bedroom door.

"You told me weeks ago that you would never stifle an artist's inspiration . . . that you would let me choose who and what I wanted to paint. Now you go back on your word!"

"That is not exactly what I said, Vincent." Father's voice was now strained, and it was clear he was finding it difficult to remain calm and professional.

"Dr. Gachet, I have imagined a third painting of your daughter. Listen to me! It will be so beautiful . . . she will sit at the church organ, a white halo illuminating her head. Tall and tapered—almost like a candle—she will rest there with her hands on the keys, the silver pipes stretching into the heavens . . . tiny blue stars in the background, swirls of gold and amber high in the nave. It will be a testament to her chastity, her musical ability . . . there will be nothing inappropriate, I assure you! I realize that I am not suitable for your daughter! I am not suitable for anyone!" Vincent's voice was cracking as it escalated.

"Marguerite will not be sitting as a model for you again, Vincent," Father said. This time his voice was firm.

But Vincent was persistent.

"I will have another relapse if you forbid it! You are my doctor—you are supposed to do whatever you can to help me heal! I must paint her!"

"No, Vincent!" Father's voice was now just as loud. "You cannot."

This went on for several minutes before I could hear Papa tiring out. Eventually he hollered upstairs for my brother.

"Paul! Please come downstairs," he said firmly.

Louise-Josephine and I had our ears pressed to the wall as we tried to hear what happened next. But Papa must have closed the parlor doors; his conversation with Paul and Vincent was muffled. Moments later, we could hear all three voices again as they entered the hallway. But the discussion was brief and abrupt. I heard the front door slam shut. Paul had obviously just helped escort Vincent out.

FORTY-NINE

Saint Cecilia

AFTER his argument with Papa no one heard from Vincent for almost an entire week. I knew Papa had grown concerned, for that evening he told Madame Chevalier he had gone looking for Vincent in the fields and at the inn, but he was nowhere to be found. It was clear from the look of worry on Papa's face that he regretted their argument, but now there was little he could do to change what was said.

"He probably just needs some time to compose himself," Papa muttered to Madame Chevalier as she knitted in the large chair in the parlor. "He'll be back soon. If he's not, I'll have to alert Theo and the police, I suppose."

But Vincent eventually did reappear. He didn't show up at our front doorstep, though. The following evening he climbed up the garden trellis to my window and knocked at the pane.

I was half asleep when I saw him. He had one hand on the ledge, the other finger brought to his lips.

I went over to the window to open it. The cool night air blew ripples in my cotton nightdress.

"Shhhh," he said. "We have very little time."

I looked around to make sure no one could hear us. "I'm not sure I should go," I said. "I will not have a second chance with Papa."

"You won't have one with me, either. Are you coming or not?"

I remained silent for a moment, stunned.

The risk of leaving with Vincent was obvious, but his offer was exhilarating. I knew I could not refuse him; his invitation was what I had been wishing for all week.

No longer was I the solitary figure in a field with no one to accept my hand. The warm sensation of Vincent's fingers slipping into mine, the feeling of his calloused palms pressed against my skin, sent all sense of reason far away. I hoisted my nightdress above my knees and began my descent.

WE tiptoed across the wet garden stairs, down to the street, neither of us taking our hand away from the other. I felt almost naked, the breeze lifting up my flimsy gown as we made our way down the street.

I knew where he was going to eventually take me. It was the only place where we could be ensured our privacy. Knowing this I asked no questions. I simply threaded my hand in his and followed. Down the rue Vessenots we traveled, the moon high in the black sky, the white stars dazzling like ice.

We arrived at the church nearly twenty minutes later. "I have yet to be inside," he whispered as he pushed open the heavy doors. A few candle tapers still burned from the evening mass. The tabernacle had been put away, but the decorative cloth was still draped over the altar.

"Go sit at the organ," he ordered. "We don't have much time."

I ran, though my feet were now filthy and blistered, and sat down.

He pulled four stretchers out from his rucksack and a square of cotton cloth. He stretched the canvas right there before me, tacking each corner with a small hammer and nail.

He painted with the canvas unprimed. He did not speak another word to me, as his eyes darted between his palette and the easel. It did not take longer than forty-five minutes before he announced he was done.

"We must go now!" Again he barked at me, commanding me in a voice I had never heard before.

I had only a few seconds to look at the wet painting. Me in my nightdress. You could see the flesh of my legs through the white paint. The organ pipes in pale ocher, the dark wood of the instrument in purple and red.

I appeared celestial. Like a Madonna in a medieval painting, my head before a saucer of gold. He held the painting so the fresh pigment was turned outward. A few droplets of pigment landed on the cold stone floor, as Vincent motioned for us to leave.

I rushed behind him. Had you blindfolded me, I would have still known how to get where he intended to take me. We left the empty church and started down the main road. For over thirty minutes we walked. Vincent carried the wet canvas on his hip, some thin paint dribbling down the side. Now the organ pipes looked as though they were bleeding. Thin fingers of amber slid along the right edge.

We arrived at the limestone cave behind the Château Léry.

"Follow me," he instructed. Vincent no longer had a free hand but was busy adjusting his rucksack and the still wet painting of me. I nodded my head and followed him inside.

He put the painting down at the lip of the cave and reached into his smock to retrieve a candle. "Come," Vincent said as he lit the match.

I wondered if he wanted to make love to me again. The damp, musky smell of the cave brought a flood of memories to me and I closed my eyes for a moment, so overwhelmed was I by the sight of the powdery white walls and the intimacy of the candlelight.

But Vincent walked ahead of me, determined to do something I had not expected.

"It will be safe in here," he announced. "No matter what happens, it will always be here."

He propped the canvas up on one of the ledges that lined the walls of the cave.

"Marguerite, it will always be here for you."

The painting stood there like an altarpiece on a podium of cold, gray stone. My face, my body, illuminated by swirls of gold and amber paint.

"This way, you'll always remember how I've envisioned you."

I went to kiss him. My hands trembled as I reached out to touch him. My fingers touched the fabric of his shirt, and felt the bony ribs down his center. He pressed against me so that his breath was hot on my neck. I was crying as I lifted my face up to his. I no longer cared what was right and wrong, I wanted to be with him.

"Marguerite," he whispered. His lips hovered over mine and I could feel my mouth quivering in anticipation.

"Tonight you are Saint Cecilia, so things between us must

remain pure." He took hold of my wrists and turned them so my palms now faced upward. He bent down and pressed several kisses into them before bringing them close against his cheeks. And I wept as I looked up at him. For I knew the painting and the kisses were his way of saying good-bye.

FIFTY

An Approaching Frost

DAWN was approaching as Vincent took my hand to lead me out. The pavement now felt like sandpaper. My toes were covered in dry earth; the soles of my feet were now cracked and raw.

With the darkness beginning to soften, I was more certain of my bearings. I told Vincent it would be safer if I returned home alone.

He stood there watching me, a lone figure as the dark sky lifted behind. I remember taking one last look into his eyes. They were staring at me intently, the radiant stars slicing white light against his cheek. Somehow something told me to savor that look of his, store it deep inside. It was as if I could sense the summer ending, a frost lurking behind the shadows and the sun. I knew, when winter arrived, I would need something to keep me aflame.

* * *

I NEED not tell you what happened several days later. Up in the fields, not far from the cave, Vincent placed his easel by a haystack, went behind the château, and shot himself in the chest.

Monsieur Ravoux alerted Dr. Mazery, the local practitioner, who in turn alerted Papa.

"The bullet passed below the fleshy tissue." I heard Papa reading the message, which was delivered to him by a local boy.

It was nine o'clock in the evening and Papa was in his robe. Paul and Madame Chevalier were in the parlor and Louise-Josephine and I were upstairs in my room.

"He's still alive . . . ," Father reported as he finished reading the note. "He's at Ravoux's. He was able to drag himself back to his room." Papa's voice was rough with concern. "Paul, go get me my surgical bag, I must go at once."

I was sick with worry when I overheard the news. Louise-Josephine had to hold me back with both arms, for I was insistent that I had to be at Vincent's side.

"You cannot go," she said. "There is nothing you can do now." She held me tight in her arms. I must have writhed there for nearly a half hour before I finally collapsed onto the floor.

WHAT happened next has now become the stuff of history books. Vincent lasted nearly thirty hours in his bed until his brother Theo came to his side.

He lay there as placid as a monk. His white face ashen, his once high cheeks sunken like dried prunes.

"This is as it should be," he told Theo. The brothers' hands remained entwined as Vincent slipped into unconsciousness.

That evening, Papa told us Theo had turned to him and asked him to sketch Vincent as he lay on his deathbed. Papa took a pad and a piece of charcoal and drew Vincent with his head propped up on the small white pillow, his eyes closed as if caught in the middle of a dream.

It was an image I could not erase from my mind—Papa sketching Vincent in his final hours. He must have relished the honor, holding that twig of charcoal in his hand and sketching the man he knew had such genius.

"There was something exquisitely poignant," I heard him tell Paul years later as the two of them copied one of Vincent's paintings in the garden. "He painted me in a pose of great pensiveness, and later on, I was the last one to sketch him in a moment of rare calm."

THE night he died, I was sitting in the parlor with Louise-Josephine when Papa and Paul returned home. It was nearly two in the morning, and Madame Chevalier had already retired to her bedroom.

"How is he, Papa?" I asked. My face was streaked with red from crying, and I could not help but think about how the paint had dribbled down the canvas of the last portrait Vincent had painted of me. Even at the time, it had reminded me of tears.

"He's passed on, Marguerite." Papa's voice cracked. "It was a bullet to the chest and there was nothing I could do."

My voice cracked, too. "How can that be, Papa? You're his doctor!" I was weeping now. "What good were all your tinctures then if they couldn't prevent this?" My words flew out angrily in between my sobs.

"They were a few herbs, Marguerite. Not miracles." He sat down in his chair, exhausted.

"Monsieur Lavert, the town carpenter, has offered to make the coffin," Father said, his face half covered by his palms. "It is a kind gesture. Vincent painted his two-year-old son only two weeks ago."

After a few minutes, Father stood up. There were tears in his eyes. "The funeral will be tomorrow afternoon. There was nothing I could do, Marguerite. I am telling you the truth."

THE funeral invitations were printed that morning in Pontoise and announced the service for 2 P.M. Because Vincent had committed suicide, the village priest denied the use of the local hearse and forbade the service from taking place in our church. When I heard this news, I thought of the symbolism of Vincent's painting of the church at midnight and it haunted me like an apparition.

In the end, a hearse was borrowed from the next township but still no church service was provided. As was the custom for women, I remained at home, unable to attend the funeral.

I wore black anyway that afternoon. Louise-Josephine tried to comfort me as I cried for hours in my room.

"You could not have known," she said over and over again. But I continued to replay our last moments in my mind. She was wrong. In some way, I had known. But I was too cowardly to admit it.

* * *

PAPA dressed in his black suit and matching top hat. Paul looked even more like his identical twin as the two of them set out in the carriage for Vincent's burial.

"I want to stop and fetch some sunflowers," I heard Papa say on his way out.

I remember looking out the window as the two of them descended the garden stairs. Behind the neighboring rooftops, I could see the stretch of meadows, the fields of poppies and sweet peas that Vincent had painted over the past two months.

It was a warm, radiant day, the sun the color of crushed marigolds. But now the chestnut blossoms were on the ground and the lime trees provided little shade. I thought about how the earth was so dry from the summer heat. Only a day before, I had been on my knees in my garden, and my hands had felt like parchment when I dusted off the pebbly soil. Now when I closed my eyes, I saw the ground cracking into myriad tiny fissures as the shovels parted the earth for Vincent's coffin.

ACCORDING to Paul, Papa's gesture of bringing sunflowers inspired everyone else to go out and return with yellow flowers.

"It was his favorite color," Paul said, and I nodded, knowing full well. "The coffin lay in his room in the inn, his last canvases nailed to the walls. Papa's sunflowers were placed beside his coffin, and then hours later, bouquets of yellow dahlias, jonquils, and other yellow field flowers were everywhere. Near his coffin, Theo arranged Vincent's folding stool, his brushes, and easel to rest next to him."

I was still in a state of shock as Paul described how he, Papa,

Theo, and many of Vincent's friends from Paris walked behind the coffin as it was taken to the new cemetery in Auvers. He said Papa tried to say a few words but was so overcome with grief, he could only utter a single sentence.

"What did he say?" I asked.

"Something to the effect that he was a great artist and an honest man. 'Vincent had only two aims: humanity and art.' He then planted a tree on the grave."

"A tree?" I questioned. "What sort of tree?"

Paul shrugged. "Papa told us it was an ornamental one . . . one that would flower and thrive in the soil. . . . I thought it a touching gesture. So did Theo. He wept when Papa knelt down and planted the tiny sapling in the fresh mound of soil."

I held my hand over my mouth, but my sobs escaped me.

My brother continued, "After the funeral, Papa told me that it would be my responsibility to ensure the grave is always properly maintained. He thought it proper that I have the task, as he is getting on in years."

"Shouldn't Vincent's family be responsible for that?" I asked, looking up at him through my tears.

"Of course, but as they are quite a distance away, Father assured Theo that he will hold himself personally responsible for Vincent's memory here in Auvers. 'When I go, my son, Paul, will take over,' he told Theo. 'Vincent will always have sunflowers on his grave.'"

I took my handkerchief and blotted my eyes.

"Yes, and in appreciation, Theo told me that I could take a few paintings of Vincent's . . . after all, there were so many in his room!"

Paul straightened his back and a small smile slid across his face. "So even though he never painted one of me, I will have several of his paintings. I hope to study his technique and learn from them." Again, Paul smiled. "There's a certain satisfaction in that!"

"Is there?" I asked quietly.

But Paul did not hear me. Papa was calling his name.

"We need to collect the canvases now," I heard Papa holler.

It took Paul only a few seconds before he was scurrying down the stairs.

FIFTY-ONE

The Collection

THEY collected over twenty-six paintings and eighteen drawings of Vincent's that afternoon, returning home after several trips to the inn with their arms loaded with canvases and a portfolio brimming with sketches. Years later, I met Adeline Ravoux in the bakery and she told me how shameless Papa was after the funeral. "He took so many," she said. "He went into the closet and underneath Vincent's bed, and ordered Paul to collect all the paintings from the walls. Your father and brother behaved like vultures."

"I was told Theo offered them," I said, trying to defend them.

She shook her head. "They didn't need to take so many."

Her words were hurtful, but I knew they were true.

I remember how Papa returned home after the burial and although he seemed visibly upset, there was unmistakably a glimmer of triumph in his eyes. He carried those canvases into his office like a pirate unloading his plunder.

THE next few weeks were a blur to me. I could not believe that Vincent was no longer in our village. That I would no longer see him in the fields, that his heavy footsteps would never again barrel up our front stairs.

Over and over again, I replayed our last moments. I fingered my palm and recalled the sensation of his skin against mine. I imagined his face in front of me, the urge I had to melt into his arms, the way he refused to kiss me, knowing all too well that in a few days he would be gone. Had Papa's herbs clouded his judgment? Had I been cowardly in not warning him that I had suspicion about Papa's abilities? Should I have told him that Papa had come into his study of herbs late in life and that they had only seemed to worsen his own condition? Or, even more troubling, had our romance pushed him toward self-destruction when he realized he could never have a marriage and home of his own?

I read over and over the text in the book of Japanese prints that Jo gave me and perused Papa's office for more literature on the East. "Suicide is not frowned upon," one of the books said. "It is exalted as a means of familial redemption," another explained.

And I wondered if that was what it all came down to in the end. Vincent feeling he had to satisfy a debt he believed he owed.

I TOLD no one, not even Louise-Josephine, about my secret painting. And only on days when I finished my errands early would I sneak to the cave and look upon that clandestine canvas. That treasure of mine, the last thing that came from Vincent's hand.

THE following year, Théophile and Louise-Josephine were finally married. Papa surprised everyone by finding two witnesses to attend the ceremony. Although neither he, Paul, nor Madame Chevalier was in attendance, Papa asked the son of one of his oldest friends, Louis Cabrol, and another one of his friends from his bohemian days in Paris to attend in order to facilitate the union.

That morning, I woke up early and collected a fistful of wildflowers for her. I snipped off long ladders of lupine, blue and white daisies, bunches of sweet pea, and lavender forget-me-nots. I had purposefully wanted to get her flowers that grew outside our garden, ones that had grown free.

And as I had promised her, I helped Louise-Josephine get dressed on her wedding day. I combed and plaited her long brown hair. I buttoned the back of her dress and tied her sash in a large voluminous bow. We did not speak, but I saw her eyes in the reflection in the glass. It was a look I knew well: half sad, half brimming with excitement. It was bittersweet for her, I knew. She was marrying and she knew in her heart I would most probably never have the opportunity.

"I am so happy for you," I whispered as I kissed her cheek. They would be off to Paris on the evening train and I wasn't sure when I would see her next.

"Come live with us," she said, reaching her hand out to take mine. "Théophile wouldn't mind."

"Only if you move to Mauritius," I said with a small laugh.

"I'm serious," she said. "You could sneak out tonight. It will be as we always said it would be."

I shook my head. I could not go. Not because I didn't want freedom, but because I knew I could never leave Auvers.

I could never leave my painting.

EPILOGUE

I HAVE since learned that an improper dosage of foxglove can cause hallucinations. That it can excite one's spirit, rather than soothe it. I don't know if Papa contributed to Vincent's suicide or if Vincent saw the halos of saffron and gold because the absinthe still lingered in his bones.

Over the years, Papa became obsessed with his attachment to Vincent. He began copying the paintings he had in his collection in an attempt to learn from them. He took the same vases that Vincent had used in his still lifes, the same arrangement of flowers, and tried to re-create what Vincent had painted while in his care.

Paul, too, shared this obsession, even after his numerous applications for art school were turned down. Both Papa and he spent countless hours studying Vincent's canvases, trying to paint identical versions that would deceive the untrained eye. They would sit in the studio upstairs with one of Vincent's canvases on an easel between them, and scrutinize each brushstroke in an attempt to reproduce an identical version that more often than not came out as amateurish and awkward. A far cry from the masterpieces Vincent had created in Auvers.

I would have gone mad living with them had Louise-Josephine not returned to Auvers. Théophile's mother had become ill, and he had requested a job in Vosiers so he could be close to oversee her care.

Every Wednesday she'd come to the house with her small daughter, Violette. The girl had her mother's brown hair and amber skin, the same mischievous light in her eyes. She seemed delighted by our garden, the small animals that we kept near the shed. How it amused me when she jumped off Louise-Josephine's lap and ran across the lawn, the wind rushing through her hair! For those brief moments, I could close my eyes and envision how Louise-Josephine and I must have looked, as we ran down the road in our youth, giddy with the anticipation of meeting our loves.

Their weekly visits soothed me and I treasured the quiet moments between Louise-Josephine and me. I enjoyed the companionship; I relished the opportunity to have someone for whom I could bake. Especially little Violette, who ate up my cakes and cookies with a relish I had never seen. Papa allowed us privacy and, as her daughter played, we would sit in the garden and it would be as if nothing had really changed between us. She was still as candid as ever. She took a look around the house one afternoon and commented on how strange the house now seemed. Papa and Paul's obsession had transformed it into a shrine to Vincent after his suicide. Now his presence was even stronger within the damp, plaster walls of our house than when he had been alive.

* * *

PAPA died some twenty years after Vincent, his body withered and his mind half addled from years of the herbs that brought him little solace. Madame Chevalier had passed away five years earlier, and her absence seemed to worsen Papa's frailty. In his final weeks, I made his favorite foods and mashed them, carefully spooning them into his mouth and wiping the yarn of saliva from his lips.

In an eerie way, the palette that Vincent had used to paint Papa seemed to foreshadow him in his last days. The same puce color underscored his eyes, his mouth was ghostly pale, his skin lined like the bark of an old tree.

Sometimes, when his eyes would be pooled with hallucinations, he would call out for Madame Chevalier. He would take my hand and stroke it between his papery palms and call me his little Chouchette. And although I yearned for him to say my name, or at least tell me that he held me in some affection, the words never came. I allowed myself to be called his little Chouchette, never once correcting him, letting him believe his beloved companion was there beside him. Her name, however, was not the last thing he uttered before he took his final breath. No, that was something that even took Paul by surprise. With a raspy breath and eyes wide open, he lifted his head from the mound of pillows and stretched out his arms. He called out her name, clearly so that there was no mistaking it, the name that it seemed was closest in all our hearts: "Louise-Josephine."

MY life changed little after Papa's death. I continued to have a solitary life, where most of my days were filled with morning walks to the village and afternoons spent tending to the flowers in my garden. But when Papa died, Paul became, by default, the master of the house. He took to his role with great zeal. He rummaged through Papa's closets and began wearing his cherished smocks, his silk foulards, his nautical caps. Two years later he married our distant cousin Emilienne, someone I only remembered meeting a handful of times. She was too old to have children when they wed, and she was neither a great conversationalist nor a beauty. But their union kept the villagers gossiping just a little less about the queer activities of our household.

My brother continued our father's obsession, dedicating himself to chronicling Vincent's last seventy days in our Auvers. He sat at his desk, his hair raked between his fingers, and tried to recall every detail of the relationship between Vincent and our father. He cataloged the paintings Vincent did in our home as well as those he remembered seeing stacked in Vincent's room at the Ravoux Inn. Like Papa, Paul shunned all visitors to our home except for Louise-Josephine and her daughter, the occasional elderly artist friends of Father's, or the rare scholar who wrote requesting to see one of the paintings in our collection.

A FEW years before Papa died, they dug up Vincent's body to move him to the new cemetery in town. And when they finally unearthed his coffin, the roots of the thuja tree that had shaded his grave for so long had penetrated the wooden boards and entwined themselves with his bones. The grave diggers gossiped that the roots clung to his skeleton like ferocious brown claws. I winced when I heard they needed pruning shears to cut Vincent free.

When Paul first informed me that Papa had planted a tree on

Vincent's grave, he had not mentioned it was a thuja. That tree was a well-known source of thujone, the toxin found in absinthe. And although Papa did not plant a wormwood tree, the tree that absinthe is most often derived from, it was still an ironic choice, particularly as Vincent admitted that he had been addicted to the "green-eyed devil" prior to his stay in Auvers.

Whether it was a hidden message by Papa or a mere coincidence, I will never know. What I am sure of is that even in death the plant's lengthy dark ropes held Vincent in a tight embrace, their serpentine legs attracted to the absinthe that remained in his bones.

Even when Vincent's coffin was disinterred and reburied next to his brother Theo's, Papa still could not let him alone. He took a few seeds from the tree that had threaded through Vincent's bones and placed them in an envelope that he labeled "Vincent's Tree." A few weeks later, he planted those seeds in the front garden and over the years the tree grew strong and high. It stands there to this day, flowering yellow-green blossoms that paper the ground.

I do not like this tree very much. The image of the original roots choking Vincent's skeleton is hard to shake from my mind. To me it's another example of something taken from Vincent. How, even in death, so many people wanted to claim him as their own. Even I, with my thoughts of our stolen moments in the cave, hoard my memories of him. Fingerprints of genius touched my skin, eyes that were aflame and full of vision chose me as a final muse. Of this I am greedy and refuse to share.

PERHAPS we all are predisposed to dislike the act of sharing. As Paul's obsession with Vincent strengthened, he became more intolerant of the fact that Vincent had chosen me to be his final muse.

Vincent had painted Papa, me, Adeline Ravoux, and other faces in Auvers, but never Paul. This fact weighed on him like a thicket of scars that blistered more with each passing year.

So tonight when my brother tells me that, of all the Van Gogh paintings we own, he has decided to sell only one—the one of me—I cannot say I'm surprised.

"It's the least technically interesting," he tells me over dinner.

His wife, Emilienne, is silent, looking down at the plate of stewed lamb that I prepared for them.

"We need the money and, as the head of this household, I have decided that because that painting is the weakest in the collection, it should be the first one sold."

I look up from the table, raising my head to stare at him. *It is mine, it is not yours to sell,* I think to myself. I know that Emilienne is trembling in her seat. I feel her eyes traveling over me like two marbles sliding across an abacus.

I do not speak. I just raise my eyebrows and stare at him with icy pupils. He knows the painting he has chosen to sell has hung for over four decades in the same spot in my bedroom. That it is the image I have seen every night before I went to sleep and the first one that I awakened to each morning.

"You're a sixty-five-year-old woman," he mutters underneath his breath. "It's unhealthy to dwell on a forty-five-year-old painting of one's younger self."

I can see his body twitching uncomfortably underneath his jacket. His silk scarf billows underneath his chin, the bristles of his goatee snagging the cloth as he lowers his head.

I try to stifle my body from trembling.

"If you must, Paul, . . . then you must," I say knowing I will not win this battle with him.

And so after the plates have been cleared from our dinner, he removes the painting from my bedroom wall. Outside, the November wind howls and I am forced to look away so he does not see my tears.

MY garden has been put to rest, the beet fields are soaked in rainwater, and Vincent's painting of me at my piano is on its way to hang on a strange new wall. But even with my bedroom wall now bare, I still remember how Vincent pressed that first poppy into my hand; how I sat for him; and how he smudged yellow paint across my cheek before our first kiss. And in those lost moments of my memory, I am as Vincent imagined me: white flesh bursting crimson through taffeta, marble skin trembling under the spell of warm fingers.

Tonight Paul believes he is selling the last portrait Vincent painted of me. But he is wrong and there is a certain satisfaction in that. He does not realize that on Sunday afternoons when I bid him and his wife farewell, I make two special trips after church.

First I visit Vincent's grave. I do not place sunflowers on his tombstone like Papa once did, and now Paul does. Instead, I place a single red poppy, so tiny and delicate. Folded neatly, like a tiny red fan.

And then, I wander past the Château Léry, ending up at the limestone cave where my painting still remains. The cool air has preserved it well. It is my little secret; not even Louise-Josephine knows that it is there.

The paint is still luminous, and the colors still glow in the soft gray light. It sits there on the shelf where he placed it years before. It remains there quietly triumphant. As Vincent promised. There, for only me to see.

Author's Note

In 1999 I attended an exhibit at the Metropolitan Museum of Art that displayed the paintings in the private collection of Dr. Gachet, the doctor who was responsible for Van Gogh's care during the final months before his suicide. The exhibition was unusual, in that it not only displayed the doctor's extensive collection of Cézannes, Pissarros, and Van Goghs that were painted while these artists were either visiting or being treated by the doctor during their stay in Auvers-sur-Oise, but also the copies of the same paintings he and his son, Paul, had executed once Vincent and some of the other artists had left their village.

Photos of the interior of their house supplemented the exhibition and, through these images, it was clear how seriously Dr. Gachet attached himself to his artist patients—particularly Vincent van Gogh. There, in the black-and-white images, one could see the shrinelike atmosphere the Gachets maintained after Vincent's death. His paintings hung on every wall, and the articles he had used for still lifes were at arm's reach. The text describing the family pointed out that the Gachets maintained a guarded and intensely private existence. Gachet's son never held a job, and he and his sister lived with their father until his death. Upon Dr. Gachet's passing, his son made it his life's work to become an expert on Vincent and, with Van Gogh buried in the Auvers cemetery, the keeper of his grave.

After conducting some preliminary research, I discovered there was an even more intriguing character in this cast of eccentrics. In the exhibition catalog, Susan Alyson Stein speaks of how Gachet's only daughter "Marguerite, who never married, was the silent and respectful witness to this parsimonious life consumed by study, in a house frozen in the past."[1]

Who was this silent woman who never left the confines of her family home yet was the model for two of Vincent's paintings while he stayed in Auvers? *Mademoiselle Gachet in the Garden* and *Mademoiselle Gachet at the Piano* are two excellent examples of how Vincent used both symbolism and a multicolored palette to illuminate a painfully shy model who was kept under close watch by her overbearing father. By placing Marguerite in both her garden and at her piano—her two favorite spots and the places where she sublimates her passions—Vincent is able to show a side of her that the average person would have missed. And that was always one of Vincent's objectives: to use both paint and his artistic eye to celebrate a subject's hidden beauty.

The most astonishing item was a footnote in the catalog that suggests that the 1934 auction of *Mademoiselle Gachet at the Piano,* a gift from Van Gogh that Marguerite hung in her bedroom for over forty years, was done on the orders of her brother Paul, who had always been jealous that he had never been painted by Van Gogh.[2] Another supposition went so far as to suggest that he had been jealous of a ru-

[1]*The Gachet Donation in Context: The Known and Little-Known Collections of Dr. Gachet,* Susan Alyson Stein. The Metropolitan Museum of Art, New York 1999, p.168

[2]*Id.* At no.30. *The Gachet Donation in Context.* Susan Alyson Stein. 1999

mored affair between the two, so he exacted revenge by forcing her to sell the painting.

The question of what motivated the sale of this painting became the genesis for the novel. Had there been an affair between Vincent and Marguerite during his final weeks? Certainly the girl was of marriageable age, having turned twenty-one shortly after Vincent's arrival. Her limited contact with the outside world would have made her particularly susceptible to the charms of an artist, particularly one as well-traveled as Vincent. Not knowing the answer, I began to dig deeper into the lives of the Gachet family, particularly this quiet young woman whom no one seemed to know anything about. What I did not expect to find was that there were actually two women in the Gachet household who were kept under lock and key: Marguerite and Louise-Josephine Chevalier, who many believe was Dr. Gachet's illegitimate child with Marguerite and Paul's governess, Louise-Anne-Virginie Chevalier.

I came upon this information almost by accident. Upon my first visit to Auvers-sur-Oise, I befriended the director of the tourist office who told me that there were two women in their nineties who were alive when Marguerite still lived in the village. She arranged for me to meet them. One was the baker's daughter, Madame Cretelle, who had vivid memories of selling bread and other provisions to the quiet Marguerite. The other was Madame Millon, who was a schoolgirl in Marguerite's later years and had memories of seeing her walking through town.

While both of them proved invaluable in telling me details that could never be found in any art catalog or history book, such as the way Marguerite dressed in muted colors when she went to church, or the shy way in which she acknowledged people in the street, they also provided me with village gossip that had never been relayed in any of the English texts I had for my research. The most shocking of these revelations was the existence of Louise-Josephine, who supposedly lived in the Gachet household from the age of fourteen to twenty-three, and who no one even knew existed until the family's house was put up for sale.

Madame Millon wrote a book in French in which she was able to find a birth certificate of this child, whose father goes unnamed on the certificate. But there are other clues about her paternity. For example, Gachet signed something that acknowledges that she was not born under adulterous circumstances so that she will be able to marry at a later date. Her name, Louise-Josephine, is also similar to Louis-Joseph, which was Dr. Gachet's father's name. Also, her conception coincides with the time just before Dr. Gachet became betrothed to his wife, the mother of Marguerite and Paul, who died of tuberculosis when Marguerite was a young girl. Madame Millon, in her book *Vincent Van Gogh in Auvers-sur-Oise,* speculates that the doctor met Madame Chevalier before his marriage and continued their relationship (and financial support of Louise-Josephine) until his wife's death. At that point, he invited Madame Chevalier to come and be his children's governess. Eventually, Louise-Josephine joined them.

Fiercely guarding his privacy, Dr. Gachet refused to let the young Chevalier be seen in the village. There is no mention in Van Gogh's letters of him meeting the governess or her child, and one can assume that Gachet, fearing the spread of village gossip, intentionally kept them away from the artist.

Seizing upon this information, I began to create a framework for *The Last Van Gogh* that would give a voice to these two female characters relegated to all but footnotes in history, especially Marguerite. Using the idea that Marguerite was not only a muse to Vincent in his last days, but also a voyeur to her father's questionable medical tactics in Vincent's treatment and a victim of her brother's rage, I tried to create a narrative in which her experience is released from her only tangible legacy: the two completed portraits Van Gogh painted of Marguerite and the one he mentions to his sister Wilhemina in which she was seated at a small organ as a modern Saint Cecilia,[3] but which scholars believe was never completed.

---

[3]*The Letters of Vincent Van Gogh,* selected and edited by Ronald de Leeuw, Penguin Books 1996, p. 498.

The clues hidden in Van Gogh's paintings (such as the foxgloves in the portrait of Dr. Gachet, which is a form of digitalis that can cause side effects such as anxiety and heart palpitations and could have been used improperly in Van Gogh's own medical treatment, and the mentioning of a painting never completed) are just some of the mystery surrounding Vincent's final days in Auvers. In the seventy days he stayed in the village, he completed over seventy paintings. *The Last Van Gogh* sets out to examine the inspiration for his final one.

Acknowledgments

This book would not have been possible without the superb scholarship of Anne Distel and Susan Alyson Stein, whose catalog from the Metropolitan Museum of Art's exhibition: "Cézanne to Van Gogh: The Collection of Doctor Gachet," served as an inspiration for this novel. I am also indebted to the scholarship of Ronald Pickvance and *The Complete Letters of Vincent Van Gogh*, published by the New York Graphic Society.

In Auvers-sur-Oise, both Monsieur and Madame Cretelle peppered my research with wonderful anecdotes of the Gachet family, particularly their memories of Paul and Marguerite Gachet. Madame Millon's research on Vincent van Gogh and her fastidious details about village life in Auvers during the late nineteeth century proved invaluable as well. A special thanks should be given to Catherine Galliot at the Auvers-sur-Oise tourism agency, who introduced me to these wonderful people and also arranged for me to privately view the Gachet house, which was not made available to the public until recently.

Rosalyn Shaoul, I thank you for your tireless efforts on my behalf. You read my many drafts and translated all my French documents and were a wonderful springboard for developing so many of the intricacies of the novel. I truly cannot thank you enough and this book deserves to be dedicated to you. Meredith Hassett, Nikki Koklanaris, Jardine Libaire, Sara Shaoul, and Heather Rowland, I thank each of you for your careful readings of the book. To my husband, I thank you for your support, your patience, and your willingness to push me further with each novel I write.

A final thanks to my agent, Sally Wofford-Girand, for your belief in this book, and to my late editor, Leona Nevler, who loved it enough to give it a home.

AND NOW AN EXCERPT FROM

Swedish Tango

BY ALYSON RICHMAN

AVAILABLE SOON FROM BERKLEY BOOKS

THE first time he saw her, she had walked outside the convent to pick up the fallen oranges. Her dark blue uniform grazed below her soft, smooth knees. Around her feet, the small yellow and orange fruit nestled, and the smell of the freshly cut grass and the perfume of ripe citrus lingered heavy in the air. She knelt down and pulled out her skirt to fashion a basket, filling the cloth with the fallen fruit.

She was truly a vision. Long black hair, slender arms, and skin the color of crushed almonds. She turned her head slightly to recover from the sun, and it was then that he first caught sight of her face. He saw past the slight wrinkling of her nose, and the slight squinting of her eyes, and saw her poetic brow, delicate nose, and full, ripe mouth. He imagined the weight of her thick black hair, envisioned his hands undoing her combs, and the canopy of curls falling over his palms and spilling onto his knees. She was so beautiful that he, almost a grown man, could have wept.

He attempted to whistle, but the sound he made was too weak to reach her ears. She was lost in her activity, for this was the happiest moment in her day.

What the mother superior considered a chore, she considered a luxury. The other girls' responsibilities were far more tedious: assisting the cooks in the kitchen, cleaning the bathrooms, or raking one of the church's several gardens. Salomé was only asked to gather oranges and bring them to the kitchen, where they would later be squeezed into juice.

Here, amongst the heavy green boughs and the yellow-dotted ground, she savored her time alone. Sometimes, when the fruit was particularly ripe, she would pierce the rind with her fingernail and place her lips over the hole, sucking the juice out in one long swallow. Other times, she would cross her legs while the oranges lay heavy in her lap, and she would admire the flight of a butterfly or the silver-green fire in the wing of a praying mantis.

Little did she know that, from a balcony only twenty-five meters away, a university student stood alone with his mouth open and his heart pounding, absolutely consumed by love.

EVERY day he anticipated her arrival as she emerged, like clockwork, from the stone convent walls at a quarter past nine. He began to groom himself for her, hoping that one day she would look up and see him, a figure in the distance, standing on his balcony alone.

He wore wrinkled shirts to his classes, saving the pressed ones to wear for the few minutes each day while he watched her. He shaved before her arrival, combing his thick black hair behind his ears and patting his cheeks with a perfume he hoped would reach her by air. Weeks went by, but she never took notice of him. And then, when he had nearly gone mad with wild desperation, he finally devised a way in which they could meet.

Each night, he pored through volumes of the world's greatest poets until his candle burned out and he could find no more light. When he discovered a particular verse that captured his own feelings of love and ardor, he copied it in his neatest hand onto tiny scrolls of parchment paper he had cut. Three weeks later, Octavio had transcribed more than two hundred poems.

In the middle of the night, with several dozen slips of paper in his pockets and a small knife in his hands, he went to the gates of the convent and stood where the orchard began. He climbed the trees and rustled the branches. He shook the boughs until the oranges fell to the ground. Then, with the moonlight above him, he carved out each fruit's navel, rolled up the love poems, and inserted them within.

The next morning, he rose, having slept less then an hour. He stood on the balcony and waited for her to arrive.

She came, wearing her simple blue uniform. A wicker basket dangled form her arm. He noticed how, when she sighed, her rib cage swelled underneath her cotton blouse, how her whole body bent in exhaustion at the sight of so many oranges.

She knelt down to examine the first fruit of the day and immediately smiled as she noticed the thin cigarlike roll of paper tucked neatly within. After searching to see if anyone was around, she withdrew the first poem:

Acogedora como un viejo camino
Te pueblan ecos y voces nostálgicas

Yo desperté y a veces emigran y huyen
pájaros que dormían en tu alma.

You gather things to you like an old road.
You are peopled with echoes and nostalgic voices.
I awoke and at times birds fled and migrated
that had been sleeping in your soul.

She recognized the poem from Neruda's *20 Poemas de amor y una Canción Desesperada, "Para mi corazón,"* and wondered who would have placed it in the orange. When she knelt down to pick up another piece of fruit, there again was another scroll of writing. When she unraveled it, therein was a love poem by Mistral.

She looked around again to see if anyone was there, thinking one of her classmates had played a trick on her. But she saw no one. As she looked straight ahead, she noticed the entire ground was littered with oranges. Each one with a thin roll of paper protruding from its center. Each one with its own magic wand.

From as far away as he stood, Octavio could hear her joyful laughter, and he leaned over the balcony to gain a better view.

For several weeks, Octavio continued to court Salomé through the poem-filled oranges. In between his studies, he transcribed so many poems that his wrists grew weary and the nib on his fountain pen bent from overuse. Still, he wrote to her until he had exhausted all of his volumes of poetry. But there were so many things he had not yet said. Realizing he could no longer rely on the cushion of another man's words, he held his head for many hours, struggling to form his desires into words. He listened to his heart and poured out its contents. He wrote of her black eyes and dark hair. He wrote of her majestic gait, her long, regal neck, and her slender arms. He imagined their first kiss and the warmth he might find in her embrace. If he had been musical, he would have composed a song for her, written an aria, and created a concerto in her honor. Had he brushes, he would have tried to re-create her image in a palette of rich, creamy paint. But, as he only had pen and paper, he continued to write.

One evening, when he rested on his arms, his eyes heavy with exhaustion and his pen nearly dry, he wrote to her for the last time. "In a star-filled sky, I wish to see you. I will bring oranges to lay down at your feet. Come to me, dearest to my heart. I shall wait for you and sing you poems of love." He carefully inserted the poem into the orange, then slipped in a second paper that specified a place where they could meet.

His heart soared with wild anticipation. He only hoped that she would come.